NO WHITE KNIGHT

SECRETS OF STONE: BOOK EIGHT

ANGEL PAYNE & VICTORIA BLUE

NO WHITE KNIGHT

SECRETS OF STONE: BOOK EIGHT

ANGEL PAYNE & VICTORIA BLUE

WATERHOUSE PRESS

To my love, my life,
the one who makes it all possible:

Thomas, you are my knight,
my hero, and the man of my dreams.

—Angel

For my boys and my very special girl:
You are my everything, and without your love
and support, I would've never taken this journey.

—Victoria

CHAPTER ONE

Mac

"Okay, ladies—single ladies, that is—it's time for the bouquet toss!"

The DJ might as well have shouted "Last call" during spring break in Cabo. I smirked at the comparison—which wasn't a far stretch—as the dance floor, otherwise known as a bunch of flat wood squares fitted together across the private San Diego estate's back lawn, was packed with female lemmings hoping to catch the coveted ball of flowers about to be tossed by the glowing bride. Giggles, doe eyes, slutty dresses, and sky-high heels abounded.

I was tempted to sneer again.

Until the little throng seemed to part for her.

Her.

The tiny blonde I hadn't torn my eyes away from for the last six hours.

Damn her.

I would've been tempted to say it out loud, if I wasn't so consumed with thinking about fucking her.

Luckily, I only knew a handful of the wedding guests, or someone would've noticed my stalker moves as I navigated the party's perimeter, darting in and out of Mission-style archways and their terra-cotta shadows, angling for a better view of the dance floor. Not that I gave a rat's ass what they all thought, anyway. The only element keeping me around at this point in the party was her, the woman who'd consumed my attention from the second I'd spotted her earlier, while the wedding party had mingled with guests before the bride and grooms exchanged their vows.

Ohhh, yes. Bride and *grooms*—and the three of them still glowed with happiness now, after openly exchanging rings of commitment to their unusual style of love. *And I'm the big expert of love all of a sudden?* I did, however, know a thing or two about unusual—and that description was getting a workout today when it came to describing that stunning little number and her stranglehold on my dick.

What is this bullshit? The thrill of the hunt? There was nothing thrilling about this muck-fest. As far as I could tell, she hadn't realized I was at the wedding, let alone near this hilltop or even breathing on the same planet. Funnily, three women out on that dressed-up plywood with her had already tapped their numbers into my cell phone. Just as fast, I'd erased all three. They were invisible to me, even now.

She was it.

The quest. The prey. The big-game kill in a tiny, sassy-as-fuck body.

Damn her.

I still couldn't stop staring at her.

Taylor Mathews. Well, at least I knew her name. We'd met somewhere in the last few months, though I couldn't pinpoint the exact day and time. That shit was for people who had time to burn, and I wasn't one of them. The clock just wasn't that important to me. Things happened either before or after I operated on a patient.

Before or after I'd changed a life.

I had performed such a feat—emergency brain surgery—on the fairer of the grooms, Fletcher Ford. Taylor Mathews had been at Talia's side throughout the entire ordeal, but not just "sitting by" her friend. She'd fought valiantly for Talia, even standing up to me when she had to. Not a lot of *men* had that courage, let alone women. And from what I could glean from overheard conversations, Taylor had even remained in Chicago for most of Ford's recovery too.

So is she Talia Ford now? Or Talia Newland? That was the last name of the other groom, his dark head tossed back in laughter while watching their woman prepare to chuck her bouquet.

Maybe she'll just go for the trendy and hyphenate it at Ford-Newland. Keeping the peace, and all that. Can't be easy, since they're both such stubborn bastards—not that I noticed much of anything about them beyond the surface facts. Not concerned with the color of their fucking underwear.

Now, Taylor Mathews? I care about her *underwear. Even better, about ripping it right off her.*

My hypersensitive mind, ping-ponging from subject to subject with its regular fury, had suddenly bounced me into the danger zone. Trouble was, I didn't want to leave—especially as that blond spitfire strutted to the head of the pack on the dance floor like she owned every splinter in those wooden planks. Just the sight of her shifted me into overdrive, a very dangerous gear for me. I hadn't had anything more than a quick fuck in two years.

But Taylor Mathews was an engine class all her own.

She drew me, even now. Spoke to me without words. Awakened something inside, calling to base urges on levels

I hadn't experienced in a long time. *Who am I kidding?* That I hadn't experienced *ever*. My throat burned as if I'd just chugged gasoline, rather than the craft beer in my death grip. My bloodstream was churning pure rocket fuel. And my cock?

Right now, I was really trying to ignore that bastard. Like he was agreeing to *that* bullshit. Every chance he could take, the message got pushed at me like a telegram stamped *Urgent*. It had been like that for hours, the primal yearning to make myself a part of her, becoming a fantasy fueling the better part of my thoughts for the entire afternoon. I could even pinpoint the exact second they'd begun. I'd been watching her from a strategic vantage point, one of the tables set off from the rest of the wedding bustle, placed for guests needing a reprieve from the Labor Day weekend sun—so while I was cloaked in shadows, she wasn't. Like I said, abso-fucking-lutely-perfect— until some young hipster jackass tried making a play for her. The douche nozzle couldn't scrape together two brain cells long enough to read Taylor's body language, mistaking her surface small talk for a prelude to the winning touchdown. He kept babbling until she faked a buzz on her phone and then a nonexistent text before her "apology" about being needed for some last-minute wedding emergency. I'd grinned from ear to ear as she bounded from the idiot faster than a gazelle spooked by a lion.

But goddamn, did *I* want to be her lion.

The commotion of the crowd roused me back to the unfolding "fun" on the dance floor. I refocused in time to watch the bride, escorted by both her proud grooms, flash a conspiratorial wink at Taylor, who nodded like a quarterback about to get the key snap of the game. The crowd *oooo*ed and *ahhh*ed as Talia posed between her men, who leaned in from the sides to press tender kisses on her cheeks, freezing that way as the photographer captured their bliss on film.

After that, it was game on.

Talia flashed the group of women one more teasing look—

Before turning and tossing the ball of flowers directly to Taylor.

Pass complete. I chuckled along with the crowd as the little blonde tucked the prize to her chest, preparing to run for the proverbial end zone if needed. After a quick look around to confirm nobody was going to dare fight her for the prize, Taylor relaxed and straightened, her composure returning to regal queen status. Her face was the most fascinating part of the transformation, especially the telling glimmer in her eyes. I wondered if anyone else saw it besides me...how the reigning sovereign only existed on the outside. Inside she was still an imposter, no matter how court-worthy her jewelry or dress.

And what a dress it was. The material, some combination of firm but silky, was spun into the palest blue I'd ever seen, matching the cloudless Southern California sky at the spot where it met the horizon along the Pacific. Her china-doll skin looked even milkier next to the fabric, and I longed to run my fingers across her collarbones, where the skin seemed even thinner. The heart-shaped bodice hugged her frame, and the fabric ended just above her knees, making me wonder if they tasted as good as they looked.

Fuck.

I wanted to taste more than her knees.

A lot more.

Just like that, lust and need climbed on their mental motorbikes, churning my mind into a goddamned festival of filth. I thought of grabbing that woman by the hand then and there and hauling her away someplace private inside the house. Parking her sweet ass on a table, a dresser, a bed, *anywhere*, so I could hike up that gorgeous blue silk-satin-stiff whatever and then yank her panties off so fast, she'd gasp and writhe—urging her wet pussy up toward my waiting mouth. Then I'd taste her. Drown in her. Suck down every drop of her until she had no choice but to come for me, preparing her sweet cunt for the stretch of my aching cock...

"Holy shit." My harsh mutter interrupted my fantasies just in time. I shifted balance to get my dick back under some kind of control.

For fuck's sake. I didn't even know that much about her. All right, she was gorgeous. No. *Stunning.* She had an energy, perhaps even an edge, that made a man want to find an excuse for lingering in her vicinity—or, if he was a ballsy hipster, even trying to impress her enough to surrender a phone number. But she needed to eat more, judging by her bone-thin frame—though even her figure, what I could see of it, turned me on. She looked delicate and acted fierce. When that temper of hers was piqued, the cutest fucking Southern drawl set in too. She did it *every* time. Believe me, I knew. I swear, just the sight of me set off a dozen of the woman's hot buttons. Don't get me started on our conversations, if that was what they could be called.

Every. Single. One. Of. Them.

My dick started twitching again. Then throbbing. Just remembering her comebacks and insults, always infused with sass and sarcasm and passion, had actually forced my hand at having to follow and contribute to a conversation. *What the hell?* I didn't "converse" with people. I talked, people listened, orders were followed. End of story...

Until Taylor Mathews had started rewriting my narrative.

The woman would *not* be taken advantage of, that was for damn sure.

Not ever.

"Okaaaayyyyy, bachelors!" The DJ's shout hauled my attention back. "It's your time to shine now. Get on out to the dance floor so we can see who catches the garter from the grooms." He motioned toward Taylor with exaggerated enthusiasm. "That lucky fella gets to slide that thing up this beautiful belle's leg!"

Wait.

What?

In half a second, I forgot all about the ham's hokey phrasing, homing in on the implication of what he'd just said instead.

My hands. On her leg. Up her leg.

Far up her leg.

The crimson flush on the woman's face gave away how the concept had hit her brain like shock paddles. She'd definitely forgotten how this stupid ritual worked when making such a pro catch of the bouquet.

Well, isn't this going to be interesting?

The recognition instantly jolted my mind and body to autopilot—though it was my personal version of it, usually saved for the times a patient was split open for me on the operating table. The intensity was the universe's glaring reminder of how my knowledge and skill were the only things saving this person's life. Though the stakes were different now, they felt just as important—just as key to validating I had a purpose on this planet beyond mere existence.

Whatever.

Cosmic dribble aside, I was certain of one key thing. While this was a hell of a lot more complicated than brain surgery, I refused to accept failure.

Whatever.

That meant some key prep work. I hustled onto the dance floor, driven and determined, though kicking myself for not having my camera at the ready to capture the look on Taylor's face as I did. Our gazes locked for a few seconds, and I inserted half a smirk in place of stopping and admitting those blue depths nearly drowned me like the midnight wave they resembled, before she averted first. That didn't hide the little twitches at the corners of her mouth, making me guess at what incited them. Was she dealing with nervousness? Happiness? Excitement? Or covering up a case of sheer dread?

She gave me no time for further deciphering. The next moment, her emotions were schooled again behind a mask of gorgeous detachment. She stared with impressive blankness into the mob of guys collecting around me.

Fuck.

I had to catch that goddamned thing.

Which meant high-alert tactics were officially in order.

With a fast sweep, I wheeled in on the center of the crowd and indicated to them all that I needed a tight huddle. With arms hooked around the guys to either side of me, I leaned in and assumed instant quarterback mode. Thank fuck everyone seemed copacetic about the new pecking order.

"All right, fuckers, listen up. The blonde with the bouquet? She doesn't know it yet, but she's mine."

The guy to the right of me, flashing tatted muscles and a huge grin, nodded. "Prime choice, dude."

"Good. Because I'm going to catch that garter or will beat

down the fucker who does."

"We're behind you, buddy."

I thanked the guy with a solid smack to the back while circling my stare back around the group. "Everyone else good?"

While the rest of the group didn't do much but grunt and stare, I sensed the overall receipt of my message, especially when I straightened and clapped my hands, breaking the huddle.

Round One handled.

Now for Round Two—represented by the groom selected to perform the garter-tossing duties, a sublime and smiling Fletcher Ford. Or maybe his shit-eating grin was because his own hands had just been underneath his woman's filmy white dress, reaching for the treasure up her own thigh—"treasure" being open to interpretation. Were the woman's panties now tucked in his pocket along with the garter? Or maybe he and Newland had ordered their bride not to wear anything down there today. I snorted. I didn't know those two *that* well, but instinct told me they were the kind of kinky bastards to do just that.

My kind of kinky bastards.

The thought made it easier for me to motion Ford over. I wasn't comfortable with the buddy-buddy rah-rah act just for the hell of it, but right now I was a man on a mission, and he strode over as if sensing just that. At my motion to lean in closer, he complied.

It was time to talk like men.

"Dr. Stone."

"Mr. Ford."

"Now that we've gotten that out of the way..."

I barely gave his sarcastic chuckle a look. Humor often

seemed a waste of time to me, and this was definitely one of those occasions. "Down and dirty? I catch the garter, all right?"

"Uhhhh." Another snicker, this time more arrogant. "All right. I can't make promises..."

I rammed his shoulder with mine. Hard. More wasted time on sarcasm. "You can, and you will," I dictated from between locked teeth. "You owe me."

"That I do." He was sober now. Properly so. Probably had something to do with staring into the face of the doctor who'd made it possible for him to be alive for his wedding day at all.

"So this'll happen?" I pressed. His answering grin, which could've lit the whole San Diego skyline, came as proper confirmation.

I watched as he jogged back over to Drake, letting him in on the plan too, before swinging my attention back to the other side of the dance floor—and the adorable little blonde now comprehending how thoroughly her fate was sealed.

She gaped, eyes wide and mouth wider. In return I smirked, but just a little. She volleyed by tightening her features into a glare, realizing exactly what I was up to. I returned the shot by waggling my eyebrows, letting my lips broaden into an arrogant, evil smile.

That's right, spitfire.

I'm coming for you.

If I had my way, she'd be coming for *me* by the end of the night. At once, at least twenty scenarios bloomed in my mind. All the sinful, filthy things I could do to quench the blue flames raging in her gorgeous eyes.

Rope, tape, cuffs, zip ties...

"Three...two...one!"

At that, Fletcher tossed the garter over his shoulder, his

aim deadly accurate for my outstretched hand. Of course, it didn't hurt that the guys from the huddle barely gave their efforts a try. Victory was mine. Was it cheating? Maybe. Probably. But I cheated death nearly every damn day, making this kids' play—though I wasn't playing around at all while parting the suckers on the dance floor like Moses through the Red Sea, headed right toward the spot where little Miss Taylor Mathews still stood, jolting every nerve ending in my body all over again with her big blue gaze and her tiny trembling body.

You. Are. Mine.

The mandate was thunder in my senses, strengthened by the feel of the frilly thing in my clutch.

The words repeated as I crooked my finger. Just once. Beckoning her, as I'd been longing to do all damn day.

In return, she had a gesture involving a finger too.

"*Doooohhh!*" The derisive moan went up from every guy still milling behind me. As a few of them even applauded my spitfire's spirit, one side of my mouth kicked up again—in time to the twitch in my trousers and the rush in my attention.

Well...hell.

And...*what the hell?*

No woman was worth this much effort, was she? But when was the last time I'd bothered to find out? When a female had *forced* me to?

Could it be that this girl was just what I was needing? Someone to challenge the bastard in me—fuck, the bastard who *was* me—to stand up for themselves without it being part of a coy game or seduction.

A woman who jabbed her finger at me and meant every second of it.

A girl who gave me a reason to stay interested.

Really interested.

There's a novel idea.

A lot of the women in the crowd continued giggling at her impertinence. I turned their mirth to gasps as soon as I flared my nostrils, widened my stance, and stretched the garter in front of me, between both thumbs. The sole aspect I didn't change was my gaze upon Taylor. With a slight clench of my jaw, I focused it tighter. With intense concentration, I watched the muscles in her slim throat work down a hard gulp.

Come here, sassy girl.

Her body began moving forward. I wondered if she was even conscious of it. At the moment, I wasn't sure I cared. I was consumed by the sight of her. By the power *she* wielded over *me* with those unthinking little steps...

Behaving just as I'd thought.

Just as I'd hoped.

Just as I now knew.

Her body craved something very different from what her strong-willed mind told her it did. A something I longed to show her—and dear fuck, would have so much fun showing her—but not tonight. A tangled ball of yarn like her would take months to unravel, maybe longer—but I was in for the commitment. I was ready to sign aboard the *USS Taylor* for the cruise of a lifetime.

But first, I had to see if she was ready for a new commanding officer.

Drake came onto the dance floor with a folding chair, setting it down with a loud thud beside me. Everyone knew what this silly tradition entailed, and at that moment, the entire crowd shrank down to one knock-out blonde trembling about two feet away from me.

"Miss Mathews."

Her lips pursed. "Dr. Stone."

I twisted my own mouth, letting the sneer linger in my gaze. "Lovely to see you again."

"I wish I could say the same, clown."

"*Dr.* Clown, remember?" My reference to the first insult she'd ever flung my way had clearly lost its sparkle for her over the last six months, but I ignored her rebellious huff in favor of quirking a commanding eyebrow. "Please. Have a seat. Looks like I have something for you." I switched the garter to one index finger and then used the digit to twirl it around.

Deep inhalation. Nervous stammer. "L-Look. We really don't have to do all this. No one needs to see this, okay?"

"Oh, I think you're wrong." With smug confidence, I spun in a circle, addressing the crowd. "Who wants to see this thing through besides me? Quick show of hands. Raise 'em high." I did the same with my free hand.

Hands popped up across the room—with the last three ladies on the survey being the bride, Claire Stone, and a third woman, a blonde like Taylor, only carved from a much fiercer mold. Her name was Mary, or Margaret, or some shit like that. Wasn't important. Names rarely were to me—though their voting hands, raised one by one, definitely were.

Behind me, Taylor inhaled sharply as her besties sold her up the river. I pivoted back in time to watch visual darts fly from her eyes, sharp and blazing and so blue, only to be blasted back by a bark of laughter from Mary. *No.* Marjorie? *Shit.* Marisol?

Claire threw back her head, fighting and failing to hold back a snicker. "Margaux! *Stop.*"

Margaux. Yeah, that was it. The queen bee troublemaker even now, her face lighting up as she jabbed a teasing finger

Taylor's way. "You are so screwed, sister."

"We are *not* sisters after this." Taylor's voice rose to such an adorable octave, I couldn't control my smile. I think she even stamped a cute little high heel before redirecting her ire toward me. "This isn't funny!"

"You're right. It's not." I bowed low at the waist, sweeping my arm out before me. "Your throne, my queen."

Her glower darkened. "You've got to be kidding."

I tilted my head. "You tell me. Am I kidding?"

"*You* tell *me*," she volleyed. "Is a clown ever serious?"

I took a mental step back and clasped my hands behind me, assessing whether I was going to cut the little vixen some slack or just turn her over my knee here and now. First choice seemed most prudent, especially because my cock still rooted for the less stressful way to conclude tonight by being naked and horizontal with her.

On that note, I gently leaned over...filling her personal space as completely as she'd let me. All right, maybe a few inches more. Close enough to murmur for her ears alone, "Just play along, girl. You love your friends, despite that beautiful pout on your lips. Don't spoil the wedding fun for them."

Still, probably just to spite me, she pouted for another ten seconds. Finally, after a heavy huff, she plopped unceremoniously onto the chair.

"Not so hard, was it?"

"Just shut it and get on with it, clown."

The DJ started prattling again as I dropped to one knee before her. His banter provided the perfect camouflage for my comeback comment, again meant for her alone. "You'll apologize for that...eventually."

"Don't hold your breath." But her fast, breathless stutter

betrayed the true effect of my words on her. I liked hearing it. A lot.

"We'll see." I smiled while wrapping my fingers around her ankle. "We'll see."

I lifted her leg from perpendicular to parallel to the ground and rested her shapely calf on my knee as if preparing to fit her with the most precious shoe. Since the DJ was still narrating every inch of my movements, I could turn the moment into something more intimate for us just by keeping my voice low. And reverent. And aroused. *Fuck, yeah. That too.*

"You are stunning, Taylor Mathews. Christ...your skin." I couldn't lift my eyes from the contrast of my large, long fingers on her mesmerizing, opaque skin. "Is every inch of you so pale and fragile...and breathtaking?"

Her leg trembled. She tried to wrench away. I held her ankle in a vise grip.

"Stop. Seriously, Stone, before I remove *your* stones in front of this entire crowd."

I didn't relent an inch. Her words were harsh, but her voice was whispered and husky. A rose-colored flush moved across her cheeks.

I dug my fingers deeper into her ankle. Tugged without mercy, forcing her light frame to the edge of the chair. I caught her off-guard, forcing her to grip the sides of the seat to stop from sliding off completely.

"*Damn it*, Mac. I'm not joking. Just put the thing on and let me go."

I raised my head. "I'm not joking either, Miss Mathews. You are perfection." I didn't care who heard me in the crowd but continued, keeping my voice low so she alone could hear me— and know what she did to me. How the simple act of touching her ankle made the veins in my cock pop and the restraint in my system balance on razor wire. *Jesus God*, I wanted her.

With one study of her trembling face, I knew she wanted me too.

We both swallowed. The air thickened and crackled around us, sizzling with our mounting sexual attraction.

"Okay, you two. Ready? Remember, tradition says the new family will have one year of good luck for every inch you move that garter above her knee. Don't let your friends down, Mac Stone!"

Technically, Fletcher and Drake weren't my friends. And that ham of a DJ was really starting to grate on my nerves. But despite it all, he was giving me the excuse to touch this woman far more intimately than I might get away with at this point in our relationship.

And yeah, I'd just called it a relationship. And yeah, I believed it, despite every flame of every bonfire burning in both her incredible eyes.

I slipped the elastic band over her sexy silver T-strap shoe, moving my grip around her heel to keep my prize in place. I used my other hand to slide the garter up her calf, running my fingers against her skin every fucking chance I could.

Up, up, up, over her knee now. I had to fight a hundred impulses to lean forward and lightly brush my lips to that ever-so-sensitive crease. Her thighs were slim, with just a slight variance from her lower leg. As I pushed my fingers at her hem, my imagination took over in terrifying force. What would it be like to feel those thighs on either side of my face? To shove them apart as I licked my way up to the pink prize at their center? To feel them tremble for me as I stabbed my tongue into her heat over and over and over again?

I shifted my position. My dick was swollen against my fly now, making me wonder how I'd get up without the whole crowd knowing my train of thought. The second I gazed back up at Taylor, even that didn't matter. Her eyes were heavy, her breathing more of a rhythmic pant. She was as stirred by my touch as I was by her *existence.*

I needed this woman.

To have her. Conquer her. Revel in her beneath me, giving me more of those sweet fast breaths as her pussy clamped around me. Then to blaze into triumph as she surrendered an orgasm to me. Then another. And another...

I gulped hard, sliding the garter higher. *Higher.* I was beneath her hem now, stroking her skin lightly as her thighs tensed and fought me. Was it because her pussy was already wet for me?

"That's one year. Maybe two. Come on now. You can do better than that!"

I'm going to cut that DJ with a very blunt scalpel.

Thankfully, the woman before me dissolved all thought of any stabbing instrument but the one between my thighs. I recommitted to the task of seduction by garter, pushing the lace up a little farther.

"You heard the man, Miss Mathews." I scraped my thumbnail up the inside of her calf. "How far are you willing to go?"

"With you, clown?" She snorted. "That's the end of the line, dude."

With another huff, she tried to yank her leg back, but that was contingent on me relenting my grip. No damn way. "Really? You're going to let your friends down that way? I didn't figure you for the type to chicken out on anything." I maintained the light tone—along with the merciless grip. "I have to say I'm a little disappointed."

Her face twisted, which should have daggered me with guilt but didn't. This was dirty pool, questioning her loyalty to her friends—but was it? I had no bosom-buddy reference of my own upon which to base the supposition, but could see, along with everyone else, that these women loved one another deeply, simply from their sisterly ribbing.

Besides, the effort earned me a pretty adorable glare down a sexy-as-fuck elfin nose—right before a line spat in a Southern accent so sassy it was an instant aphrodisiac.

"Do you really think I just fell off the turnip truck, mister?"

I felt my grin spreading again. I'd smiled more in the last five minutes than in the last five years. This creature was getting to me on every level. The realization should've been terrifying, but I was having too much fun. "Not at all, spitfire. Did you know research shows it takes great intelligence to have sharp wit?"

"Do *you* know flattery usually gets a guy nowhere?"

"Do you always have a habit of changing the subject when someone makes you uncomfortable?"

"You don't make me uncomfortable."

"Then have dinner with me."

"No."

"Then come back to my hotel with me."

The words tumbled out before I could stop them. I wasn't sorry. Probably the polar opposite. *Come home with me, Taylor Mathews. Please. Let me peel that sexy dress off you, then get tangled in all my sheets with you, and then bury myself inside you...*

"Are you *fucking* serious right now?"

Her accusation was so unexpected, I was caught completely off-guard. My grip slackened, giving her the freedom to yank her ankle back, lurch to her feet, and then stomp off the dance floor without a backward glance at the clown on his knees.

Yeah, she stomped. Literally.

And it was exciting as hell.

I let my head fall forward, chuckling to myself.

Yeah, chuckling. Literally.

The whole situation was so absurd. So unexpected. Just like her. She was a revelation every time my orbit collided with hers, a delicate package concealing such a fierce temperament. She was adorable and unexplainable, gorgeous and ferocious, a rocket engine powering a cute convertible chassis...

And she wielded a complete, constricting grip over my entire thrumming body.

What the living hell was I going to do about her?

The demand seized my breath as she disappeared into the crowd, her three girlfriends following her beeline for what I presumed to be the ladies' room. But just when I assumed that'd be all I saw of them for a while, Margaux notched a glance back over her shoulder—and signaled a determined thumbs-up.

So maybe I liked Margaux.

The laughter around me died as people returned to their cake and conversation.

With a determined push, I straightened to my full six feet, grabbed the folding chair, and carried it off the dance floor. Drake Newland was waiting to take the chair and stow it against the wall. I grunted a fast thanks and was ready to leave our exchange at that, but he pulled me back over by giving me a hearty pat on the back. "Worthy effort, Doc."

I just grunted again. This wasn't going to become *Kumbaya* hour.

"Hey...the ones you have to work hardest for are the ones worth it by far."

"Oh, fuck me." Thank God someone materialized to say it besides me. That person was Fletcher Ford, looking infinitely better than the car accident victim on my surgical table a few months ago, especially when it came to his sarcastic grin. "You sound like a cross between Yoda and Dr. Phil," he razzed Drake.

The big guy just shrugged. "Guess that's what love does to a guy."

"Truth, my brother."

"Speaking of love..."

"Was just thinking the same thing."

"Let's go find her."

"Later, Doc."

"Later." I muttered it to my feet, kicking them at the manicured lawn in the growing twilight, debating whether to set up base camp outside the ladies' room or save the shreds of my dignity and get the fuck out of here. Plan B was getting a damn good lead, and I was on the brink of decisive follow-through when my tall, dark, enigma-of-enigmas cousin approached.

Joy of fucking joys.

"Mac."

"Killian."

"Good to see you." The man's words were appropriate, but his tone had no life or sincerity, betraying how he really felt.

How we *both* did.

"Wish I could say the same." *Asshole.* I refrained from my usual sequitur out of respect for the occasion, not him. Sugar coating anything in life, especially sentiments for my cousin, was highly overrated.

"So. You know any good surgeons?"

I side-eyed him. "Where you going with this?" *Asshole.*

"Well, one day you'll have to have that chip on your shoulder surgically removed. It's been there a long time, so you'll need professional help."

"Fuck off."

"Suit yourself. But you'll need to look into that if you want to get anywhere with Taylor."

"What does *our* history have to do with Miss Mathews?" I volleyed back, annoyed.

"Ouch. 'Miss Mathews'? She's iced you out worse than I thought." His onyx eyes glinted, sharpening the blade of the tease.

"Now you can really fuck off. It's called respect, not that you'd know anything about that."

Killian sipped his Scotch and roamed a long look around the patio. But beneath the lazing panther façade, he was pure, piercing vigilance. "What I *do* know is that Taylor is one of my wife's dearest friends." He motioned toward the door the women had disappeared behind. "Those four have been through a lot of hell together. She's like family to us, Mac. I won't stand by and watch you hurt her."

I growled, a second away from tossing that expensive alcohol into his smug face. "What the hell are you going on about? You think you know everything about everyone? I've met her once, maybe twice before—so back the fuck off, Papa Bear."

A laugh chuffed off his lips. A goddamned *laugh*. "Ohhhh, shit."

"What?" If words had blades, I would have guillotined him.

"Dude. Really?"

"*What?*"

"None of us is blind or dead, so rest assured, everyone *here* knows exactly what went down between you two. Further, I wouldn't be surprised if half the fucking city felt your chemistry, so you need to just cut the shit, okay?" He sliced a hand through the air when my mouth opened, not that I had any words ready to go. "I'm just giving you fair warning. There are a lot of people here tonight who would be more than miffed if she were hurt or let down."

"Fine, fine. Consider me warned. *Dude.*"

My growl made him step back, both hands up, though the Scotch was still upright. Only Kil could pull off the move so smoothly, notching my irritation higher as he kept going, his condescending grin in complete opposition to his surrendering move. I was glad when he turned his back so I could finally flip him off.

A few seconds later, his wife emerged from the bathroom and they smooched so hard I wondered where the sap spigot was hidden. I didn't spend a lot of time on the guessing, since I was more preoccupied with waiting on Taylor's reentry—but after a few minutes of nothing, I headed to the bar instead.

While nursing the beer, I realized why I still hung out, waiting for her like some fucking puppy. I wanted a chance to apologize. Maybe I'd been a little...forward. The archaic expression sounded better than "pushy asshole," so I went with it. But went where? After a while, it was clear I'd have a better chance of going home alone and watching a rerun of *Keeping Up with the Kardashians* than getting face-to-face with Taylor Mathews again.

It was time to regroup.

Because, damn it, I refused to accept this as the end.

CHAPTER TWO

Taylor

"*Tay.* Come *on.* Just stop lying to yourself—and us, while you're at it."

"Truth."

"Honey, what's the big deal? Maclain Stone is smokin' hot—and the heat between you two could strip wallpaper."

"Truth. Again."

I didn't hold back on the bewilderment of my stare, which I swung between the two girlfriends refusing to leave me alone in the lounge. The confusion wasn't because they were still here but because words that belonged to the other were coming out of their mouths. Talia, our posse's usual nodder and conservative one-worder, was now the naughty talker hitching up her wedding dress and plopping down on the sofa beside me. Margaux, usual queen of every raunchy word in the dictionary, was damn near playing Madonna and child in the chair opposite us, rocking her beautiful baby, who gazed up at her with intense eyes that matched her daddy's.

I huffed and folded my arms. "We're not going there, girlfriends. Just let me chill and regroup, okay?"

"But why?" Talia smoothed a hand down the ethereal white layers of her skirt, though the daring neckline of her couture dress was more inspiration for words right now. "You know catching the bouquet doesn't *really* mean you have to get married next."

"Yes, sweetie." I patted her hand. "I'm very aware of that. Nice connection on the pass, though."

"Don't try to change the subject."

"Watch it," Margaux admonished. "She *is* good at that."

"Shut up," I mumbled at her.

"*You* shut up," she volleyed and then winked.

Talia huffed and prompted, "The subject? Mac Stone? *Remember?*"

I fell into silence. Talia wasn't wide-eyed and naïve anymore, but that didn't mean I could share everything with her, notably the reasons I couldn't—*wouldn't*—touch Dr. Maclain Stone with a ten-foot pole. That man smelled more and more like danger every time I got near him.

And, fuck me sideways, did danger smell good.

Yes, but so did food poisoning before it came back up the wrong way—and that man was the last thing I could even think about getting involved with.

Because too much of me *would* get involved.

To the tune of ending up just like Janet, my mother.

Wasn't going to happen. Not now. Not ever.

I'd learned the most important lessons early. Probably earlier than most—I think I was around seven—but I could look back and be grateful for that now. From that first moment of understanding, recognizing why Janet was sobbing in her room after another Daddy candidate had dumped her clingy ass, I swore I'd never be so damn desperate for the "love" of a man.

From that point on, every time my mom fell hard for Mr. Right, I saw the bastard for who he really was—Mr. Right *Now*.

But Mama would persist, crooning to me about how different he was and how he'd take care of us for all time. Our lives were about to be transformed, she'd say. Things were going to be good this time, she'd also say.

But all that had ever changed was my respect for her.

How it had diminished, each and every time.

By the time I was eleven, I couldn't stand looking at the only parent I ever knew.

Once I'd hit my teens, she'd turned to alcohol. I got my driver's license just as hers was suspended because of her third DUI. The laws, especially in the South, were different then. Mama liked a lot of other lenient things about where we lived too. One of my nightly chores became dropping her off and picking her up at the Watering Hole. Or the Wet Spot. Or O'Hooligan's. The name of the place never mattered, and neither did her dutiful efforts at snagging us a new man who'd "change everything."

"Yo, baby. Are you even listening to me?" Margaux was on her feet again, rocking her sleepy infant.

"Frankly?" I retorted. "No, I'm not. But I might if you let me hold her."

"Fine. I have to pee anyway. You are *not* getting out of this conversation. Okay, sweet baby, go to Auntie Taylor."

She carefully placed the swaddled pink bundle in my outstretched arms. Instantly, I felt better. Peaceful. It was impossible to be angry when holding a newborn. I leaned down and inhaled. Baby powder and sleep. Pure bliss—especially because I'd be able to just return her in a few minutes.

No strings. No attachments. No connections that would "change my life."

Not that I'd shared any of the bullshit about my mom

with any of my girlfriends, nor did I ever plan to. At the moment and on the surface, that justified Margaux's lecture, as she continued from within the stall on the other side of the bathroom.

Margaux's speech started back up from behind the partial door that provided privacy to the toilet. "Look, Tay. Every one of us has made the same stupid mistake you're attempting now, so what makes you think we're going to sit back and let you do the same thing?"

"Truth!" Talia called out. The world order should have felt more balanced but didn't.

"Right?" Margaux returned. "Dear God, can't *someone* please learn from our errors?"

"You guys are crazy." I leaned over, kissing the flawless little tip of the infant's nose. "Isn't that right, sweetie? Your mommy and Auntie Talia are cah-ray-zee."

"Pssst." Talia leaned over, taking on a scandalized whisper. "She already knows that." She leaned in, bussing the baby's forehead. "What she *doesn't* know is how Auntie *Taylor* refuses to listen to her bestest, closest friends."

"Oh, my God," I muttered. "I have no idea what you're talking about."

"*Hey.*" The toilet flushed. "Cut it with playing dumb with us, Taylor. It really doesn't suit you." Margaux barreled out of the stall, still tugging at the hem of her fierce cocktail dress. It had to be a crime to have a killer figure so soon after giving birth, but Margaux was unrepentant. "We both know you too well for that bullshit, and you know it."

"*Language,*" Talia rebuked.

Margaux rolled her eyes at us via the mirror while washing her hands. "You getting kickbacks from Claire on the swear jar now, Mrs. Thing?"

"Strictly my civic duty." Talia flashed a sweet smile.

Margaux passed up snapping at her again to eye me instead, nodding via the mirror once more. "Sweetie, just listen to me. You know we all love you, and we just want you to be happy..."

"And here it comes," I groaned.

"But for that to happen, you have to stop running from the obvious. And that guy out there? He's the big fat obvious. What harm would it be to just go out with him? Everyone needs a good fuck-buddy up the street, right?"

"*Language*," Talia rebuked again. "And an editorial correction."

Margaux frowned. "About what?"

"He lives in Chicago, remember?"

"Shit." Margaux shook her head, tousling her long blond waves. "I didn't." A shrug and then a pouty pop of her crimson lips. "Okay, so all of this is now a moot point. Unless you think he'd be open for a good clear-the-cobwebs fuckfest?"

"*Language!*" The new censure belonged to Claire, who entered the lounge area just as Margaux came in from the sinks. My stunning redhead of a boss swept kisses to her niece's silky cheeks before propping both hands on her hips and glaring at Margaux. "You said you'd try to clean it up for the girls. You're not even trying."

Margaux indulged her third eye roll in just as many minutes. "Bear, take a chill. They're, like, two fucking months old. Unless one of them is the next Mozart in the making, I think we're good for a little bit longer."

"And what if one of them is?" Claire rebutted. "They're like sponges right now."

"Did your ten million books say that?"

"And if they did?" Claire topped out at around my height but could still straighten into an imposing silhouette in Mama Bear mode. "They're seeing and hearing and absorbing absolutely everything. At this rate, Iris's first word is going to be fuck!"

"Oh." I brightened. "You've finally decided on a name?" Though they could have been talking shower mildew removal and I would've run with it. As long as the subject wasn't me anymore...

"Yep." Margaux beamed. "Iris Diana Pearson."

"Beautiful."

"It satisfies my need for unique, though Michael's happy too because his mom will be honored."

"Took you long enough," Talia inserted.

"Greatness can't be rushed, but the timing *is* a good thing too." Margaux looked my way. "The christening is only two weeks away. You're still on board for godmother, right?"

"Fuck, yeah, I am."

"*Language!*"

As Talia took care of the castigation and Claire rushed forward to cup Iris's ears, Margaux pushed out a weary sigh. "You need a sedative, sister. As usual." Sensing her mama near, little Iris started fussing. Margaux carefully took her from my arms while still addressing Claire. "So what's the scoop from Kil about Dr. Feelgood?"

"Ohhhhh noooo." I dropped my head into my now empty hands.

"You're right," Margaux muttered. "That was bad. So we'll come up with a better one, since he might be sticking around for a while."

"No." I snapped my head back up. "He is *not*."

"Just warm up to it, sweetie." She reached to pat my arm, enjoying every second of the not-so-subtle taunt. "It's going to happen. I just know these kinds of things."

Claire took a seat, nodding sagely. "Sorry, Tay, but she really does."

"Just give in and accept it now," Talia piped in next. "It'll be easier."

"Like you two did?" I cocked my head, pinging a disbelieving glance between them.

"Well, it was different for me," Claire explained, motioning at Margaux. "We were in a very different place when Killian and I first fell in love."

"Understatement of the century," Margaux agreed in a terse mutter.

"And things were different for me too," Talia offered. "Two guys, one girl, orthodox family, multiple cities..."

"Only a *few* complications." Margaux chuckled.

"But in the end, you were still right," Talia replied.

"That she was," Claire concurred.

"That I was." Margaux preened.

"Riiiiigggggghhhhht." I scuffed at the tile floor with my pointed silver shoe. "Damn it. You all suck. Bunch of traitors." But looking at my foot reminded me of how Mac's fingers felt around it. And the heat he spiraled through my body. And the blood he sent straight to my pussy. And the way he made me flush, exactly as I did again now...

"But you're thinking about him again—as we speak." Margaux spoke with soft, steady certainty. "Aren't you?"

"No."

"Bullshit."

"You totally are," Talia chimed in. "Look at your face!

You're remembering how he touched you out there."

"Mmmm 'kay, *that* was hot." Claire fanned herself.

"Stop!" My voice, cranked by the red alert on my senses, erupted much louder than I intended, startling poor Iris. "Shit. I mean, damn. So sorry I scared her. I'm just so upside down about this, and you bullies aren't helping."

Margaux accepted my apologetic grimace with a wry smile, which widened as the other two giggled. I tried to join in, but my rioting nerves made the feat impossible. I knew the three of them meant well, but I couldn't take any more of their "good intentions."

I started for the door. None of them tried to stop me. But just as I was about to yank it open and go, Claire cleared her throat and announced, "So...I asked Killian a bit more about Mac."

Wench.

I diverted my path, just a little, to "check my makeup" in the vanity mirror near the door. In the reflection, I had a good view of the whole lounge area, including the knowing tug of Claire's teeth on her bottom lip. She saw right through my stall tactic but was kind enough not to call me on it, instead going on as if Margaux and Talia were just as puzzled as me about the mysterious but obvious feud between Mac and Killian. Come to think of it, maybe they were. Margaux was Killian's sister, and Talia had just married Fletcher, a former patient of Mac's. A tangled web, and none of us were quite certain how it was all woven yet.

"What did he say?" Margaux helped Iris latch on for a nighttime snack. After everything was settled, she covered the baby's head for some privacy, likely hoping the infant would also drift off to sleep.

Claire seemed grateful for the pause, her expression giving away a search through mental notes. "Well, it all seems ridiculous," she finally began again. "But most family feuds do, right?"

"Unless your last name is Perizkova," Talia mumbled loud enough to be heard.

Claire spread an indulgent smile, rubbing Talia's back as she continued talking. "Best as I can gather from Kil, the real problem seems to be Mac's mother."

"Oh, great." Margaux grunted. "A mama's boy? I knew that shit was too good to be real."

"That's not it," Claire returned. "Not exactly."

"What does that mean?" Talia echoed the question in my own head. "Not exactly?"

"Apparently, Constance Stone is a real piece of work. Like all batshit crazies, she's got a laundry list of issues but has always been convinced everyone else is the problem."

"Mommy Dearest, is that you?"

Everyone, including me, laughed at Margaux's joke, despite the chilling seriousness behind it. Andrea Asher, Margaux's adoptive mother, was still a criminal at large and would likely plead insanity when the Feds caught up with her.

"So how does she affect the relationship between Killian and Mac?" So much for remaining uninterested in the conversation, though I was thankful once more when Claire scooted over and patted the space next to her on the love seat, as if we were settling in for a PassionFlix binge instead of dredging Stone family baggage. It certainly was never a dull day when the Stones were in town.

"Constance and Willa, the woman Killian's called mother most of his life, are sisters."

"But Willa Stone isn't the woman who gave birth to him, right?" I asked, just to make sure I remembered the story, which had become the stuff of a major business world scandal a couple of years ago.

"Right," Claire concurred. "And that's where most of the bad blood comes from."

Talia nodded, seeming to be connecting the dots. "Constance has been sitting in the same camp as Trey Stone—"

"May he rot in hell," Margaux inserted with saccharine in her smile and murder in her deep-green eyes.

"Where he'll still be bitterly jealous about Killian being given the opportunities due to Josiah Stone's blood relatives."

Claire sighed deeply. "Never mind the fact that Kil has run Stone Global better than anyone in the family, Josiah included, *and* that Mac's talents were clearly destined for the operating room, not the boardroom."

I released a thoughtful frown. "So deep underneath all this, the beef isn't really Mac's? It's his mother's?"

Claire shrugged. "It certainly sounds that way, from what Killian told me. But you know how it goes. Years of programming by a parent, especially if it's pounded in during childhood, and the child becomes a minion of the parent's point of view. I'm not sure what Mac would really say or do if given the chance to act on his own accord, but he's a loyal son. And right now, she still resents Killian, so *he* resents Killian."

"Logical." Talia shook her head. "More than a little codependent and messy as hell but also really, sickeningly, logical."

"Can we vow, here and now, to not be fucked-up parents?" Margaux stroked her daughter's fuzzy head while looking up at Claire.

"Couldn't agree more," her friend responded. "The world is a pretty tough place all on its own. Why add so many more problems?" They locked pinkies to seal the deal—so much better than a handshake and twice as binding. Their maternal moment gave me a few seconds to ponder everything that had been said—and then finally voice the curiosity that resulted from it.

"I'm still thinking back to the way they treated each other in the hospital in Chicago. And it seems like there must be more to it." I finished in a mumble, "Or maybe it's just me."

Or maybe it was how Dr. Maclain Stone affected me.

No doubt about it...the man did crazy things to my circuit boards. The mental *and* physical ones.

"Hmmm." Claire shook her head, causing her copper chin-length bob to fall artfully around her face. "Killian's pretty straight with me, especially since we've had Regan. After we lost the first pregnancy, something changed between us. I didn't think we could be closer than we were, but after that..." She drifted off for a second, her expression traveling to just as misty a place. "Yeah. Something changed for us. There's nothing between us now. Like this is him, and this is me." She held her hands up, palm to palm, pressed together as if to send up a thankful prayer. Her lips quivered as she looked at their clasp, without a sliver of light passing between them.

Talia and Margaux let out a tandem sigh. What Claire described—hands joined, souls melded, connection so deep not even light could get through—was what they'd all found with their men, a bond every girl dreamed of...

Except me.

Not a single damn sigh from *this* side of the couch. Instead, I went ahead and voiced my true inclination, clearing my throat with a dramatic gagging sound.

Talia burst into laughter.

Claire rolled her eyes.

Margaux smiled through a knowing chuckle before murmuring, "Ohhh, little grasshopper, I was once like you too—but my day came. Fate scooped me up, balled my heart into a neat little wad, and then sent it to Michael Pearson with a pretty first class stamp. Your day is coming too. Mark my words." She paused a few seconds, setting up for maximum dramatic effect. "Or should I say, Mac my words."

Claire, Talia, and I were in agreement about reactions this time. Groans erupted all around, until I glared over at the preening mama and her "gotcha" smile.

"Mary Stone, you may have nicely recovered your cute little figure, but your pun game is still waaaaay off."

"And throwing the spotlight back on me won't get you off so easily now, bitch."

"*Language,*" Claire and Talia snapped.

She *pffft*ed them and then volleyed at me, "Oh, and if I wasn't holding this sweet angel, I'd make you pay for using that name. You know that, right?" Her finish was classic, fake-sweet Margaux—which I flung back with perfect precision, beaming all my pearly whites at her.

"Let's just say I picked my moment, darling."

"Bitch," she grumbled.

"Margaux!" Claire unleashed a full glare at her sister-in-law, though it wasn't the full distraction I'd hoped for. "Not so fast, sugar." She yanked me back down to the couch before my ass cleared two inches of an escape. "We're not done with you yet."

I notched up a brow. "Excuse the hell out of me?"

"That's not everything I've got to say about Dr. Clown."

I openly gawked. "You mean there's more?"

Margaux snickered. "Dr. *Clown*?"

"It's her affectionate nickname for Maclain Stone," Talia explained.

I sneered. "Trust me, that's not affection you're vibing on, girl."

"And Edwin in the SGC mailroom doesn't have a creepazoid thing for you, either," the bride drawled.

"Edwin?" Margaux gaped. "The one with the monkey hands and the serial killer eyes? *He* likes Tay?"

"Oh, my God." I huddled as close to the arm of the love seat as I could. "This is ridiculous."

"Oh, hell, no," Margaux protested. "This is getting *good*."

"Don't you all have husbands who need attention? And why haven't they broken down the door, looking for you?" I whipped a pointed look over my shoulder toward said door. "Especially the marine."

"*Former* marine," Talia clarified. "Thank you very much."

"Well, once a marine, always a marine, right? My guess is he has no trouble ordering you around, Miss Perizkova."

"Aannnnd score one for the mistress of deflection."

Leave it to Margaux to call me out on my shit again—and to Claire to flush all of it away just as efficiently. "Okay, back to business," she instructed, making the three of us giggle as only girlfriends could, though her demeanor didn't relax by an iota. With our gazes meeting over the new handclasp she insisted on initiating, she stated, "You need to be *careful* here, Taylor, okay?"

For a moment, I was genuinely confused as to what she was talking about. For the next moment, I battled to pretend that didn't bother me. "Careful...about what?" Okay, maybe I pretended for a little longer.

"About that man, honey. Mac Stone. Dr. Clown. Dr. McHunk. *Whatever.* Kil told me, in no uncertain terms, that the guy might be brilliant at fixing brains but doesn't know the first thing about hearts and souls. He has the total reputation around Chicago."

"Total reputation...how?" *Yeah, still pretending.*

"He's basically a dickhead. Treats women like they should be grateful he gives them a minute of his time and then gives them just about that before he's out, off and done." She wrapped her grip tighter. "You know the type I'm talking about, yes?"

"They're called *douchebags*, Bear. You can say it," Margaux teased.

"I don't have to." She assessed me carefully, tilting her gaze. "You *do* get it, Taylor? Right?"

No. I wasn't sure I did. I mean, yes, I'd heard her loud and clear and even believed every word of her testament about Mac's lothario ways back in Chicago—but when he and I stepped into the same atmosphere together, that wasn't the guy who greeted me. And smiled at me. And challenged me. And ignited me. And stared at me like I hung the damn moon. And touched me like I was a diamond resting on silk...

And how many other idiot females have recited the same drivel to themselves about the man?

The same lunacy Janet used to tell me about every horny asshole she'd ever brought home?

"Yeah." I said it to Claire from the middle of the ice bath she'd just dunked me in. "Thanks." And gripped her tighter in return to tell her how much I meant it.

"And on *that* note..." Margaux rose carefully, holding

Iris tight so the baby wouldn't wake. "I love all of you, but this mama is beat. I need to find Michael and get on the road. Andre is visiting his family for the entire month, and driving in this town sucks an entire bag of dicks."

"And now that." Claire slapped her hand to her forehead. "Right in her precious ear!"

"She's sleeping, Bear. What the fuck is she going to 'absorb' in her *sleep*?"

"Why don't you just play NWA on the drive home, then?"

"Nah. Thought I'd throw on some Bruno and have my man do me reverse cowgirl while I did all the steering—if you know what I mean."

Even Claire couldn't resist joining us in the giggles from that one, and we laughed all the way out of the bathroom. Each of the girls quickly found their spouses, leaving me to realize I didn't know what to do with myself anymore. Absently, I started picking up empty cake plates. I'd never been good at being idle, and a cursory look around didn't turn up any catering staff, so I got busy.

I had a stack of at least ten plates when Mac approached. By approached, I mean that we saw each other across the room before he pushed away from the column that had nothing on him in the rock-hard, tall, and imposing category and charted himself on a direct, determined path across the large room to me. But once he was there, about three feet away, he paused and held position, almost as if racking his brain for the proper password to enter my clubhouse.

"Hey." As passwords went, it was weak. He made up for it with the intensity of his eyes. They were green but not overpoweringly so, like the watchful gaze of a great beast of prey. Their allure came from the strength behind them, not from surface glamor or dazzle. They were the kind of eyes inviting weeks, months, maybe years of study, only to lead an onlooker right back to where they started—with his honest exposure.

And that was more than enough of that.

"Hey," I replied, keeping it as neutral as possible—not easy when his mere presence made the air feel more special, every moment that much more significant.

No. No, damn it.

"Need some help?"

"I can manage. Thanks, though."

Eight words we'd spoken. *Eight.* I'd counted as if they all mattered. As if I wouldn't remember every moment of them for hours—or the sweep of motion after that, when he reached for my shoulder as I turned to head back to the kitchen.

"Take your paw off me, clown." My voice sounded acidic, even to me. Since my other choice was a simpering sigh, the acid treatment it was.

"Stop this."

"Stop *what?*"

"Don't be like that."

"Like *that?*" I spun back around, plates clanking in my hands. "Like what, exactly? Because it's not like I know you or even like *you.*" I licked my lips if only to regain some composure but quickly recognized my mistake as soon as he homed that possessive stare right in on my mouth. "You—you don't know me from Eve, okay, so don't act as though there's some easy rapport between us because you just had your hand up my skirt."

He stepped—stumbled?—back a bit, hands held up as if I'd just pulled a gun. "Christ, girl. Relax a little." The edges of his mouth quirked, but that was as far as he got with the smile. I got the impression he wasn't comfortable with the whole concept in general, which was probably why he began picking up dishes too, despite what I'd just said. "Are you always this... uuuhhhh...intense?"

"Are you always this dense?" I tilted my head, openly baiting for an answer.

"I'm many things, Miss Mathews, but dense isn't one of them." Again with the smiling-not-smiling thing. "My IQ makes most humans cower."

A laugh spilled out before I could help it. "That so?"

"Oh, I can assure you." He nodded. "It's so."

"Wow." Once again, he left me speechless.

"That's a strange response."

"To your IQ or your douchery?"

"Douchery. Is that a word?" He had the balls to actually chuckle on top of that one.

"It is now." I paused, trying to not let my anger get the best of me but failing. "Tell you what, Dr. Stone. You finish up here while I go cower in the corner with the other humans."

In a rush that was nearly clumsy, I piled every one of my gathered plates into his arms, the china discs sliding this way and that, making a crumb-and-icing mess all over his white dress shirt. During my stomp back inside, I was tempted to look back but staved off the urge. I made my intent all about finding my purse and makeup bag before I could contemplate punching him in his smug face. Talia and the guys would understand why I'd bailed without saying goodbye.

Right now, Maclain Stone needed to be the mountain range in my mental rearview—a spectacular memory I'd look back on with a sigh, wishing I'd had the right equipment to climb while I was visiting, despite knowing that adventure would've been the painful death of me.

Instead, in the name of self-preservation, I'd driven on—knowing in my deepest soul that I'd thank myself for it.

Eventually.

Hopefully.

CHAPTER THREE

Mac

"We should get going, Fairy. Our sweet baby girl will be missing her mama."

"With the way you've been rocking her to sleep every night, Mr. Stone, I think she'll be missing her daddy more."

I eavesdropped on my cousin and his wife from the other side of the hedge separating the outdoor bar and the main wedding reception area. While nursing an imported beer, I'd just found the best reception entertainment of the day—the taming of the wild Killian by his fearless woman and a round of sickening sweet nothings. The whole ritual would have made me want to lose my lunch, if I'd eaten any. Stalking Taylor had taken up too much of the day to bother with food.

So how sickening does that make me?

Even the warm beer didn't hold much appeal anymore. I pushed it away, preparing to blow this taco stand for good and return to the hotel, when Claire asked Kil a question that plunked my ass solidly back on the bar stool.

"Why do you really think Mac isn't married?"

I stole a quick look through the break in the bushes in time to witness her mooning stare at Kil, all big brown eyes and open adoration. Those two factors I could write off with a grunt—but the third aspect of her expression, genuine concern, turned the beer to acid in my stomach. My name wasn't Oliver Twist, and I sure as fuck didn't need any porridge from Killian Stone or his wife—a sentiment Kil himself conveyed, leaning his tall frame back in his chair, arrogant as all fuck.

"You've met him, right?" He finished the growl by crossing an ankle over the other.

Claire smacked him on the arm. Silently, I urged her to make the blow harder. *Dickhead.*

"Come on," she chided. "Seriously, baby. He's a smart, good-looking guy. And he must make good money."

"Hey." He sat forward again, giving her a dominant look of warning. "You trying to make me jealous now?"

"You know my sun rises and sets with you, mister." Her purr eased him a little. "But I was just thinking about Taylor."

"Why?"

"Well, they clearly have spark together, and—"

"No."

"*Killian.*"

"*Claire.*"

"She needs happiness too."

"And he's not the one to give it to her." My cousin would make his word the final one, even if he claimed the sky was green. "Trust me, Fairy. He's *not* the guy for her."

"Why?" she persisted, making me like her a little more despite how she'd been easy on the asshole with the shoulder punch. "*Why* are you so sure of that? You were there too. You felt the chemistry along with the rest of us. They're hot together, baby. Crazy hot."

Kil rubbed his stubbled chin in thought. "Yeah, I was there," he capitulated. "But sometimes, things require more than heat."

"That's not what you said when *we* first met."

"You mean when my soul ordered me to never let you go?"

She mooned again, kissing the tips of his fingers. "Why doubt others can have our happiness?"

He tugged her hand up, kissing her knuckles in return. "Fairy, no man in the fucking galaxy can be as happy as you've made me."

I clenched my own jaw. It was that or really give in to a full vomit. Christ, he was whipped.

And I was jealous as fuck.

"I don't know," he finally went on, responding to his wife's open skepticism. "It's just..."

"What?"

"Taylor's so—fuck—tender? Fragile? You can't say you don't see it, babe. She doesn't parade that crap for the rest of the world, and that's her business, but the girl has seen shit. There's cracks there, lots of them, and Mac is—well—Mac. He'd destroy her." He scrubbed his jaw again. "It'd take a ball buster like my sister to handle a guy like Mac."

Claire snorted. "You've met Taylor, right? Taylor *Mathews,* the one we all like calling firecracker?"

"Because you're all respectful of her act too and let her keep the shields up." His gaze narrowed, as if surprised he had to point out the obvious. "You do all know that's all an act, right?"

"I know I've spent a lot more time with her than you."

With perfect diplomacy, Kil chuckled. "Suit yourself. But take it from someone who used to live behind a lot of shields. I know them when I see them."

"So...Mac's never been serious about anyone?"

Killian erupted in a sharp laugh. I almost joined him. His

woman was like a dog with a bone. I definitely liked her. "Only once...I think," he replied. "Though again, I don't know if it was serious or just lip service."

"What do you mean?" Claire leaned forward.

"He was engaged for a brief time, during his med school days. I remember my mom making a comment when the announcement came in the mail."

"And what happened with that?"

"Clearly, it got called off."

"Why?"

"You ask as if I know or care. The guy isn't my BFF, Claire."

"I think you *do* know but just don't want to tell me."

He raised a single dark eyebrow before growling, "I don't keep anything from you. You know that."

At once, her head dropped. "You're right," she murmured. "I shouldn't have said that. I just want to figure him out. I think there's more to him than he lets on."

Kil let his own head dip and pinched the bridge of his nose with two fingers. "Please don't make this your next project, Claire. I'm begging you. Constance Stone is not a person you want to tangle with. She would easily give Andrea Asher a run for her money. *Easily.*"

"Do you think that's what happened with his fiancée? Was his mother the issue?"

"Wouldn't surprise me." He paused for a minute or two before surging back to his feet, gently pulling her along. "Come on. Let's go home. I need to forget this bullshit by burying myself between your gorgeous thighs."

"Now *that's* a worthy project."

"I'll have the car brought around."

Her long, savoring moan was the response to that—

and I watched over my shoulder, like a damn pervert, as Kil lowered a kiss on her that gave serious new meaning to the term sucking face. Thank God it was over in seconds, when my cousin released her with a satisfied smirk on his lips and a wolfish fire in his eyes. As soon as he strolled off toward the front of the house, Claire headed toward the bride and grooms to say good night.

My cell phone had enough battery left for hailing a ride back to the La Valencia, the hotel in La Jolla where I was staying. I had a job interview on Wednesday at a local hospital, a last-minute decision to humor an old college buddy, but thoughts of living in San Diego had definitely put down roots this weekend, aside from the obvious reasons.

Chicago winters sucked. Even as a child, I'd hated them. While the other kids had bundled up and gone playing in the snow drifts, I'd stayed inside with my Lego and Nintendo GameCube, with the driving simulator games topping my list of favorites. I'd clock lap time after lap time, always figuring ways to push the onscreen vehicle to perform just a little better than the turn before. The laws of physics literally made my blood pump faster. It had become a passion of mine as an adult, and racing was something I could do anywhere the world but most especially in car-crazy Southern California.

Except, it seemed, when it came to the vehicles assigned for my rides around town.

I cringed when the ride app flashed a message about my driver, a kid who looked about twelve, and the domestic compact he'd be arriving to transport me in. Sure enough, the young ginger rolled the vehicle up with an eager grin on his face to match the "gumption" I was sure the car got marketed with.

I was tempted to offer to drive so the guy could take a break in the passenger seat while I got myself back to my hotel in one piece. Besides, he'd surely been out delivering pizza in this thing earlier, judging by the pesto and Parmesan scent still clinging to the car's interior. This would be the last trip I didn't reserve a rental ahead of time, only to be told at the counter that they were all sold out.

"How's it going?" Incredibly, his smile cracked wider.

"Fine. Do you mind if I ride up front? I feel out of control in the back." And more likely to give free rein to the mental ping-pong balls, which would create every possible scenario from the gophers in this thing's engine blowing up to a random hurricane taking us out. Hurricanes *were* possible in California. Rare, but possible. *When was the last time the state was really hit by one?* I was sure I knew, but—

"Not at all," the kid chimed, cheerier than an episode of *Barney*. "Wherever makes you comfortable."

"Awesome." I pivoted at once, striding purposefully toward his side. "In that case, I'll drive."

"Uh..." His face contorted, at once looking like one of the gophers under the hood. "I—uhhh—I'm sorry. That's, like, totally against corporate's rules. Sorry, man."

I shrugged. "It was worth a try."

His expression mellowed, and the grin returned. "Well, have no fear. I grew up in San Diego and know my way around with my eyes closed."

"Please don't do that."

"Don't do what?"

"Just...keep your eyes open." I added, as a prudent afterthought, "*Please.*"

He flashed a confused stare until the gears clicked into

place. "It was a figure of speech."

"Yes," I snapped. "I know. And I was joking."

"Oh. Ummm...gotcha." As he overcompensated with a hearty laugh, I examined the dashboard. Unimpressive and plastic, but it gave me something to do besides mourn the waste of my dry humor or make an attempt at conversation. Human interaction meant the ping-pong balls would start to bounce again, and I was too damn tired to think of any balls except the ones still aching to be slammed against Taylor Mathews' sweet body.

But when the dude just sat there, expectantly looking over at me, I was backed into the proverbial corner. "So what school do you go to?"

Apparently, those were the magic words. As he woke up the gophers and put the putt-putt into gear, he answered, "State. I'm in gender studies."

"Isn't that a bit confusing?" I kept my tone noncommittal.

"Oh no, I'm totally clear which gender I most identify with. I mean, usually."

"I meant which college you go to. Isn't there both San Diego State University and Cal State San Diego?"

"Ooooooohhh, I'm at SDSU. You're kinda confusing, you know?"

Yeah. I *did* know.

At that point, I dug out my phone and dove into checking emails. This conversation was headed for potential debate territory, and no way would I come out ahead against a twenty-something kid obsessed with his gender, so it was best to get caught up on what the world had been doing while I'd played like Don Quixote and my impossible Dulcinea.

Except that my phone was about to die.

And did...

Just as I caught sight of an incoming email from my mother.

Shit. Mom.

The hotel wasn't far, and I could respond once I plugged in again, but the mental jolt took me back to the conversation I'd just eavesdropped on—and the way my nerves were still clenched about it.

And how thoroughly none of my unease made sense.

Killian had, in essence, spoken nothing but the truth to Claire. I'd put an engagement ring on a woman's finger once— and when it had all fallen apart, I'd sworn I'd never do so again. *Winnifred Nelson.* I'd loved her to the roots of my soul, and she'd returned the passion with every smart, funny, beautiful ounce of herself. We'd fallen hard and fast and maybe a little foolishly considering the demands of med school alone, but I didn't care. She was the one for me, and I was ready to forge any necessary key to lock it all down. I wanted her. Everything about her. She was *it...*

Until she met my mother.

It took me years to realize that was the point it all started falling apart—but slowly, the pieces snapped together, revealing Mom's careful, calculated plan.

"She's not right for you, Mac. You cannot just give the Stone name away to anyone. We're prominent. We're leaders. You need someone who was raised for our *world. God only knows if Killian will select anything but trailer trash..."*

She came up with different versions of the message for Winni, of course—but slowly chipped away at her too. Planted enough tiny seeds of doubt that our young, insecure minds caved like sandcastles beneath the strain. By the time I called off the engagement, I all but hated the woman I'd once cherished—and poor Winni had no idea what she had ever done so wrong.

I'd devastated her.

Worse, I hadn't justified any of it with any explanation except that I had fallen out of love.

And I called Killian *an asshole.*

Even more lame? The fact that I couldn't blame anyone but the master puppeteer I called Mother. She was a master manipulator, the queen of emotional poker—and a year later, when I realized it, I cut every string she'd used to control me, vowing I'd never be her instrument of hurt again.

Swearing she'd never hurt *me* again.

I'd considered reaching out to Winni. Maybe attempting an apology, an explanation of what had really happened. But what good would that do? By that time, I'd become such a cold-hearted dickhead and such a legendary lothario, she probably wouldn't have answered even an email from me—and for good reason.

"Here we are." Ginger boy parked the car in front of the hotel's stucco entranceway. "Enjoy the rest of your time in San Diego."

"Thanks. Good luck in school. And pick a new major if you ever want to actually get a job." I slammed the door just to let that truth sink in to the kid, my lips twisting in the beginning of a snarky smirk. As I strode past the ornate Spanish gates and down the breezeway, I muttered beneath my breath, "Yep. You're an ass."

With that uplifting statement, I crossed the hotel's lobby. The La Valencia was a historical boutiquey place with an underlying scent of age and sea salt, but that was pretty much every place in La Jolla—a "unique and distinctive experience" for which every property in this town charged top dollar too. But it was easy to forgive the price tag once the marine layer burned off, exposing the vast ocean views. The Pacific was literally a stone's throw away. The waves made a fantastic lullaby.

At once, their magic began to take effect on me. I relaxed enough to admit at least one immediate truth. It had felt fucking good to be a dick to that kid on the drive home. That was my comfort mode now, the man I knew how to be. The man I'd been trained to be, courtesy of my mother's systematic destruction of my world.

Now, the other guy? The kind, caressing sap who emerged around Taylor Mathews? *He* worried me. He was heartbreak bait. He was going to get hurt. The Mac Stone I'd learned to be had rebuilt himself from the ground up. He was a fucking warrior, who could take anyone and anything on and win. He could stand toe-to-toe with any man who dared and fuck any woman he wanted.

Except Taylor Mathews.

Yeah, she was a hot piece of ass—that much was undeniable—but even thoughts of getting her naked, pretty legs and pert tits and all, weren't worth going back to the Mac of this afternoon. He existed in a cold, dark, terrifying place...a no-man's-land of insecurity. And God fucking forbid if my mother ever discovered I'd gone back there for a second. If she even caught a whiff that I felt that deeply for a woman again, she'd stop at nothing to ensure that woman's destruction.

Taylor didn't deserve that. Especially if she had, as Killian claimed, "seen shit" horrible enough to give her "cracks."

No way in hell would I subject her to even a minute of

Constance Stone's insidious wrath.

Which meant that, as far as Miss Mathews was concerned, I'd forever be nothing except Dr. Clown.

CHAPTER FOUR

Taylor

"Nooooo," I whispered. "Behave!"

Like my jalopy was going to listen *this* time. True to form, her sputtering and popping made several heads turn in the Scripps Green Hospital parking lot, even after I turned the key and shut her off.

"Attention whore," I muttered while checking my makeup in the rearview. I swore the noise got worse in certain zip codes, especially the closer I got to the Pacific. Being in La Jolla inflated the snobs' annoyance factor, but I loved my car. She'd seen me through some rough times, like the nights I'd had to sleep inside her when I couldn't make rent for a few days. Nobody knew that part, not even the three besties of my mini tribe.

Nobody knew *all* the parts.

And that was the way things would stay.

Janet and her lifestyle had taught me that lesson too.

My car was the only one who probably knew everything, and I trusted her to keep the confidence now that I could at least wrangle funds for regular oil changes and car washes. Besides, my old Nissan even earned me hip factor with the teenaged gearheads for keeping the classic scene alive. I always found it funny when some of them slipped me their numbers, reverently murmuring shit like the car was a true "drift missile," whatever the hell that meant, and how if I ever wanted to sell her, please call them first.

One of those numbers flitted from the passenger seat to the floor as I turned and grabbed my purse. I watched it land with a rueful smile. As if buying a new car was an option I could possibly entertain. I made great money at Stone Global Corp, but after the bills were paid each month, I had little left to splurge on extras. When I managed to get ahead and save even a little, Murphy's Law kicked in without fail, and I'd have to bail Janet out of her own rent crisis. Or medical bill drama. Or post bail...again.

Stop.

Enough morose thinking. It was too perfect a day for that, especially this close to the water. Early September in Southern California meant hot days and cool nights. This one was falling right into the norm, though it wasn't sweltering quite yet. Another twenty minutes, and the bake fest would begin. I'd damn well enjoy every second until then.

With that in mind, I stretched my sunshade across the cracked dash and then slid out of the car and headed toward the enormous RV at the other side of the hospital's parking lot.

Scripps Green was well-known in San Diego, occupying some of the most prime real estate in the southwest, where its campus overlooked the ocean. On top of that, its care was renowned. Patients came from all over the world to be treated there, though that wasn't my purpose on campus today. I believed in donating blood as often as possible. They were always in critical need, especially for donors with type O positive blood. It was just a small thing I could do to help other people, and it made me feel good in the process. I didn't mind the needle stick or the momentary dizziness afterward, and the cookies at the end were the best kind—guilt-free because I'd just done humankind a solid. So, yeah...*sold.*

The sign-in sheet sat on a table outside the camper, but the pen was missing in action. I dug through my purse and found an extra I could leave behind for the next person and then grabbed the forms to fill out and have ready when they took me inside. Since I had a frequent donor number, most of the spaces could be left blank.

"Hey, Taylor. How's it going?" A friendly face peeked out to see if anyone was waiting.

"Hey, John. Good. How are you?" I smiled up from the paperwork.

"Can't complain. Do you have an appointment? I don't remember seeing your name."

"I do. Eleven twenty. I'm a little early." Because being early was my superpower.

"Oh, yep. There you are." John checked the list tacked to the back of the RV's door. "Let me get set up, and we'll get you started."

"No worries. Not in a hurry. I'm off today."

"Cool." He smiled again, a little wider, before scooting back into the Blood Mobile, leaving me to pass the time by scrolling my phone for emails—and ditching some residual guilt about the reason behind his increased charm. John had worked with the San Diego Blood Bank for years and had asked me out sometime last year. I'd said yes because he was funny and buff as fuck, and maybe things might've worked out, but they hadn't. Nothing had ever clicked for me, not like I think he wanted it to. John was beyond nice and would make some lucky girl really happy one day, but it wouldn't be me.

There just hadn't been a spark.

Not like there'd been with...

*No. Just...*no, girl. *Forget it. You're not going there.*

But I couldn't *not* go there. Two nights had passed since Talia, Drake, and Fletcher's reception—two nights in which I'd woken sweaty, throbbing, and needy from the hottest sex dreams of my life. Two dreams—with only one starring man.

Maclain Stone was getting damn hard to keep slamming into the "not going there" file.

Why had that smug bastard gotten under my skin—and into my dreams? Oh, God, *those dreams...*and how he'd taken me, used me, wrung me out in them. No way could the real thing ever measure up to those fantasies, not that I'd have the chance to find out now. He'd probably already returned to Chicago and was back to being doctor-God-clown of his own bustling little universe. He probably didn't remember my name, much less his illicit invitation from the middle of the dance floor while his hands had been wrapped around my damn leg. He sure as hell didn't care about the cold sweat he'd caused me to wake up in this morning, just as I was damn sure one of my "Mac visions" had made me come in my sleep.

I'd never, ever, *ever* orgasmed from a damn dream.

But I'd never, ever, *ever* met a man who affected me like Maclain Stone.

"Okay, hon. Come on in."

Shit. Why was John calling me "hon"? *Oh, please, please, please, mister, just tell me you've found another nice girl and moved on.* The last time we'd met for drinks, I'd made it pretty clear I just wanted to be friends.

Fortunately, there were two other donors in the RV, already reclined in the chairs, red tubes coming from their arms. Laura, the pretty brunette who often helped out at this location, was also working today. *No real possibility of things getting too awkward with John right now, thank God.*

"Hop up here, and Laura will get you started. I did all your paperwork. Just need to test your iron real quick and get your signature here and here." He made marks in two places with Xs for me to sign, waiting while Laura stuck my finger with a lancet.

"Looks good," Laura said after placing the small red drop into the receptacle at the end of a handheld device. I signed the forms John placed in front of me and handed the pen back to him, and as he accepted it, he sneaked in a quick wink. I managed to grit out half a smile, hoping he was up on his subtext skills this morning. *Not happening, buddy. I woke up with wet panties after dream-screwing someone else, and I'm not sure the asshole won't be scrambling my subconscious again tonight.*

The actual process itself took about twenty minutes. Afterward, Laura gave me a color-coordinated bandage for my puncture, told me to choose my snack and juice, and have a seat outside for at least fifteen minutes. I wouldn't be able to leave without getting cleared by her or another staff member, though I really hoped it'd be her and not John.

I smiled, nodded, and grabbed some juice along with a package of Nutter Butters, my favorites, before heading outside to read a little on my phone. I'd downloaded the newest book from one of my favorite romance authors and was deep into the story of a billionaire in disguise flirting with his secretary on a tropical vacation when a deep voice startled me. A deep, all-too-recognizable voice.

A voice making my nerves jolt more than the picnic table

did as he straddled the seat right next to me and leaned in close.

Unnervingly close...

"Shit!" I managed to blurt.

Maclain Stone, on the other hand, looked as unperturbed as the seagulls riding the wind over our heads. "That must be pretty good." He looked over at the text on my phone screen. "I called your name twice."

Shit. Only my mind said it this time. Correction. Screamed it.

It was him.

He was here.

Why the *hell* was he *here*?

"Well. Maybe I was ignoring you, clown." I scrolled to the next page, though the words were now blurs. Focusing on the arrogant hunk in the book was pointless, now that I had a real-life version beside me.

Quickening my breaths...

Sharpening my awareness...

Torching my freaking bloodstream, even if it was down by a full pint.

Damn. *Damn.*

"You don't mean that." He pushed over by another inch.

"The fuck I don't." I backed away from him by two.

He grunted, and damn it, even that was enough to light up my nerves again. "Well, praise Jesus, you do eat, at least."

I forced my gaze to stay locked on my phone. "Hmm. I wouldn't have guessed you for the Jesus type."

"No?" His deeper inflection sent vibrations to my toes.

"No," I confirmed, finally jerking my gaze up to confront his. "You're more of a Satan guy."

He threw his head back and laughed—and again, I avoided

admitting how good he looked in the sunshine, with the wind teasing at his hair. "I suppose so. Especially when inspired properly."

"What's that supposed to mean?" My retort was more to cover up the meaning my *body* derived already, but the words were barely out before Mac stood and marched for the Blood Mobile. He threw open the door and stepped in like he owned the place before emerging a few seconds later with both arms full of assorted snacks. The load was mostly cookies, but he'd jammed in a few packages of crackers and chips too.

Once back at the table, he spread his arms like the bucket of a front-end loader, dumping the payload on the table in front of me.

"What the..." I trailed off as he plopped back down beside me. My gawk never left the determined lines of his obscenely square jaw.

"Eat," he ordered.

"Whaaa?"

"See? You're so hungry you can't form a coherent sentence." He had the audacity to wink.

"For the love of Pete." I shook my head. The man had the social graces of a gnat and the balls of a bull.

And now, the glare of a rhino as well. "Who's Pete?"

"No one. It's just an exp—"

"Your boyfriend?"

"No!"

"*Pete.*" He spat the name now. "So he's the one who lets you starve like this?"

"Mac. *Stop.*" I pushed him and the pile of processed garbage away. "I'm not starving. And I don't have a boyfriend." And why the hell I'd just offered that tidbit up so eagerly, I had no idea.

"Huh." His comeback barely hit the range of a mutter. "Well...good."

"Excuse me?"

"*Eat.*" He tossed a pack of Fig Newtons in front of me. I grimaced. "Ew. No."

"I touched them for a second. And I don't have cooties."

"But those do." I scrunched my nose tighter.

"Huh?" His own grimace was instant. And adorable. "Who the hell doesn't like Fig Newtons?"

"*I* don't," I protested. "All those odd little seeds. They stick in my teeth."

"Fine." He snorted. "What, then? What are you eating there?" He stretched his neck so he could see what I'd been nibbling before he arrived. "Peanut butter. Okay. So you'll do these." He shuffled through the pile, getting to a pack of orange crackers with peanut butter in between. Without looking away from my face, he tossed them to the table in front of me.

"Would you stop throwing food?" Before I could rein it back, my voice jumped by an octave. "Holy shit, you're rude."

His eyes gained glittering backlights, as if I'd just told him he rocked my world and had the dick of a god. "But I'm also right. You need to eat more. You're underweight."

I pivoted a little more in his direction, just to gain a better angle for giving him even more shit. One, because he probably hadn't gotten taken down by a few pegs enough in his existence, and two, because I couldn't sit by and let that cock-o'-the-walk look run wild. My new positioning had *nothing* to do with how his dark-gray suit was perfectly tailored to every delectable inch of his body or how tempting his rugged neck looked beneath his loosened silk tie. It sure as hell had nothing to do with how alluring he smelled, like high-end resort soap mixed with a cologne brand that never went out of style. He was probably an Aramis guy. On him, the "old man" cologne was new again, in all its woods-and-leather complexity.

"Is this your version of flirting?" I leveled. "You're a freak."

"This is my version of caring." He looked genuinely confused about what I'd said, increasing my own crazy mix of emotions. A little guilt at calling him out. A good deal more disappointment, that I'd misread his move so thoroughly. "I mean, I guess that's what it is." His brows crunched in. "I'm a doctor. I'm concerned." His clinical once-over took a nanosecond. "And there's no way you can tell me you aren't underweight for your height."

"I'm done here." I quickly grabbed two more packs of Nutter Butters from the pile he'd brought. "*So* done." I stashed them into my purse during the same sweep of motion it took to spin and then stomp away from him.

And, at once, to regret every rash moment of it.

The world spun. My vision narrowed to a black tube as my knees turned to quicksand.

Instantly, something caught my fall. No. Some*one*. Mac. Right. He was there once more, his arms like some massive piece of steel construction equipment.

"Sit down," he dictated into my ear.

I flailed at him. Well, tried to. "N-No."

"Shut *up* and sit *down*, Taylor. Now."

His commanding snarl accomplished its quest. Instinct kicked in, and I responded like a child, sitting down without looking what was beneath me—which was nothing but air. The front-end loader arms were there again, thank God, sweeping me right off my feet and back toward the RV's door, to which he dealt one fast forward kick before bellowing, "Open up!"

Only two seconds passed before John emerged. When he saw me in Mac's arms, he blanched. If I didn't feel so shitty, I would've broken into a small victory dance. The dude surely got the message now. I had my arms wrapped around Mac's sturdy neck, and my head rested against his firm shoulder. *Wow.* His muscles were even better than his clothes let on, and I wanted to confirm that fact by burrowing even closer. And goddamn, he really did smell so good...

Wait.

No.

This was *not* the torrid island from my book, and he was *not* the sultry-eyed dreamboat man from those pages. This was nothing but my life, and he was nothing but Dr. Clown.

What the hell was I doing?

I echoed the words, more or less, in the form of my fuming struggles. "Put me down, damn it!"

"She almost fainted out front," he explained to John as if I'd merely mouthed the words. "She needs to lie down if you have a spot open."

"We'll make one. Put her here," John responded, clearing supplies off one of the recliners. "I can take it from here. I'm a tech."

"That's great, junior. I'm a *neurosurgeon*. So how about I take it from here instead? Get a cool compress for her forehead. And give us some privacy."

"Mac. *Fuck*. This isn't necessary. I'll be fine. I give blood all the time. I just stood up too fast."

"I'm the doctor here." His voice rumbled from so many parts of him, I felt every reverberation too—and fought the fresh wave of dizziness brought on by the awareness. "I'll decide what's necessary and what isn't."

I groaned and then giggled. "But if you put me down, King Kong, you can *really* give that chest a good beating." *And what an incredible, beat-worthy chest it is...*

"When was the last time you ate a proper meal?"

"Oh, my God. Are we back to that?"

"Yes. We are."

"I had breakfast this morning, Daddy." Another tiny laugh. "Three eggs and bacon, since you're demanding the fucking details. And yes, clown, I eat bacon. Greasy, nasty, artery-clogging bacon. And toast—with real butter. None of that fake-ola crap because I'm from the south and that shit is just sacrilegious."

I finished by widening my eyes, daring him to chastise me again. Since he'd been busy during my diatribe, gently lowering me into the chair, he was now free to answer by simply boring an unflinching gaze down at me. His gaze was the color of rich jade, and half a smile grazed the lush balance of his motherfucking sexy mouth. I shifted a little, fighting the effect of that smile on the deepest layers of my pussy. At once, I yearned to drag him down to me and kiss his smile away. Then I imagined him obeying me—only to dip that beautiful mouth directly between my thighs...

He blinked and whipped in a harsh breath, as if granted a front-row ticket to the movie in my mind, before leaning down until his lips were wickedly close to my ear. "You're a feisty little she-devil, aren't you?"

I took a bunch of shallow breaths of my own. Shook my head to fight the intoxicating effects of his playful accusation. *Feisty.* It had always been one of those stupid words reserved for the heroines in my books and the puppies at the mall.

Mac Stone's growl transformed it into breathtaking poetry.

Literally.

I gulped, wondering if I really would ever breathe again, as he dipped in even tighter, pressing his mouth to the curve of my ear as if there weren't five other people openly staring at us in the confines of a glorified tour bus.

"Yeah, I said feisty...and I meant it in all the ways you can dream of and more, Miss Taylor Mathews. All the ways *I've* been dreaming of it too...for the last two days. Do you know how many times you've made me hard as a fucking rock? That I'm getting that way right now, just looking at you lying beneath me and wondering how many ways I can touch you to make you scream?"

"Stop." A whisper I didn't mean, joined with an equally ineffective bat at his shoulder. I was so woozy, a butterfly could've done a better job at smacking him than me.

"Do you want me to, love?"

"I'm *not* your 'love.'" But did it matter? As long as he kept up the murmur that turned deep sound into wanton sensation through my whole body, what did it matter what he called me? I'd take Mildred or Rapunzel right now.

"Deny whatever you want, Taylor—except the one thing you know you can't. This. Us. What's going on here. The pull. The heat. The connection. The need. You feel it too...in more than a few places. I've been around the block enough times to be able to read a woman's body, and yours is calling my name, little one, loud and clear."

"*Stop.*" This time I meant it. He was too close. Too hot. Too right.

He pulled up and away, the smile back on his mesmerizing lips—kicked up in a wolfish gloat this time. "I'm glad you grabbed those extra cookies out there," he murmured. "You're going to need to carb up for what I have planned."

His wink of punctuation, as if he'd just told me a nursery rhyme, brought a flood of heat to my face and a rush of need to my pussy. I fought to fling him a new fume but just lay there like a gasping fish on a wharf, yearning to banish everyone from the RV and jump him then and there.

Oh, my God, I am in trouble. A deep, beautiful river of it.

But maybe this could be a good thing. Why was I blowing it all up so big? Maybe if I cleared the cobwebs with him, as Margaux had so poetically put it, that would be the trick to flushing Mac Stone out of my system. I could walk away unscathed. No more Dr. Clown porn dreams. An itch scratched.

Again, as if he'd taken a peek at the film playing in my mind, he cleared his throat and asked huskily, "Do you have a car here, love?"

Forget correcting him now. I showed my irritation with the snark in my retort. "That's usually how people get from one place to another around here. California, remember? The land where freeways are an art form? And you call yourself a brain surgeon?"

The pause he took to answer wasn't exactly filled with a romantic gaze, making me stiffen just before he leveled matter-of-factly, "Well, that's two."

"Two? Two what?" I wasn't following. And was even more tense about it.

"Two very smart remarks you're going to pay for."

I felt my vision narrowing and my sex reacting. But I didn't back down from anyone, even the hunk who woke my senses in ways I'd never imagined possible. "You're threatening me?"

He silently, slowly shook his head. And once more, never broke eye contact. "Not at all. But I *am* going to drive you home."

Moisture flooded my pussy. Unavoidable, when the man's offer of a ride home was so gruff and greedy and growly. He was a dangerous beast, and he wanted to end this night by tearing me open and devouring me.

And I longed to keep poking the beast.

"You'll do no such thing," I forced myself to say instead. "Wait a second. Why are you still here in the first place? And why are you *here*, at Scripps? Shouldn't you be back in Chicago?" I jerked my head higher. "Are you stalking me?"

I tossed it out only as provocation—so my shock was *really* a shock when his mien didn't vacillate. "Do you *want* me to be stalking you?" He tilted his head, invoking even more wolfish candor. "I think maybe you do. Your pulse just ticked up."

My jaw dropped. "How did you notice that?"

He leaned back in and dropped his voice so low, only I could hear him. "Because you're so fucking sexy and pale, I can see your veins through your skin. I can literally see your heart beating"—he grazed his fingertips over the major blood vessel in my neck, just beneath the collar of my flowy peasant top, bringing on a flurry of new shivers—"right here."

My head spun again. Violently. Holy shit, what he did to me. Though right then, I was having trouble admitting if it really had been him or the blood loss or...

Did it matter?

My libido was in a whirlwind. My thoughts were in a tailspin. Stars still flickered in my eyesight, and I wasn't sure I ever wanted them to leave. But they had to—and so did he. As in, five minutes ago. Danger. Beast. Me. Prey. The end result of that sequence wasn't lost on me. Sleeping with Mac Stone wouldn't be just scratching an itch. It would alter reality—just like he already had right now.

"S-Stop d-distracting me," I finally stuttered out. "I'm serious, damn it. You know this *is* like level five creepy stalking, don't you? Stop laughing." When it was again obvious my words were as good as silence to him, I pushed myself to my elbows.

With a forearm, he easily pushed me back down. "Uh-uh. Lie back a bit longer, or I'll be forced to carry you out to the parking lot."

"*That* shit isn't happening again."

"No?"

"No."

"Well, I wouldn't mind." He dared to do the winking thing again. *Arrogant fuck.* "But your watchdog over there might piss himself." He nodded at John. "Not that I'd mind that, either."

I shook my head. "God, you're an ass."

"So did you date him?"

"You trying to change the subject, stalker?"

"Damn. You did go out with him. Shit, Taylor. Give yourself some credit. He's way beneath you."

"Shut up. He's nice."

"You deserve better than nice."

"So...who? Somebody like you?"

"Definitely like me." His head dipped closer. "Who's changing the subject now?"

I lolled my head back and shut my eyes. Talking to this man was like talking to a classroom of kindergarteners. And, as with five-year-olds, that meant consciously shutting him out.

"I had a job interview."

Until he blurted stunning shit like that.

"What the..." I shot up, despite instantly seeing stars again. After falling back on my own, I rubbed my temples.

"You okay?"

"Not...sure." I peeked out with one eye. "I've never had this much trouble after donating before. Not sure why I'm not bouncing back."

I turned my peek into a meaningful glare, implying the obvious difference about *this* occasion, but once again the implication flew right past the man's perception. He eyed me clinically.

"Are you having your period?"

Oh, yeah. Dr. Matter-of-Fact had checked in for duty again. "I...beg your pardon?"

"Are. You. Menstruating?" He repeated the words, one at a time, slow and clear.

"I know what you said, asshole." I shoved at him in furious confusion. He was a Jekyll and Hyde in designer wear, turning my pussy to aroused magic one second and then referring to everything down there like a broken back hoe the next. "You don't just ask a lady that. Seriously. Were you raised by a fucking pack of wolves?"

His gaze narrowed. "Do you kiss your mother with that mouth? Though your accent's adorable when you're pissed."

"I don't kiss my mother. *Ever.*" And there spilled more of my "adorable" accent, in acidic form.

"And I would've rather been raised by wolves." His words were just as bitter, though more softly uttered.

We fell into silence. Our smartass comments had unintentionally hit nerves inside the other, leaving the conversation with nowhere to go.

Well...shit.

Finally, I couldn't bear the stalemate. "A job interview, huh? For you?"

"No. The queen."

"Fine." I stood up, grabbing the arm of the chair just in case, but the room stayed steady this time. "I'm really done now." I waved in John and Laura's direction, unwilling to commit to anything more after the display with Mac. "Thank you, guys, for the extra TLC today. I'm going to get out of your hair."

Without any more hesitation, I pushed past Mac and rushed out of the RV. In the parking lot, I headed straight for my car.

"Taylor."

If he could pretend I hadn't spoken, I could sure as hell do the same.

"*Taylor.*"

"Not listening anymore, dickwad." I spewed it beneath my breath.

"Wait. Please."

I stopped. Instantly hated myself for it. But fucking hell, something about his plea, a combination of urgency and sincerity, fish-hooked the center of my gut. *Please.* I sensed—maybe knew—it wasn't a word he used often. Or easily.

I spun around. "What the hell do you want from me?"

He released a heavy breath. The heat had started to encroach on the day, making him sweat a little in the suit. It was beyond sexy. *Damn it.* "I really do want to drive you home. Forget all the shit I said in there, if it makes you more comfortable. I just wouldn't feel right if something happened to you."

I shifted from foot to foot, beyond bemused. From Dr. Wolf Child to Rumpled-and-Sincere Man... He was driving me insane in the best *and* worst ways.

"I don't need any help, okay? I'm fine on my own. Always have been and will continue to be."

"I understand that." He moved in by another step. "But I *want* to help you."

He looked so good. He smelled so good.

He pulled at me...like no one else ever had...

I swayed. Just a little. Giving in to the strange force gathering between us. Raw energy arced, pulling us tighter together as he reached up and stroked my cheek. It was just a light brush of motion, the back of his knuckles against my overheated skin...

It felt like everything.

My vision telescoped again. In all the best and most delirious ways.

"You *sure* you feel okay, love? You're really warm."

"Please...stop with that."

"Saying you're warm?" Though he whispered it, I felt every syllable. We stood almost chest-to-chest. I wondered what it would feel like if we were naked...

"No," I forced myself to answer. "What you said...before that. It doesn't matter. And no, I'm not okay. I feel odd. I—I don't know what's going on."

"You need to sit down again."

"No." I wrapped a hand around his elbow. It flexed beneath my touch, and I didn't doubt he could support my entire weight if needed. But I couldn't need him. I couldn't need anyone. "I-I think it's you, clown. I felt fine until I saw you today. Well, no, that's not all the way true, either. There were the dreams."

He inhaled sharply. "What dreams?"

"I-I'm not making sense, huh?" I smiled, letting my eyes drift shut again. The sun felt good without the glare.

"Taylor." His growl was lower than before. And so much sexier. "Fuck." After I responded with nothing but a woozy sigh, he gritted, "Now I'm really not taking no for an answer. Where's your car?"

I waved in the general direction of where I'd parked. When I reopened my eyes, everything was fuzzy around the edges. Mac repeated his curse right before gathering me up again. With a blissful sigh, I burrowed my face into his neck. *So much for resisting him. As if that was a possibility in the first place...*

"*Taylor.*"

"Hmmm?" Belatedly, I realized he'd probably tried the command a few times already.

"What kind of car do you drive?"

"Drift missile," I muttered. "You smell really good for a wolf."

A weird choke erupted from him. "You have a Nissan 240sx?"

I lifted my head and looked him in the eye. "How do you know that?"

He shook his head. A new half smile tempted his lips. "I'll explain another time. When you don't have low blood sugar and low blood pressure."

"'Kay."

"Is this light-blue one yours?"

"Ah...yep."

"And do you have any water in your car, love?"

"*Stop* calling me that."

He snorted. "Water?"

"In the trunk."

"You shouldn't keep water bottles in your trunk."

"You're a nag. Better than not having any, right?"

"I guess. Where are your keys?"

"Purse."

He lowered me gently, letting me lean against the car while fishing the keys out of my purse. After lowering all the windows and dropping the passenger-side seat all the way down, he helped me slide in. A moment later, he returned with a bottle of water, helping me sit up to drink before putting the lid back on and placing it in the cup holder.

I turned a little in the seat, trying to get comfortable, though that was officially impossible as soon as I caught sight of Mac through my lashes, dashing around the car's hood like a kid beholding a new playground slide. As he slid in, that joy intensified. Stalker man, wolf boy, and Dr. Clown had vanished, leaving only one persona to define him now. Sexy Happy Man.

I liked it. A lot.

"I can't believe you have this car." He ran reverent hands over the steering wheel. "I'm in heaven right now. You have no idea. We're going to have to have some fun with her one day, the second you feel better."

I couldn't help cracking a little smile. His energy wasn't just lust-worthy. It was contagious. "I've had it since it was brand-new. One of my mom's boyfriends bought it for me."

"Well, it's in great shape."

"It is?" I was genuinely stunned.

"Oh yeah. Little crack here on the dash, but that's unavoidable in this heat. What's your address, love? I'll put it in my phone so you don't have to worry about telling me directions."

I resettled, pushing up a little. "I can guide you. Really. I'm feeling better again. I don't understand what's going on. Maybe

I have a bug. Wearing jeans on a heat alert day probably wasn't a good idea either."

"Drink as much of that water as you can. It'll help."

I complied with the command as he started the car and headed toward the parking lot exit. "Head south on the Five," I instructed then. "You'll want to hit the Eight east, into Mission Valley. Try to keep it under eighty. The steering wheel really starts to shake."

"Sounds like you need your wheels aligned or balanced. Maybe new tires. Or all of the above."

"No shit, but that all costs money." I took in his profile with a little laugh. "So are you a mechanic as a side hustle? The whole brain surgery thing not covering the rent?"

He grinned. The expression was nearly as alluring as his confident grip on the wheel. If it was possible, I swore my car purred more smoothly, as if feeling the force of his adoring touch. *Damn.* Even my car wasn't immune to Mac Stone's powerful presence.

"I've loved cars since I was a boy. It's a hobby. Well, more than that. A passion. I race and collect now."

He shrugged as though those were normal things to tell someone. My gape didn't alter that.

"You *race?*" I finally got out. "Like, cars?"

"Uuuuhhh...yeah."

"Like, on a track?"

"Where else? Hey, you okay? Why are you even paler?"

"I—well—" The seat jerked beneath me as I yanked the lever to straighten back up. "I think I'm just embarrassed."

He scowled. "Why?"

"Well, poor Sally has a self-esteem problem to begin with, and now you're behind the wheel."

His gaze bugged. "You named a 240sx Sally?"

"What's wrong with Sally?" I put my hands on my hips, though admittedly it wasn't the most intimidating pose when delivered from the passenger's seat and after almost passing out twice in the past thirty minutes.

"When you see what this car can do with the right driver, you'll want to give her a different name."

"Never." Though watching him navigate the car down the freeway like threading silk through a needle certainly inspired some new perspective. "But maybe we can talk nicknames. Like an alter ego?"

"That works." He flashed a devastating grin and rubbed a confident hand atop mine. I liked looking down at how his grip engulfed mine. It wasn't a consummation I'd enjoy forever, but right now, in my dazed state, it was nice to be cared for, protected.

It was damn nice...

"So, do you know what drift missile even means?"

"Hmmm?" I was still too busy admiring his hands. They were filled with such powerful elegance. His fingers were long but not girly. His nails were manicured squares. "No. It never seemed important."

"You've never googled it? Or looked at drifting videos on YouTube?"

"I'm a *girl*, Mac. That stuff makes me more nervous than anything."

"What does being a girl have to do with anything? Women make great drivers. Small feet. Better pedal control."

I just stared. *Honestly, how is any of this even happening?* An hour ago, I was preparing for a day of running errands and crossing shit off the to-do list. Give blood. Pick up dry cleaning.

Get a christening gift for Iris. Scrub the toilet. Shave my legs.

Now, I was discussing car driving with my very own panty-melting clown. Being personally cared for by aforementioned clown. Thinking about the fifteen different ways I'd like to fuck, kiss, or suck several parts of his fascinating, not-an-inch-of-softness body.

But most of all, panicking as I realized there was no way Mac Stone could see the inside of my crappy apartment when we arrived there in five minutes. I needed to come up with an artful way of sending him home without inviting him inside, though my body had craved nothing more from the second he'd plunked down at that picnic table with me.

God...what am I going to do?

"This is it, right? So where should I park?"

CHAPTER FIVE

Mac

What the hell is going on?

In the span of a few minutes, everything had changed. Our conversation, effortless as whipped cream, had become the consistency of a steak, and now we were trying to cut the damn thing with a butter knife. I glanced over, at once noting the flushed rose hue of her normally snowy skin, as well as the shallow breaths lifting and dipping her chest.

"Hey, what's up?" I glanced between her and the road as I pulled in to the aged apartment complex. "Do you feel faint again?"

"Uh...yeah," she replied all too quickly. "Yeah, that's it. Exactly. Whew. I better just go on in by myself. Thanks so much for bringing me home, though. I really, really appreciate it. You can just call a car back to your hotel, right?"

I turned my glance into a frown. "I'd better walk you to your door at a minimum. The wolves raised me with a few manners at least." And no way was I letting her out of my sight even after that, considering what had happened at the hospital as well as her bizarre behavior now.

"I'll be fine. I've imposed enough. Spot seventeen is mine. Right there, third one in." She pointed out of the windshield with a long finger. Christ, even her hands were gorgeous.

"I like your nails." Maybe distracting her would help.

"Wh-What?" Yeah, I'd thrown her—and maybe that was a good thing.

I pulled into the parking spot. In the space to our left was a piece-of-shit Dodge Caravan. To the right, an Iroc-Z28. *Whoa. The eighties called and wanted their gems back, minus the minivan, of course.* Trouble was, I was ready to fight them for Taylor's car. But more than that, for the woman herself.

"I said I like your nails. They look pretty."

"You..."

"What? It's not a lie. They've got those white tip things. It emphasizes the shape. Kind of sophisticated." Except for when I imagined her hand wrapped around my cock. Then all bets were off on sophistication.

She huffed out a laugh, relaxing enough to flop back against the seat. "You're an odd guy, Mac Stone."

"You're not the first to say that."

"Yeah, but as a compliment?"

"That wasn't exactly a compliment."

"Wasn't *not* one." She smiled, rivaling the sun for brilliance, taking my breath away. I used the pause to get a better look at it, leaning back in my seat too.

"Well, it was certainly a first, at least."

She returned my mock suspicion with a confused scowl. "A first what?"

"You used my name without referencing a circus performer."

She looked ready to chuckle again before apparently stopping herself with some internal smack. That left her ready to hurl another insult—triggering an answering instinct in me. Before I could stop to question it or stop it, I let the impulse drive me through the space between us until I covered her lips with mine. I was pretty sure I shocked myself as much as her, but I was damn glad I'd made the move.

Fuck. *So* glad.

Her lips were soft and yielding, but I resisted the urge to plunge my tongue all the way into her mouth—barely. Instead, I focused on meshing our lips where I could and savoring the sweet, sunshine smell of her for as many long seconds as possible. She was so damn graceful. So delicious...

When I pulled back, her eyes were still closed and she swayed toward me. I smiled a little, exalting in her attraction, and cupped her rosy cheek. It was one of the few times I saw color in her skin. It was fucking intoxicating.

"Wh-What was that for?" She still didn't open her eyes.

I let a low hum vibrate up my throat. "Didn't want you to spoil your streak."

Her blue eyes finally popped open. "One time isn't a streak," she murmured with a grin.

"You have to start somewhere."

"I wouldn't count on it, cl—"

I put my finger across her lips. "Don't ruin the moment by talking." And regretted the words before they were finished. The douchebag routine was sheer habit—not a fact I remotely wanted to embrace right now, especially in the two seconds it took for the light to die in her eyes and the dreamy softness to turn back into her narrow scowl.

"You're such an ass. Goodbye." Before I could process the end result of *that*, she yanked the keys from the ignition, swung from the passenger side of the car, and slammed the door. Her sandals made distinct clacks as she stomped down a walkway between a couple of the complex's buildings toward what I assumed was her unit. I figured she lived in apartment seventeen to match her parking spot number, but at an older place like this, that wasn't a given. And yeah, I meant *old*. The complex was small and clean but not one of the amenity-rich, luxury communities seeming to outnumber Starbucks shops all over San Diego. And at this point, I *was* an expert about that shit, having done my research about the area's real estate offerings as soon as Lawrence had reached out with the job offer at Scripps. Rentals were much more affordable in these older, less glamorous developments, which were tucked into the canyons and river walks of the city and its suburbs.

"What neighborhood is this?" I asked, managing to keep at least a visual on her after bolting from the car and racing to keep up with her. Her shoes still made those click-clacks along the winding walkway, almost like an erotic pied piper to my mindless rat of a cock. *How can such a sharp noise be so fucking cute?*

"One a person with your last name wouldn't be caught dead in," she called back. "You'd better run along, mister."

Sure enough, she strode up to a door with a worn number seventeen on it. I caught up, moving beside her while she frantically searched through her keys. The descriptor wasn't empty. Her fingers shook as she peeled from key to key, prompting me to snatch the whole cluster away. With an equally decisive move, I grabbed both her hands in one of mine and then waited until her head jerked up and her glare confronted me again.

I had words ready, though they came out rougher than I'd expected. "I'd appreciate not being compared to my cousin at every turn," I stated. "You barely know me—and Killian's hardly a fucking saint. Nor is he suffering in that castle of his in Rancho Santa Fe."

For a second, her features softened a little, and I thought—perhaps hoped—she'd read through the veneer of my bitterness to the pain underneath. But it was only an instant. "Why, Dr. Clown," she quipped, yanking her hands down and popping her hip out to one side. "I wouldn't have guessed *you* to be the jealous type." She added a coquettish head tilt, once more seeming tempted to take her thoughts deeper, but then straightened with a lurch, snatched her keys back from me, and deftly opened her door.

Once inside the threshold, she whirled around and winked. The proverbial "W" for winner was practically stamped across her forehead.

"Bye now."

She gave a bratty smile, swinging the old wooden panel toward the doorjamb.

I rammed one hand into the middle of the door.

Whump.

Who's got the "W" now?

Flush with victory, I stepped into the foyer—if it was legal to call the three-foot-square space of tile a foyer—which also crowded every inch of me against her. The spoils of war had never felt so good.

"You really need to be taught some manners, Miss Mathews." I closed the door without looking back, the warped wood lurching in complaint, while never letting an inch of space develop between our bodies. Not wasting another moment, I pressed my palm flat against her sternum, backing her against the wall. My spread fingers spanned her upper chest, making it easy to feel her heartbeat, thundering at a tumultuous cadence.

Tentatively, I rubbed. She mesmerized me. Her slight body held such a ferocious, fiery spirit. Did one beget the other, and if so, how? What drove her? Inspired her? Hurt her?

Arouses her?

Her cheeks were pink again, burning beneath her paper-thin skin.

Very pink.

Goddamn. She *was* aroused. And now, so was I.

Before even thinking of talking myself out of it, I leaned forward slowly. I only stopped when my mouth reached the apple of her cheek. I gave her the smallest nibble there, resulting at once in her sharp inhalation. She did it again, pulling in air through her nostrils, but didn't move. Most importantly, she didn't tell me to stop. I wasn't hurting her. I would never hurt her. I just wanted...

To consume her.

To sample every delicate inch of her.

To taste her in every way I possibly could.

Starting with this...

When I stepped back, she raised her hand to the spot I'd just bitten. Her fingers curled in, lightly stroking where her skin was still shiny from my saliva, though her big blue eyes remained hidden beneath her closed lids.

I watched, entranced, as she spread the moisture around the red mark I'd left.

"You...bit me," she breathed more than spoke.

"Just a little." One side of my mouth kicked up.

"Why?" Again with just the breath more than volume. Fuck, it was a beautiful sound.

"I like biting." As I shrugged, I bent closer to her again. Let my own voice drop to something like a breath. "The truth? I want to eat you alive, Taylor. I want to taste every fucking inch of you."

"Mmmmm." She still kept her eyes closed, while her moan blasted open all my nerve endings. "I...I want that too."

"So..." My constricting throat roughened my voice. "I didn't hurt you?"

"No." She swallowed. "I liked it."

I pushed closer. Stepped a little wider so my thighs braced the outside of hers. "How much?"

Her lips parted. "H-How much...what?"

"Did you like it?" The syllables practically rumbled from me now. "Are you wet, Taylor? Right now...are you wet for me?"

She dropped her chin to her chest. *Damn. So beautifully submissive...but not giving a discernible answer.*

"Answer me."

"I said I liked it, didn't I?" Her fire flared back with a gorgeous, brilliant vengeance.

My cock responded in matching degrees, surging and stiff. *Dear fucking God, this woman is going to be fun to crack open. To break into screaming, sobbing pieces.*

"But that's not what I asked you."

At last, she popped her eyes wide open. Through gritted teeth, she huffed, "Just stop talking, clown. It sucks the hot out of things."

"Oh no, little sass. It turns the heat up a thousand degrees if you let it. But you'll learn that over time too."

She spurted a laugh. "Excuse me? I'll *learn*? Over *time*?" Her adamant head shake made her hair catch the light, almost distracting in its radiance. "You know that's BS too, right? That there *is* no 'over time' here, buddy. Don't get me wrong. I can already tell you'd be a seriously fun once-and-doner. You live in another state, for Christ's sake. Nothing better than that for anti-cling-on insurance. But the 'over time' nonsense, in any form, will *not* be going on here." She motioned back and forth between the two of us with a finger. "Besides"—the finger stabbed into the middle of my chest—"you're a douchebag clown, and I can barely stand you. Though I admit, there *is* the whole 'looking at you' portion of things." She went on, as if my glower hadn't just torqued by at least a dozen degrees, "Dude, seriously? You're definitely *smokin.*"

A few more beats passed. I worked my jaw up and down, buying time while I tried to make sense of a single word she'd just said. *Fuck me.* How could a woman have such a gorgeous yet disrespectful mouth?

Finally, I stated, "I truly have no idea what you just said— except that there's a good chance we're going to have sex, and I like that part. But the rest was in Californian, and I just don't speak that yet." I was going to make more of a point about that, before my gaze roamed across her small living room. "Whooooaaaa. Do you play?"

In a curved alcove along the opposite wall there was a table set up with a very old chess board. The set was intricately carved from marble and well taken care of. The pieces were positioned in midgame, and at first glance—then second and third—it looked like the white king was in a terrible check situation.

Unable to resist, I crossed over to the board. Taylor was at my side so quickly I was reminded of Louvre security guards as soon as someone dared to reach for the *Mona Lisa.*

"Do not touch a single piece."

I inched back, tossing an amazed side-eye. I never would've pegged the woman for that strident a commanding hiss, but in my line of work, a guy learned to embrace the unexpected, no matter how confusing.

"Okay." Drawing out both syllables, I backed off by a step.

"It's—it's just that it's an antique set," she rushed like a kid explaining a milk spill, "and I-I just don't have very many things that are valuable—as you can probably tell."

I backed off by another inch. Replied quietly, "I've had a narrow focus on the scenery so far."

She didn't want to enjoy the compliment. Her pressed lips and averted gaze proved it. "Well, I'd hate for anything to happen to this."

"Of course." I said nothing else, not pressing the matter. If she wasn't lying, I was a goddamned cyclops, but right now, there were more important matters at hand. Like revisiting the part about having sex.

"Well, that's too bad," I said easily. "I was hoping you played."

"You do?"

"Since I was a boy. Killian's father taught me. It's been a while, though. It'd be nice to have someone to play with again."

"What about Killian?"

"And what about we keep the subject in the realm of reality?" I scooted in on her again, fitting the fingers of my left hand through the soft digits of her right. "So, a 'once-and-doner,' huh?"

She shook her head again, trying to pull her hand away. "I shouldn't have said that."

I didn't let her free. Just the opposite. With a sweep of dedicated movement, I used my hold to lift her hand and then turned it palm up. The fleshy part of the human hand, right where the thumb connected to it, was very sensitive if stimulated properly. Yeah, I liked knowing that—and yeah, I liked using that knowledge on her, dipping my head and kissing her there. I lingered with my lips, warming her skin with my breath and licking the flesh slowly with my tongue. Small circles, letting my taste buds memorize her heady, creamy taste...

"Mac." It was a weak protest at best, and she made no effort to get free. I smiled against her milky skin and kissed it again—before sinking my teeth into her palm.

"Ahhhhh."

I stopped about three seconds after she made the sound, knowing she could take so much more and was reacting out of surprise and arousal than true pain—though I also sensed this beauty would enjoy real pain if she ever consented to try out its transformative power. No. *Once* she consented. I needed to see that stunning moment for myself—though it wouldn't be tonight. Down the road sometime. *Way* down.

And goddamn it, if I had any influence on the matter, our road wouldn't be finished after tonight.

I lifted my eyes to watch her reaction as I licked the dark-red stain I'd made on her palm. The sight of the mark—*my* mark—fueled my blood with dizzying lust.

"So, this is your thing?" she said, sort of stuttering after sucking in her breath as I licked her. Still, her undertone was accusatory. "Biting?" she emphasized. "Like a toddler?"

I slid a devilish grin. "Do you want it to be my thing?" I dragged my lips along each of her fingers, finishing each caress with a warm suck to her fingertip. "You seem to like it."

Her spine went rigid. If it were even possible, she looked a little prim. "I...I do like it."

Yeah. Screw that rod up her spine.

Her confession was all it took to unhinge my composure again. I yanked her to me hard, crushing her lips in a brutal kiss, softening her *Anne of Green Gables* act inside ten seconds. I did it that way because I knew she craved it this way—and God knew, so did I. No tender duel of tongues or other poetic crap. This was a full-on declaration of war, a battle of mashing lips and hungry breaths. The victor would have the fewest bruises, and damn if I didn't want to wave a white flag just to feel her ferocity unleashed on me in this way.

I was hooked on her already. I couldn't get enough of her passion, my custom drug of choice. As I sucked her tongue into my mouth, I imagined what her clit would be like in its place. As I ran my free hand along her side, I cursed the clothes that kept me from the treasure of her pale, perfect body.

A groan punched the air, and I vaguely recognized it as mine. I was a creature outside myself, though never had I been more connected to every fucking inch of my body. That beast repeated his moaning war cry while finding the closest wall and ramming Taylor against it, at once parting her legs in order to grind his throbbing cock into her flat belly.

Fuck.

Fuck.

Fuck.

She was pliant but vicious, fierce but needy, radiating heat but shivering to the ends of her limbs. I lifted her with the force of my thrusts, and it still wasn't enough. I wanted to split her in half with every shove. Fill her until she could taste me with every lunge. She would know who claimed her when we were through. She turned me into a man possessed, crazy with lust, needing her smell, her taste, her simple essence. It had been a long damn time since I'd felt this way. Years. Long ones. I thought I'd gotten over the foolishness of needing to consume a woman, but Taylor Mathews blew that theory into the damn cosmos.

"Take me to your bed, Taylor," I all but begged into her ear. "I need to fuck you."

"No."

I froze—damn sure I'd misheard. She stated her answer so simply, getting the syllable in between our wet kisses.

"Uh...what?"

"I said no."

"What the hell do you mean?" I wasn't about to let up on her. Dragging my mouth along the seam of hers, I demanded, "I know you want this too. Why are you denying us this?" Why, indeed. We were on fire. I was stunned the building hadn't gone up in flames from our lust.

"I'm not fucking you, Mac."

She literally gasped it now, between all of our horny and desperate kisses.

I growled back, "You're making me crazy, woman. I don't understand." I bent in, biting her neck particularly hard, leaving a mark she wouldn't be able to hide even if she had a few turtlenecks in her closet. I liked that idea. I rejoiced in the idea of her blushing when her friends saw or guessed at the source of the marks on her body. *It was me. Read the evidence and weep...*

"No. *No.*" But the words tumbled out of her anyway, even as she grabbed me by the hair and pulled me down for another hot, open-mouthed kiss. "You d-don't understand...at all. You don't want to do this. I'm way too fucked up for this. For *you.* You...you won't be able to—"

I silenced her with a kiss meant to punish, and it did just that to us both because I craved her now to the point of pain— and not the good kind. "You don't get to decide what I can handle and what I can't," I finally snarled against her lips. "But tell me your cunt isn't drenched for me, sassy, and I'll walk the hell out of here."

No confession of the sort—but she did kiss me again, forcing her tongue halfway down my throat.

Yeah. We'll see exactly what I could handle, damn it.

I twisted the button on her jeans and slid the zipper down. Spread the two halves open wide, like I wanted to fuck her with her legs wrapped around my rutting hips. I stood back, making her watch as I pushed her jeans down to her jutting hip bones, roughly pulling her sexy cotton panties along with them. As soon as I bared her beautiful pussy, her arousal infused the air and my cock nearly tore a hole in my pants.

And holy Christ...her pussy.

Mother fucking hallelujah, the last female on the planet who hadn't shaved or waxed off all her pubic hair stood before me. There was a god, or Santa Claus, or pubic hair fairy after all.

"Jesus...*Taylor*." I buried my face in her neck, instantly starting a new trail of love bites into her delectable skin. From behind her ear, I dug in down her neck, across her collarbone, and out to her shoulder, where I really sank in. That one was going to leave an actual bruise, and I reveled in the high little shriek she let out as I delivered it without mercy. At the moment she seized hardest from the pain, I plunged my middle finger up into her cunt. Her cry turned into a moan loud enough to give her neighbors some juicy dinner table gossip.

"So good, love." I meant every husky syllable. "So damn good."

"God. Mac." She swallowed hard. "Oh, my God."

"Mmmm. You're so fucking wet." I pressed on her clit with my thumb, adding my ring finger to the penetration alongside my middle finger. The heat inside her body made my head spin. The clench of her channel made my knees weak. "Fuck. *Taylor.* My God. Take me to your bed, sassy. Let's do this the right way."

"Stop. Talking." She'd managed to undo a couple of my shirt buttons, now digging past that barrier to my abdomen. Her other hand clawed the back of my head. "Just finger-fuck me, clown. Please. *Please.*"

It was close enough to an order to be taken as one—normally a dynamic I never agreed to in the bedroom—but her voice was a million strands of heated silk around my dick, all yanked tight at the same second. My pleasure was now inexorably wound with hers. I didn't just want to make her come now. I needed it. Whether I was inside her or not.

I needed the explosion of her pleasure like I needed my next breath. Maybe more.

I rubbed her clit a little harder while slowly pumping my fingers in and out of her. "How's that? Enough? Do you want more? Tell me, Taylor. Tell me what you like. Tell me what you need."

"More. *More.*" She sucked on the skin of my neck, burrowing her nose into me like a little kitten. "Just...more."

"More what? More pressure? Faster? Fuller? Tell me, love. Let me give you what you need."

"More fingers." Her voice was a whimper as she gripped my shoulders, grinding down on my hand.

I gladly slid my index finger in with the others. Her pussy was so wet and pliable and soft and aroused, I'd probably be able to get my whole fist up inside her. Precome leaked from my tip at the image that thought conjured.

Another day, big guy. Another day.

I was genuinely counting on that. Something told me there wasn't anything this little sass couldn't manage. And nothing I didn't want to push her to take.

"Spread your legs wider, Taylor. I'm going to fuck you harder."

She instantly complied, and I rewarded her with a bite on top of the first I'd already given to her shoulder. The dark-red mark there was already so fucking sexy, I was drawn to deepen my claim on her once more. "One-and-done" was going to be the one she'd never forget.

"Oh, God! Mac!"

I pumped harder and faster into her pussy, reveling in how her juices dripped between my fingers. Maybe I'd make her lick her essence off me after she'd orgasmed—another image causing my cock to scream at me from its confinement, while her desire was a living, breathing entity on the air now. A goddess of a creature, possessing us both as she slammed her head back against the wall, closing her eyes again and panting hard.

"I'm—I'm going to—"

"What?" I bit it like a profanity. "God*damn* it, Taylor. Tell me."

"I'm...I'm going to come."

"Yes." And just like that, I was on top again. Commanding *her* again. Controlling every tremor, shiver, sigh, scream, and molecule of sweat, arousal, and juice her body had to give. All for me. All *because* of me. "You *are* going to come. And you're going to do it hard, sassy—for me."

"Okay." She swallowed hard. "Just please...don't stop. Please, please, please don't stop. Just like that."

"Feels good, baby?"

"B-Better than good. Oh. *Ohhhh*."

I angled forward, trying to find just the right spot deep inside her quivering body. Every woman was just a bit different, but there was no doubt about it—when a guy hit it, he knew. He just *knew*.

"Ohhhhh!" She shrieked so loud both my ears rang. I smiled, deepening my caresses over that little strip of sensitivity inside her cunt. "*What* are you doing to me?"

I leaned in, scraping my teeth along the curve of her jaw. "You want me to stop?"

"No!" Another long moan. "Dear God, *no*! Ohhhh...hell..."

Apparently, no one had ever hit her G-spot before, but watching her fall apart had to be one of the best damn moments of my life. I pumped her through the shattering orgasm, keeping my fingers deep in her channel while she fluttered wildly around me. My free arm, still around her waist, remained in a tight hold until she was finished with all the residual shivers. When she slackened against me, I slid to the floor and gathered her close to my chest.

We sat there, silent and sweaty, in her tiny apartment, wordless and, in a way, even weightless. Time was sure as hell not a consideration, nor were her jeans and panties, still haphazardly pushed around her thighs.

She purred in my lap, completely content.

And strangely—wonderfully—so was I.

For perhaps the first time since we'd met, we were at peace. I liked the feeling. A lot. What a treat it was to stroke her silky blond hair while she relaxed in my arms, finally not defensive or combative. Just simply...Taylor.

Taylor. The most captivating, curious, mystifying woman I'd ever met.

Literally. Ever.

CHAPTER SIX

Taylor

Lord. Help. Me.

It was, without a doubt, the best orgasm I'd ever had.

But the man's horrid—*heavenly*—biting habit needed to stop. Or so I kept attempting to tell myself—and failing. My shoulder throbbed but in the most tantalizing way. The pain brought back every second of the memories...the moments I never wanted to forget. There'd be an enormous bruise there, and I'd wince at that—as every inch of me glowed anew with erotic warmth. It would be my badge of honor. The ultimate sign that I'd tamed the beast known as Maclain Stone.

And what a beast...

That thought brought out my inner preen, inspiring me to be more snuggly than usual on the outside. With my head burrowed against his chest and my body drenched in a post-orgasmic high, I finally muttered, "Hey...clown?"

"Hmmm?" he murmured, still sounding sexy and growly.

"We need to talk about you getting a chew toy."

He laughed from so low in his throat the sound vibrated through his body and rumbled through mine. I was still draped across his lap like a rag doll, my pants hanging low around my thighs like some harlot's, though at this moment, I was okay with the comparison. Sometimes, careless harlot felt good.

Not true, either. Harlot had *never* felt good for me—until this. Until him.

"I think I've already found the perfect one." He tugged a section of my hair a little harder, just in case I'd missed the obvious reference. My preen button given a rocket boost, I didn't even want to muster a protest. I tucked my head beneath his chin and sighed. No. Not a harlot at all. A treasured kitten. I said as much, practically meowing into the spot where his pulse thudded so firmly, at the base of his corded throat.

After a few seconds of that, another low vibration moved through him. "Taylor," he husked, swallowing solidly.

"Mmmm?"

"Let's go to your room. I'm not done with you."

"No." Once more, I issued it with soft simplicity.

"Huh?"

"You're done, mister. Trust me."

"Little sass, if you think that's all there is to a night with me, you are sadly mistaken."

His sensual drawl nearly made me give up and kiss him again. Long and hard. I resisted by huffing, "I'm sure your sexual prowess is mighty, Super Clown, but I'm not about to test your strengths one by one." I summoned the strength to straighten a little. "No offense, but I have to get up for work in the morning—and regardless, I'm sure my neighbors have called nine-one-one after that last trick."

Feeling I could accomplish a full rise, I swung my feet to the floor and pushed up. Mac helped, carefully supporting me, while getting himself upright in a single smooth motion. The man was so naturally agile, he bordered on daunting—but that wasn't where the word stopped with him. As I yanked my jeans back up and then refastened the button, no way could I miss the bulge in the front of his dress slacks.

The impressive, *unnerving* bulge.

"Dude." I winced. "Sorry."

"Don't be." He shifted closer at once, reaching without hesitation for my waist. "We really aren't done here."

It took more willpower than I thought to swat his hand away. "No. We really are, Mac. You know the saying, right? *No means no?*" I tilted my head up, daring to confront the dark jade lust in his gaze. "You're not a dense man. You did make it through medical school, after all."

To my surprise, a grin broke past his lips. "Make it through? I graduated top of my class, love."

I rolled my eyes. "Of course you did."

"So, definitely not dense."

"Of course not."

"So if I say something is going to happen? It happens. And this?" He motioned back and forth between us though let his hand stray once it reached me, stroking a defined path across my shoulder blades...and then down between my breasts. "This is going to happen." His tone roughened, matching the slower intent of his touch. My heartbeat clamored toward his mesmerizing fingers, throbbing like a cobra beneath the spell of a masterful charmer. "This is intense, Taylor Mathews, and we both know it. Stop trying to deny it."

I swallowed, knowing he noticed but unable to hold back. My nipples pebbled inside my bra. My lungs scrambled to claim nonexistent air. And holy shit, my pussy began to respond too. Yes, already. Yes, to the point of agony. Yes, seeping into my panties and my jeans.

"Y-You're crazy."

The edges of his mouth lifted again. His eyes dropped,

watching every inch of my face. "Maybe a little of that too. But there's one thing I'm not, Taylor."

"Wh-What's that?"

"A liar." His tone was nonchalant but direct, almost as if we were negotiating business. The contrast between that clinical sound and the visual strip-down from his gaze... Yeah, I was wet again. "I'm not a liar, Miss Mathews. Ever. With me, you'll always get the truth—even if it's not what you want to hear."

His conclusion gave me an opening for insouciance. "So... is that some kind of mystical warning?" My confusion wasn't a lie. While I might not have graduated top of my class, I wasn't a daft person, either.

"No. I'm just telling you something about me." He shrugged as though that wasn't an odd thing to just announce—spinning me into even deeper puzzlement.

"Okay, what's going on here? I barely know you, Maclain Stone—only today, you magically show up in the exact same place as me, instantly going Mr. Pushy about my eating and then taking over Sally like—"

"You *really* need to name her something other than Sally."

"Shut up." I slammed both hands to my hips. "Now you're in my crappy apartment, damn near dictating we're going to sleep together, and I feel like I'm watching a lost episode of the *Twilight Zone*." By the time I realized I'd added my tapping toe to the posture, fulfilling every nuance of his—and not altogether awful—nickname for me, his fresh grin said he had done the same math there too.

"Like I said, sassy, you'll never get anything but the truth from me. As I said back at Scripps, I was there for a job interview. My buddy from med school, Lawrence Ball, works in the Neurology Department there. He called a few weeks back about an opening they have, right after I booked the flight to come out for the wedding. I gave him some dates, and he hooked me up with the department head and chief of staff." He shrugged again, his broad shoulders moving with no effort, toppling every inch of my hard-won attitude from distraction. "It was a complete stroke of luck that I ran into you in the parking lot, but maybe that was a good thing too."

"Yeah?" I refocused and rallied, tossing him a look that was drollness on crack. "And how do you figure that?"

"Because you really *do* need to eat more and probably need someone to tell you that. And maybe that someone is me." And just like that, he reclaimed the upper hand—literally—by using that easy grace to hypnotize me as he stepped back in, crowding my space once more. With the same flow of motion, he leaned over and pressed a thumb right into the bruise on my shoulder. "Believe me, love...you need all the help you can get to keep up your strength."

He smirked as I squirmed, shamelessly wicked about his gloat. When I wriggled harder, he yanked me around the waist, pulling me against him.

"Mac. What're—"

"And this isn't a crappy apartment." His statement—command?—matched the green iron spikes that entered his gaze. "It's charming and full of personality, much like its sassy little occupant."

"Oh, my God." A new eye roll. I didn't care if I got another thumbprint on my bruise for it. And the man really expected me to believe his "calling it like I see it" BS now?

"Go clean yourself up." Again, he went on as if my words were Teletubby babbles. "And we'll go get a pizza or something.

I'm starving—and I wasn't joking when I said you'll need energy for what I have planned for the rest of the evening."

I started the toe tapping again—considering it preparation for kicking him. "Why the hell aren't you listening to me? You are *not* staying here."

He stepped back. Only by an inch. Jogged his jaw at me by an equal amount. "Let's settle it on your chess board." He started back toward the table with the marble set on it, in a little alcove to which I referred as the "office."

"I told you I don't play."

Glancing over his shoulder, he countered, "And I'm calling your bluff. Six moves to checkmate. Whoever gets there first decides if I'm staying or not."

"Six?" I raised my eyebrows. Damn it. Damn *him*. I couldn't resist a challenge, not one like this—and I could almost taste the sweetness of victory on my lips. It'd feel so good to beat his ass. "You're a dead man, clown."

He thought for a second, and I ignored how hot he looked doing it. "Then don't you mean *you're a dead clown*?"

"Oh-ho." I nodded with a knowing smile. "So you're a grammar Nazi too?"

"I have many talents, little sass. You'll see." He leaned against the corner where the alcove began. "Another one of them is a lockbox memory—meaning I'm going to overlook your lie about not being able to play. That makes three things I'm looking forward to punishing you for...when you're ready."

I gave an inner groan. Maybe a soft outer one too. I might have been able to let the new mention of his mysterious *punishments* fly by unnoticed, but he had to add that last part, once more in that presumptive growl. *When you're ready.* Like he completely expected I *would* be...and that I'd even enjoy it...

though not nearly as much as him.

And why did the idea of *his* pleasure even matter—let alone bring such a deep wash of heat to my bloodstream?

This ended now. The second I checkmated his ass, so I could toss every hot-as-hell inch of it away from my temptation forever. "Cute," I retorted to him while tugging the table and board away from the alcove. "But you can just tear up your little 'infractions' list now. It's never going to happen."

Mac eyed the area from which I'd just yanked the board, right next to the small credenza where I kept my computer and printer. The board was handy for when I played opponents online, so I could move actual pieces as every move was made onscreen. Sometimes—many times—chess wasn't just the logistical but the tactile. The actual weight of a piece in one's fingers, lending psychic insight for the next move, was sometimes the difference between rote strategy and insightful victory. Of course, none of my friends knew this about me, and I preferred it that way. It was best for everyone that Taylor Mathews remain her sarcastic but sunshiny self, not the pensive chess player with the laundry list of trust and codependency issues. Yes, best for everyone and way easier for the nerd recluse—who once more snapped on her audacious mask while scooting toward the breakfast bar, the best place to put this thing for his little suicide match.

But as I moved, there was no physical way to avoid contact with the smirking man. He couldn't move out of my way because of the couch, so our bodies were pressed achingly close against each other. I tried a deep breath for self-control, but that only reminded me how good he smelled, the old-school cologne colliding with all that virile musk, and...*shit*.

Mac himself did nothing to ease the situation. With just

one subtle move, he dipped his huge frame over me, giving him the perfect vantage point for fitting his lips to my ear again.

I froze.

He murmured, "I promise you will beg me to punish you."

The board trembled in my grip, making the pieces dance.

The waltz betrayed my growing excitement. My clamoring arousal.

Though it was ridiculous, right? That a threat—a *promise*—like *that* would make me feel this way?

"I-I think you're taking the drugs you prescribe for people."

Yes. Ridiculous. But ohhhh so unbelievably real.

"I don't prescribe drugs for people, silly girl. I fix people so they don't need drugs."

"Oh, my God." I plopped the board onto the breakfast bar and dropped my head into my hands in disbelief.

"Chess, then?"

He slid onto a bar stool, already looking triumphant. I lifted my head, yearning to smack the smugness off every inch of his sexy face. I opted for a hard glare instead.

"Let's do this so you leave me in peace."

His lips quirked. "Let's."

"Hope you're not a sore loser."

"We'll see who's sore in the end, sassy."

I said nothing—and since I was feeling charitable, I pushed the white pieces in his direction, giving him first move. In a game of just six moves, that already gave him the advantage—technically speaking. The psychological warfare was different. *Take the edge, clown. You'll need it.*

We each made quick work of setting up our pieces, and I sat back to await his opening move.

Which consisted of him stretching a hand across toward me.

I stared down at those extended fingers and ordered myself not to remember what those talented digits were capable of doing to my body, my brain. "What?"

"Good luck." His smile doubled his natural handsomeness—as well as the devil behind his easy charm.

"Sure." I smiled and shook once. Nothing wrong with giving in to the cordiality of a good-looking stud, if it was just for a few seconds. "You're going to need it."

Twenty minutes' worth of tense silence later, he plunked his bishop closer to my queen—and I instantly recognized the foolishness of the move that had preceded it. I'd thought I had him beat and gotten lazy about studying the entire board. As a result, he was able to fill the air with one soft but deliberate word.

"Checkmate."

I blew out a long breath—as my heartbeat quickened with a bizarre mix of dismay and anticipation.

Have I actually...wanted to lose all along?

No. I'd given the match my best—though now that my gig was up, the loss wasn't so hard to take. My nerves sparked hotter. My skin prickled, antsy, agitated, and anticipating. It was difficult to stand and not look jittery, but my hand was steady as I offered it to him. "Great game."

He didn't reply. Instead, he stood, took my physical yield with a determined grab—and hauled me against his body with an audible thud.

At once, his scent surrounded me—and his muscles enervated me.

"You're a very good player," he said, too damn controlled

about every syllable. "I thought for sure you had me at the end."

"Well, you beat me," I managed, not nearly as polished. "Straight up. So what's your prize going to be?"

A dark chuckle, bordering on a growl. "You have to ask?"

Deep gulp. "I guess I don't."

"You know what I want, Taylor. But I won't force you to do something you don't want to do. So how about we start with dinner? I'd really like to see you eat something besides cookies."

"And eggs, bacon, and toast." I slanted a challenging eyebrow. "This morning. Remember?"

"Aaahhh, that's right. With real butter." He winked, and I struggled not to grin. I wondered if he used those winks as part of fixing his patients. They could be prescribed as effective therapy. "So...if I stay overnight, can I expect the same breakfast of cholesterol champions?"

"Depends on how well you perform tonight at the circus, clown." I looked up, taking in his gorgeous face, trying for a flirtatious look of my own. Perhaps it was time to start fighting fire with fire.

"Well, it'll be all three rings for you, Miss Mathews...trust me."

Trust me.

Did he have any idea how hard it was for me to take those words seriously?

But this wasn't a moment for that dysfunction. This was an opportunity to let my eyes slide shut, glorying in the expert rolls of his hips, savoring every inch of his erection grinding into me. He tucked his mouth against my jaw, his breath heavy and purposeful, steaming my mind's dirty recesses with dark, illicit promises. He felt so damn good.

So. Damn. Good...

This man would be the certain death of me if I wasn't careful. Sharp wit, sinful sexuality, and a body built to bring it all to life... Yeah, my self-restraint was already halfway toasted. My most erotic fantasies played ring-around-the-roses right in front of me, and we were all about to fall down—right into my bed if I wasn't careful.

"Food."

His deep voice brought me back to the present. "Hmmmm?" I sighed back, voice gritty with need. "What?"

"Food first," Mac reminded, scooting back. *Damn.* "Sex later." He finished it with a more wolfish version of the wink. *This man.*

"Yes. Food. Then we'll see." Without his cock mercilessly taunting my sex, I sounded a little more like myself. Thank God.

"Whatever you say." His tone made it seem like he didn't think my resolve was very strong. "Let's call for a car. That way we can have a few beers—or whatever you like to drink."

"I like beer."

"Another plus." He kept me captive in his arms while we chatted.

"Where are you staying, anyway?" I had to tilt my head back pretty far when I spoke to him. I guessed he was over six feet tall.

"Ummmm, La Valencia? In La Jolla. Yeah, that's the name of it."

"Oh. The place on Prospect?"

"I have no idea." The self-effacing version of his grin was just as gorgeous as the others...perhaps more so because of the way it crinkled the corners of his eyes. One man, so many facets and so many ways to captivate my attention. It was thrilling. And scary.

I finally managed to toss out an indulgent laugh before asking, "Well, does it seem to be the main drag in town?"

"Yes. The traffic is ridiculous. I'm glad I don't have to park around there."

"Yeah, that's it. I love that place. The ocean right out back, and I've eaten at their restaurant a few times." When Claire or Margaux were treating. "There's a beachwear store across the street that I love too." And had actually shopped at, when I had a little cushion in the bank account and felt like splurging.

"Yeah. Great for sleeping."

His comment couldn't have been more "man blunt" if he were quoting football scores—and upped his adorable factor by another notch. I had to admit, dating guys who knew more about thread counts than me was a little strange.

"I'll bet it is," I murmured, using our clasped hands to urge him back toward my door. "So...wouldn't you rather go back there after dinner?"

His brows pushed together. "What's wrong with here?"

"Besides the crappy and cramped part?" *And the fact that you fill too much of the air in it? And that I'm beginning to like that?* But I was also uncomfortable in the not-so-good ways. Observing him here, in his luxury threads, his precision-cut hair, and his confident stance, seemed to make my humble abode that much more...well...humble. But right now, it was all I could afford for comfort while still socking away funds for Mom's "emergencies." Sure, I'd have rather lived on the coast along with many of my friends, but Janet Mathews raised the term "bail money" to a whole different level of meaning.

"I told you before," Mac all but growled back. "This place

doesn't bother me." He went on, disregarding my protesting huff, "This place has *you*. And a chess set. And even a thermostat I don't need a degree in rocket science to operate."

I narrowed my eyes. "I thought neuroscience was nearly the same."

"In some ways, sure. Just don't ask me to bump up the heat by a couple of degrees in a hotel room." He mock-shuddered, spurring my soft giggle. "Those big, fancy places... They're impersonal and cold. And the people... Way too many for my liking."

"So...wait." I scowled deeper. "Are you telling me Mr. Bigshot Brain Doctor Dude doesn't live in one of those sparkly new buildings in Chicago?" I gave a hard huff. "Who do you think you're kidding right now, mister? Just because I sound like a hayseed doesn't mean I am one."

His expression tightened. "Okay, I just explained this shit to you. I'm not a liar, Taylor. I live in a medium-sized condo in a nice neighborhood. Parts of Chicago have become pretty dangerous, so I pay for the address, but I'm not attached to it."

"Which was why you considered your friend's job offer?"

He shrugged, his ire shifting to nonplussed—another new expression for me to absorb. "One of the reasons...among many."

"What are the others?" I genuinely wanted to know. From what I'd been able to fathom when spending all those days in Chicago Memorial Hospital with Talia, the man was close to a celebrity in Chicago's medical scene. *What else could inspire him to leave such a sweet gig?*

"Well, I'm not a fan of the weather," he quickly conceded. "I often don't get to pick the two seconds a week I'm not working, so I'm at the mercy of the elements, which are often up to delivering humidity or snow for some fun fuckery. I'm not certain which one I hate more." He paused, as if weighing the two for their merits. "No, definitely hate the snow more."

I nodded, connecting the dots of that obvious conclusion. "None of that can be fun for a guy who likes driving and collecting cars." But still, the dots seemed unreal. Was I really having a conversation about car collections when I'd be begging Sally for another day of her best effort tomorrow morning?

"Bingo." He tapped my nose, an affectionate show that turned me a little gooey inside. "Nice cars get ruined in that shitty weather, and idiots drive like bigger idiots in heavy rain and snow. I've fixed more skulls from bad-weather accidents than I care to count, meaning I've paid my damn dues on that front. I'd love to live somewhere like this, where every day is a top-down kind of day."

I paused for a second, letting the smile he induced in my heart break free on my lips. The man was transformed when talking about his passions, and I couldn't help but feel changed with him. Caterpillar, meet butterfly—and the big, beautiful wings were preparing to take flight. I couldn't imagine anyone not getting swept up in the glory.

"Have you ever driven a convertible?" The question was a good follow-up and bought some more minutes in the presence of his glow. I was entranced with the commitment he gave to his favorite subjects...so similar to the way he'd plunged into the act of fulfilling *me*...

Ohhhh, my God...

"I've driven one but never owned one," Mac answered. "Though it'd be a must-have in a climate like this. Weekly drives up the coast just to smell the ocean air..."

"During your two seconds off?" I teased.

He chuckled. "Time worth finding."

"Bingo." As I returned his affirmation, I used a knuckle to buss his nose before nodding in agreement and saying, "There's nothing like coming home to San Diego after you travel. The minute you get off the plane, even on the gangway, you can already smell the ocean in the air as you walk toward the terminal. It tempts me to tear up every time I come home from a business trip."

"Do you travel a lot?" The sincerity in his voice was obvious. He was truly interested in my contribution to the conversation—such a change from the usual guys I dated.

"It's not too bad," I explained. "Maybe once a quarter. Depends what SGC has going on."

"Whoa." He started as if I'd set off a firecracker in his face. "*You* work for my cousin too?"

I quirked a frown. "How did you think I knew Claire and Talia?"

"Same hairdresser?" He joined me in a laugh, but tension still clamped his features, which were now infused with annoyance. "So...the guy employs all of San Diego."

I batted his chest. "Don't tell me you really didn't know."

"Guess I didn't care." Just like that, as he held my fingers over his heart, his tone mellowed like mist over a sunset sea. "I don't think things completely through when it comes to you, love. I'm usually too busy being distracted by you in general."

Sweet, freaking blister bug in a pepper patch. How's that for the sexy side of honesty?

It was fine. *Very* fine. I grinned like a fool and didn't feel a morsel of shame for it. And for some reason, he was grinning like a fool too.

"All right, all right," I drawled. "You win, mister. Let me go shower really quick, and then we can go eat. TV's over there," I swung a finger in the vague direction of the sofa and television. "Remote's on the table if you'd like to watch something."

His stare, not leaving me, turned the shade of a lagoon in the middle of my sweltering pepper patch. "You *know* what I'd prefer watching, firecracker."

I rolled my eyes. "And isn't that a shocker?"

His expression took on a hopeful Boy Scout ardor. "You really sure you don't need some help?"

Okay, make that a naughty Boy Scout. I had no idea they existed, but he proved the point with blaring clarity. "I think I can manage. Thanks, though."

"Can't blame a clown for trying."

"Indeed."

He gave my rear a swat as I turned to retreat into the bedroom. When I swung back around to scold him, he whirled me close again, kissing me soundly enough to suck out my breath. As a result, my senses spun and I desperately grabbed the boulders of his biceps for purchase. His groan was my response, reverberating through my mouth as he swept inside with his skilled tongue. My entire head swirled again. It was the most blissful vertigo I'd ever known.

Is he seriously this good at everything?

The question was a funny hum in my head, even after he stopped. No way was I about to let him go, since my brain was still twirling like a three-year-old ballerina.

In a flash, the solution to that struck me.

"Hey. Did you drug me?"

Confusion stormed across his face—until my gist clearly sank in, making him succumb to a deep, hard laugh. "Oh, sassy girl." He smacked my forehead with a sound kiss. "You haven't seen anything yet."

"Christ Almighty." I mumbled it under my breath, but he chuckled again, making sure I knew he'd heard.

"Shower." He spun me toward my room, lightly pushing me this time. No more swats. *Bummer.*

Despite his leniency, I nearly faceplanted before catching myself on the doorway. I rested my head on the stained wood trim for a second or two before pushing open my bedroom door and then closing it behind me—and instantly flattening my back against the portal as I struggled to catch my breath.

Like a damn three-year-old ballerina at her first recital.

No. A virgin with the star quarterback in the next room.

No. Worse.

A woman dying to throw open the door and let that man barge in here, throw me onto the bed, and slam his long, incredible thighs right between mine...

"Get a grip on yourself," I ordered from between clenched teeth. "Nobody gets in here, Taylor."

Nobody.

Not *this* room. Not my sole sanctuary left on earth. This was mine, just like the protected room inside my soul too. The place nobody got to see—because that way, nobody got to hurt it, either.

Nevertheless, this was all getting embarrassing—and my hide-and-seek act wasn't helping. The man's ego was already out of control, meaning he must be thinking I'd escaped for not being able to handle him.

And isn't that partially true?

Maybe more than partially?

Not that Doc Stone himself needed to know that—or have his damn fire fueled any more.

With that thought, I took a lightning-fast shower, ran a

quick refresh to my makeup, and declared myself ready to go despite five wardrobe changes.

Why this outfit selection stuff was so hard, I had no damn idea. Finally, knowing we were just going for pizza and beer, I kept it super casual. Lightweight skinny black overalls were paired with a white crop top underneath, with block-heeled sandals finishing off the look. My jewelry was simple, since I owned little of it in the first place.

After one last once-over in my closet door mirror, I grabbed my bag off the dresser and went back out into the living room. As soon as I reemerged, Mac stood—his stare raking me from head to toe with appreciation he didn't bother to hide. With strides emulating an approaching lion, he sauntered over, going straight for another kiss—though this time, he took my mouth with an admiring kind of reverence.

"You're gorgeous," he finally said in a soft snarl. "And you smell good enough to eat."

"I thought you wanted pizza?" Yeah, that was me deflecting with humor. Compliments were uncomfortable for me to accept, even when they came from people who didn't want anything from me in return.

Mac tilted his head, seeming to comprehend exactly that—though he countered just as easily, "Hmmm. I may have changed my mind. What is that perfume? I love it."

I laughed lightly. "You're a strange clown, if I've ever met one."

"Do you know a lot of clowns?"

"Guess it depends on how you define clown." I punctuated that with a small shriek as he lowered back to the faded couch, pulling me down with him. "Hey! What's this?"

"Comfortable." He secured me on his lap by practically

engulfing me in his arms. "Wouldn't you agree?"

The question was rhetorical. Sort of. His grip relaxed when I only fought half-heartedly to get back up. I blamed that on getting to caress little circles into his forearms, exposed now that he'd hiked up his dress-shirtsleeves. *Damn.* Even the man's forearms were hot. Just the right amount of rough hair and hewn muscle.

"Why do you think you can just manhandle me like this?"

"Because you let me," he supplied. "And you like it."

I shook my head—and refused to give him the all-too-true assent to that. Instead I said, "Believe it or not, the perfume is Allure, from Chanel. Margaux gave it to me because she didn't like it. But I think it's nice."

"And why do you say believe it or not?" Again, he seemed genuinely curious about my answer—a luxury I ordered myself not to get used to.

"Because I would never spend that kind of money on perfume. It's silly. I usually just use lotion that smells good. Whatever's on sale."

"But you should treat yourself to something nice once in a while. You work hard. I'm sure my cousin pays you well. He's a cocksucker, but he's not unfair or stupid."

I spurted out a little laugh. "First, I'm pretty sure Killian Stone doesn't suck dick. I think Claire would've mentioned that." I grinned even thinking of such a thing. "Second, he pays me very well. And third—" My lips compressed. I dashed my gaze down, glad for the distraction of his all-too-awesome forearm. "Well, third isn't worth talking about because we're having a nice evening."

"And nothing you can tell me will ruin that evening."

Christ. He really was a Boy Scout. But if he wanted to

earn this merit badge so badly, I might as well let him. He was the one into honesty, after all.

"All right, then." I straightened my stare, locking it directly with his. "I'm the 'adult child of an addict.'" I air-quoted the words, though the somber understanding in his eyes made them unnecessary. "And, needless to say, my mom has the awesome habit of playing with the trouble fairy. When their shenanigans get out of control, I'm pretty much it for her financial, physical, and emotional rescue." A deep whoosh of a breath later, I concluded, "Annnnd if you want to run for the door, it's right there. No harm, no foul."

The breath I'd just been indulging now clogged and tangled in my throat. *No harm, no foul.* I'd meant it when I said it, but the reality of possibly following through wasn't as easy to accept—which was why so few people in my life were allowed behind that door. Beyond that portal, I was soft. Exposed. Open to be wounded.

Or healed.

Which isn't what I expected from Douchebag McHunk, is it?

Then why am I still staring at him...holding my damn breath? And why did it feel so freaking good when, a moment later, he pushed me gently off his lap like I'd merely admitted my mother collected yarn and liked doing sock puppet shows for local school kids—neither of which was true but was a small fantasy to consider for one pretty moment...

"Come on, woman. I'm starving," he declared before standing. "I called for a car, and they should be pulling up in a few minutes."

While we walked back out to the front of the complex, he slipped his hand just inside my overalls, pressing it over the bare skin at the small of my back. While the move made me feel valuable and cherished, I couldn't resist canting a saucy look up at him. "Uhhhh...Dr. Stone?"

His eyes glinted like a grab bag of green gemstones. "Yes, Miss Mathews?"

"Aren't you being a little forward?"

"Maybe. Probably. But I can't seem to keep my hands off you, firecracker. So what do you propose I do about that?" While I floundered for a comeback full of brilliance and wit, he turned fully toward me. "Seriously speaking, do you mind the contact?" His gaze searched my face. "I don't want you to be uncomfortable."

Well, there was the opening for my wit again. With a dramatic flourish, I glanced around the lawn. "I'm sorry, sir. Who are you, and what did you do with the clown I had to myself for the day?"

He laughed but quickly sobered. "He's with you in public now—and the wolves taught him that different rules apply here. What we do in private is a different story—I can and will push you to every limit you have then—but I'm not into humiliation." His head cocked. "Unless *you* are?"

Now I almost laughed—but caught myself at observing his earnestness. "And if I was..."

"Then I'd have to do some research on it first," he replied easily. "But I'd be up to speed soon so your needs are fully met."

My needs. The term crashed into the walls of my mind before detonating into shards of pure shock—along with the others he'd been using with me, so foreign yet so amazing. *My comfort. My pleasure...*

Holy hell. This man.

Yeah, the same one I'd written off as King Ding Dong

Douchebag just a few hours ago.

Seriously, who the hell *was* he? And what planet had he come from?

"No, no," I dismissed him in a rush. "You're saved from homework. Codependent, remember?" I pointed back to myself with my thumb. "Have already logged those frequent-flier miles."

The car pulled up then, and we climbed inside. But as soon as the driver, a friendly enough guy who liked smooth jazz, stepped on the gas pedal, Mac's low grumblings began. First, it was about the compact car itself, and I smacked his thigh. Next, he started in on how the guy wove in and out of traffic. Smack number two. When we exited and hit more condensed traffic, he swore we'd end the ride with a trip to the emergency room. Smack number three, as well as a concerted effort on my part to hold back my laugh—as well as a serious mental note to never get behind the wheel in his presence.

When we finally got out in front of the little pizza place in Hillcrest, there were actual beads of sweat on the good doctor's brow.

"Sweet corn on the cob," I muttered, letting the accent get a good stretch. "You are a mess."

"I'll be fine."

He jerked away in order to thank the Kenny G fan and was shockingly cordial about it. When he walked back over, I was still busy biting back a giggle. "You have got to be the worst backseat driver I've ever seen."

His shoulders settled but instead of a protest, he said, "I should've sat up front. It's worse for me in the back seat."

"Then why didn't you?" I pressed a hand over his cheek, which was still pale in the neon glow from the restaurant's sign.

He leaned his face into my touch. "I wanted to sit with you."

My heart swooned—just before I let the laughter burst out. As in knee slapping, doubled-over laughter.

"What's so funny?" He smiled past his defensive tone.

"You. *You're* so funny." I straightened and swiped the tears from the corners of my eyes. "Is this a control thing?"

He chuckled "I suppose so. I just can't deal when other people drive. I've operated on so many auto accident victims..." Sobriety crept into his composure. He jammed both hands into his slacks pockets. "And I've lost plenty of patients too." He shrugged and kicked one expensive loafer at the sidewalk. "It's just too real for me."

"Yet you love to race cars," I pointed out.

"Yep." He nodded firmly, exposing the brawny cords in his neck. Sometime between the Blood Mobile and our intimacy on my couch, he'd ditched the suit's coat and tie. By now, he was gorgeously rumpled. "Yep, I *really* love racing cars."

I shook my head and stated softly, "You are such a dichotomy." And let that rest while staring at him. Dear God. He was pretty magnificent. *How the hell did I get here?*

"A *what*?" My tag had clearly disarmed him.

"I don't know." I shrugged. "I...don't know. You're just... interesting, I guess." I just shook my head again.

He kicked the sidewalk while pushing a hand through his hair. "You're making me self-conscious."

"Maybe you should be," I riposted. "You're pretty put-together for a clown. But now I know you have a fault. I may have to go to the media with the news. Facebook at a minimum. Insta and Twitter too."

"You wouldn't dare." He shifted his hands up to his lean

waist. Moved in toward me, useless in his effort at appearing menacing. Yeah, I was positive of that. The wattage of my snark was clear proof.

"Well, I can be bought."

"And I'm *very* interested in knowing your price." He lion-crept closer, into that space where our heads had to bend to accommodate the twine of our stares, his dipping low, mine arching back. "So what do you say let's go inside and discuss your terms over a big, greasy deep dish?"

"Thin and crispy, and you've got a deal."

"Thin and crispy?" Once again, I'd exploded an invisible firework in his face. "Are you fucking serious?"

"As a heart attack." I folded my arms. "Which is what deep dish will give you, after gulping down enough of that dough."

He snorted. "That's what the gym is for."

"Uh-uh." I raised a hand, palm out. "Allergic to the gym."

"Sassy. I'm from *Chicago*."

"You're in the land of fruits and nuts now, buddy. Time to assimilate."

"What have I gotten myself into?" Though he groaned it, his grin was brilliant as he swung open the door for me. I stepped through, certain mine matched—because the bubbling bliss in my heart dictated it.

Ohhhh, shit.

We were stumbling into very dangerous territory. The emotional equivalent of penetrating enemy lines, where landmines and tripwires lay hidden and deadly for the unwary—and the stupidly grinning. Yeah, the kind of stuff that blew up in someone's face, rocking their entire world when they least expected it. The kind that destroyed entire villages and burned their civilizations to the ground.

Meaning, if either of us had any sense, we'd abort the mission immediately.

But the communication link to my brain was nothing but static.

Blissful, giddy, sexually charged static.

CHAPTER SEVEN

Mac

Finally, we were back at Taylor's. She'd seen the wisdom of doing things my way, and I planned on continuing that trend all the way into her bed and then between her incredible silken thighs.

As soon as fucking possible.

I was confident about accomplishing the quest. Like in chess, victory was about strategy, and mine had begun before we took our first bite of pizza. The plan hadn't been tough to execute. Being with this woman was invigorating... intoxicating. And unless I was misreading every one of her signs, the sentiment was very much reciprocated. Now, our stomachs were full and our happy buzzes still going—but best of all, there was a sexy blonde still tucked under my arm.

Oh, yeah. That was definitely the best of all.

She fumbled with her apartment keys, though I wasn't making the task easy with my ardent kisses behind her ear. Could I be blamed? Never had I been with a woman possessing a more hypnotizing neck. Every time my lips came near it, I longed to go full beast mode, riddling her white skin with my ravenous bites.

"Open the door already." I nuzzled her earlobe before biting it hard.

She gasped but then giggled out, "Sssshhhh! And stop that, or you'll make me scream."

"And that's a bad thing?"

"My neighbors will turn the lights on." Another sweet giggle. "Hmmm. That actually might be fun. Showtime, folks!"

I joined my low laugh to her string of snort-snickers. Jesus, her little shaking body felt so good against mine. *Intoxicating* might have to be escalated. She was jacking me to the realm of high. *Euphoric.* And reveling in every second. I hadn't expected her to be so silly after a few drinks, but her giddiness was a sheer delight, heightened by the ticklish spots I kept finding all over her body. Her slender frame seemed filled with them, and I'd stopped trying to control my hands from launching search after search for them all. Why stop heaven, when it existed in the form of her girlish little squeals?

And yep...there was another one. The middle of the back of her arm. I stroked her there again, just to be sure...

"Mac!"

I answered her gasp with a savoring growl. "I love the sound of your laugh." I finally took the keys from her hands before pinning them low alongside her thighs. As an easy silence thickened between us, I pressed my forehead to hers, waiting expectantly for her gaze to angle up.

"Look at me, girl," I dictated, threading my low voice with sexual promise.

She swiveled her head from side to side. "I don't want to," she whispered into my chest.

"Why not?"

"Because it hurts."

"To look at me?" I punched it with incredulity.

"You're too handsome." A she-devil's grin spread across

her lips. "For a clown, I mean."

I was tempted to retort a number of things, but in the end I just repeated, lower than before, "*Look at me*, Taylor."

It was hard as hell to stay the course on serious when she wanted to keep up with the sexy and playful, but it was time to gauge her readiness for this—to verify that the arousal flowing off her in tidal waves was true craving for me, not just a product of the cold beer and the steamy night. I wasn't taking our earlier activities as any indication she wouldn't bolt now. Confronting bald realities, especially when it came to claiming her own fulfillment, seemed to be a missing chip in this woman's mainframe.

Finally, she looked up with those enormous blue eyes. Her lashes were fresh and long, her skin dewy and flawless without makeup. As I studied her, it hurt to breathe. I forced words to my lips anyway.

"So perfect," I told her, stroking hair off her cheek with the backs of my fingers. "And so damn pretty, little love."

She opened her mouth, clearly at work on a protest, but I stopped her useless words by pressing a kiss to each of her eyelids. She kept them closed, making it possible for me to sweep my lips over the fans of her lashes before brushing back over the tip of her nose...and tenderly nibbling her a little there. How could I resist? She was like dessert to me. One delectable taste deserved another...

"Mac..." The word left her on a serrated breath. "That feels...so..."

But if she had a word in mind, I stole it from her with the solid mesh of my kiss. She moaned as I fitted my mouth over hers, pushing my way inside her mouth in my next hot sweep of motion. She tasted as sweet as honey, infused with slight bitterness from the lager we'd drunk with our pizza. *Fuck. Pure ambrosia.*

I could have sampled her all night like this—but so much more was in store. At least I hoped so. Prayed so. "Shit, sassy. Beer tastes really good on you."

"Mmmm," she hummed, her lips curving with dreamy languor. "You too."

I kissed her again but deliberately truncated the move. Sucking face like that first time wasn't wise if I wanted to keep us from being her neighbors' popcorn attraction for the night. Besides, I had something substantial to say.

"Hey."

"Hey yourself." She reopened her eyes, those gorgeous lapis depths lending me boldness.

"I have a cool idea."

Her lips quirked. "No, I've not read the *Kama Sutra*, nor am I interested in doing so."

Thinking better of telling her I'd studied the thing a number of times, I stuck to my original subject. "Let's go to Oktoberfest next month. I bet they do a pretty decent one around here somewhere. Maybe a few." Just like that, the ping-pong balls in my brain activated. "Though officially, Oktoberfest starts in September. And you're supposed to wear a fuzzy hat. That's the status symbol at the festival. The fuzzier the hat, the wealthier the drinker, you know. Though that's in Munich, where the average temperature in late September is only—"

"Whoa." She giggled it out. "Uhhh, clown?"

"I'm going to regret asking what, aren't I?"

She grinned, alcohol obviously still soaking her with more courage. "Oktoberfest? Errr—Septemberfest?" She waved a dismissive hand. "Okay, whatever. Doesn't matter. Big, un-overlookable detail, dude. You live in another state."

"Minor detail."

"*Minor?*"

I narrowed my gaze while lowering my head. "So, they have this modern-day thing called an airplane. Crazy contraptions, really." I kissed her again, lingering this time, licking ardently at the seam of her closed lips. When she wouldn't succumb, I growled, "Open."

She jerked back. "No. Let's go inside. Mrs. Franklin just appeared in her window. You'll give her a heart attack with that obscene hard-on."

"Think it's obscene, do you?" I swiveled my hips into her belly. She sighed, appearing on the edge of letting me do much worse, Mrs. Franklin or not, but then pivoted, keys back in hand, and feverishly opened her door.

The second we were inside, I kicked the warped wood back into place with one foot while using the other for leverage to shove her backward, into the opposite wall of her "foyer." *Score another point in the "plus" column for the small apartment.* In two seconds I was all over her again, ramming my mouth to hers, taking over without asking permission—though she willingly granted it anyway, opening for me with a rough sigh, letting me plunge into all the recesses of her sweet, hot mouth.

We easily found a rhythm, our tongues twirling, sucking and tasting for several incredible minutes, until I finally forced myself back from her.

"Show me your bedroom." Honestly, my intent was to make it a question, but my roaring senses turned it into a heated demand. My cock clamored with just as much need, stretching my fly to capacity, already preparing for the heaven ahead.

"No."

Her breathless pant made me rear back. "No?" A heavy breath escaped my lungs. "Are you *really* saying—"

"No." She threw it out but huffed hard, shaking her head. "I mean *no*, I'm not saying no."

"Huh?"

She aligned her hands on my chest, at both sides of the heart using my chest cavity as a punching bag. "I couldn't say no if I wanted to, Mac. I'm just saying...not in my room."

Clearly, she meant it as an explanation. All it served up for me was more confusion. "Damn it, woman. How many ways do I have to say it? I don't care if shit is messy, or the bed isn't made or it's covered in weird little stuffed animals."

She openly grimaced. "Stuffed animals?"

"Or whatever," I mumbled, grabbing for her waist again.

She smacked at my hands. "It's not that."

Christ.

"Okay." It was an impatient bite but much better than the snarl begging for release instead. I stepped back, scrubbing a hand across my head and then pacing into the living room to attempt clearing things up more. "Want to tell me what's really going on here? You have some creepy grandma in there? Is she sitting in the corner in a rocking chair, knitting cobwebs into baby booties for your stuffed animals?"

"Stop!" But she laughed it out, balancing the tension in the air a little. "I don't have stuffed animals, okay? *Or* a grandma, creepy or otherwise."

I waited for her to go on. She only shook her head and let silence take over once more.

"So tell me what's going on." Now I meant the demand in my voice.

She tossed her gaze to the floor. "I—I just don't have sex in my bed. I don't want to talk about it, and I sure as hell don't want to explain it. It's just my thing. You can deal with it or call for another car. I'm—I'm sorry."

"Don't be." I meant the leniency too. Hell, I wanted to push her, not force her. "What's going to make this right?"

Anything but asking me to leave...

"We can do it out here. On the floor. On the sofa. Wherever."

Maybe anything but that.

"Taylor."

"Mac?"

"You're serious?" I returned her nod with a disbelieving grunt. "For fuck's sake, I'm not making love to you on the *floor* of an apartment you *rent*."

Shitty thing was, it really *was* for fuck's sake. I couldn't get down with this plan—bad pun included—for twenty different reasons, despite how stridently my cock battled to raise my consciousness above the situation. *A* for effort, *Fail* for execution. Number one, and most importantly, she deserved better than to be screwed like a hooker on top of fifteen-year-old shag pile. But how the hell did I explain that to her?

"You aren't making love to me, period. We're *fucking*, all right?"

And suddenly, "explain" went out of the door as a realistic verb. "Fine," I barked. "I also refuse to *fuck* you on a sofa older than both of us. *Combined*." I jerked my head toward the monstrosity still daring to call itself livable furniture. "You know there's probably more DNA on that thing than on the floor of a liquor store bathroom, right?"

She held both hands up. "Okay, okay. I get it. The germs

thing is an issue. You're a doctor, and—"

"I'm a *human*." I blew out heavy air. "Honest to shit, am I really the first guy you've brought home to have an issue with this?"

"How many people do you *think* I bring home?"

"I didn't mean—" Or maybe I did, which was unnerving on an entirely new level. It wasn't just the idea of her on that couch with someone else. It was the vision of her porcelain body tangled with *anyone* else's, period, let alone some loser asshole, that had the edges of my vision turning red.

"All right, let's just relax. If it makes you feel any better, I don't usually come back here with guys."

Her tone was so nonchalant, the red changed from a thin haze to a crimson mass. If I didn't know any better—and thank God I did—I'd think my incredulity had become a goddamn hemorrhage. "So where does that leave us?"

"Why are you making such a big deal about this? You've killed the mood."

"*I've* killed the mood?" I raked my hands through my hair, exasperated as hell and still horny as fuck. "Says the girl who won't have sex in her bed?"

"You want a bed?" She spread her arms. "So let's make one out here."

I blinked the red from my sights. Clarity swept in, along with relief. "You mean, drag your bedding and lay it down here instead?"

She smiled with adorable ease. "Like a campout. With better s'mores."

"You're good with that?" I had to be sure before giving my cock permission to hope again.

She nodded, tossing cute chunks of hair into her face.

"This is an amenable deal, clown," she declared, not bothering to shoo the strands away. That was good because I wanted to do it. *Fuck, do I want to do so many things to her tonight...*

"Thank God," I growled, grinning as she giggled. I shot into action, not giving her the chance to think twice or back out.

"Nest." She repeated it with a note of whimsy, biting her bottom lip. "Yes. I like that." Less than one second skipped by before her next protest was issued. "Wait!"

Just as I reached for her bedroom door knob, I froze with her command. "What is it now?"

"I'll get the bedding. Why don't you grab us something to drink?"

She was really serious about this bedroom thing. The very realization should've had me making excuses to get out of here, on my way to the hotel and a cold shower, because clearly this woman was carting more crazy on the brain than I had time or sanity for—but right now, I was just scarily thankful the whole night hadn't gone up in flames. At least not the crappy kind of flames...

She burst into her bedroom, so hell-bent on accomplishing her higher purpose that she didn't even flip the lights on. The light from the living room illuminated the space well enough for her to grab most of the bedding. She headed back for one more load, snaring a couple of pillows, the bed's second blanket, while I stood speechlessly watching her frenzy.

In the living room, I had placed two fresh beers on the side table and then spread the comforter across the floor, already making a more welcoming scene. I could see the pattern of her comforter—a simple leaf pattern in shades of green, perfectly matching her soft but strong character.

I let the pillows plunk to the area near my feet before toeing off my shoes and leaving them near the door. When I turned back to our little "nest," Taylor was already sitting in the middle, her shoes kicked off, her bare feet tucked under her sexy little rear. As I approached, her teeth sneaked out over her lower lip.

I stopped at the edge of the comforter.

She lifted her head, locking her gaze to mine.

With our stares still tangled, she unhooked each side of her overalls, letting them fall around her hips. The white T-shirt she wore beneath was imprinted with some sort of band or clothing logo—who the fuck cared at that point—and her perky tits pushed against the thin fabric, distorting the image more. *Damn.* If the band—or whoever—behind that shirt could see her now, she'd be signed as their fucking spokesmodel, after they got past my dead body. Because as long as I was alive, I wasn't sharing a moment like this with a single other person on the planet.

My dick completely concurred.

I had to rub the aching length right through my pants, hoping for some relief, though even that effort was useless as she popped free the silver buttons that held the overalls at her hips. My breath congealed into a hard ball in my throat as she lifted to a tall kneel, scooting the pants down to her knees. At once I dropped to the blanket, mirroring her pose. Now she was just inches away, and I was a bull seeing nothing but a red flag. I reached, unable to resist her milky skin a second longer—but just as I brushed the paradise of her warm body, she eased backward onto her bottom again, pushing her overalls off the rest of the way.

"Jesus," I groaned.

Her legs were bent at the knee, her heels flat on the floor, just a strip of taut porcelain skin between her little white half shirt and her insanely sexy cotton panties. The only part missing from this fulfillment of my dirtiest fantasy were athletic knee socks, the kind with two red stripes around the top. Yeah, she even wore an impish, almost virginal grin on her full pink mouth.

"Hmmm. Not sure he's around," she murmured in response to my call on the Almighty.

"No?" I countered. "Well, look harder, because I'm damn sure I've died and gone to heaven." My cock was raging now. Leaking. Swelling. Needing. *Does the woman have any fucking idea how mesmerizing she is?* Yeah, she probably did. My crotch was a damn circus tent now. My stare felt like it was on fire. My mouth, hanging open, likely made me look like a baboon on LSD.

"Are there other clowns in heaven with you, or are you there all by yourself?"

"No. Just me. This clown doesn't play well with others."

"Why am I not surprised? But...a one-clown circus?"

I winked. She liked it when I did that. The new hardening of her nipples confirmed that right away. "Damn straight."

"Sure you can handle all the entertainment yourself? That's a lot of tricks for one little clown."

I palmed my crotch harder. Our banter had just rounded a new turn—mental stimulation that took instant effect through my body. No other woman made me leap through flaming verbal hoops like this. My brain reveled. My body raced.

"Little?" I volleyed with a snort. "You may want to reconsider your word choice, missy."

Taylor pushed to her elbows and jerked up her chin,

confronting my gaze with all the boldness of her beauty. "Why don't you make me, mister?"

I snarled low but gave her no more words—at least not while standing and then unbuttoning my slacks. Watching her as she watched me was a sight I'd remember on my damn deathbed. She knew my cock would deliver and had even commented about it earlier, but the awe in her gaze brought a stirring mix of humility and victory.

Time to put you in your place, sassy girl.

I celebrated the words in my head while dropping my pants and boxers to the ground and then quickly stepped out of them. With a fast kick, I sent them flying across the room, against the sofa. With matching eagerness, I freed my shirt buttons and then tossed the thing in the same direction. I had no issues with being naked. Never had. I knew I had a decent body. I worked hard at it, and genetics had been good to me. Now, with cock in hand, I walked toward where she sat frozen in place.

"So," I drawled. "You were saying, Miss Mathews..."

"That you're beautiful, Mr. Stone." Her voice had turned raspy...and sexy as hell. "But you already know that, don't you, Doc Smug?"

"Not smug." My own tone was brazen velvet, blending with the cadence of my slow strokes to the length of my dick. "It's confidence, firecracker—and it's what's going to take your night from *meh* to *fucking amazing.*"

She laughed, fully and musically, as I raised my free hand like an evangelical TV preacher. "Oh, I like that category," she said, beaming up at me. "But the night wasn't *meh* before."

"You won't say that after I'm done with you, sass."

"Well, in that case...I'll take 'fucking amazing' for the Daily Double, please?"

"Uh-huh. That's what I thought."

Her laughter faded to a sigh as I dropped to my knees between hers, spreading them wider to accommodate my body. Leaning forward on all fours, I took her mouth in a slow but hungry kiss, nibbling and licking before thrusting in with the full force of my tongue. Taylor moaned as I followed that with more starving kisses, working my way down her neck until I was tugging at the neckline of her T-shirt.

"Sit up," I directed her in a low, lusty tone. "Let's get this fucker out of the way."

As soon as she obeyed, I pulled the little band-designer-whatever shirt over her head and then took a blessed second to be still, admiring the glory of her pale beauty clad in just a scanty bra and basic white panties.

Fuck. Me.

So this was what it felt like, to force oneself to take a breath. I knew breath control and used it all the time when my fingers were the difference between a human being able to speak or think or dream or live again, but for the first time, the breathing thing was flipped and my lungs were in control.

No. They were slaves to my cock, just like the rest of me. And they sure as hell couldn't be blamed. Not with this incredible woman consuming my vision, my attention, my senses...

I took another deep breath while tracing a finger along her collarbone. Continued down her sternum, across her concave belly, and then over to her hip. After a journey down her thigh to her kneecap and then back again, I tucked a couple of fingers under the band of her panties. "These too." I brought up my other hand in order to tug on both sides now, watching goosebumps take over her thighs as I grazed her skin, pulling the underwear away.

"Sweet Jesus," I rasped. "You, my little sass, are the beautiful one here." I caressed the tawny hair on her warm mound. "And I am so fucking happy you haven't shaved yourself clear off." She didn't have a full bush but was trimmed with enough left for a sexy, feminine look. Simply flawless. My mouth watered. "Sit up a little more."

I smiled in approval as she complied. As adorable as she was in brat mode, it was a nice treat to have her listening so well. When she was upright, I reached around to unhook her bra, sliding the straps down her arms and then tossing the lacy thing off to the side. During the same pause, I took time to stack the bed pillows up behind her, readjusting things so she'd be inclined a bit.

"Perfect," I murmured, easing her back onto the soft pile. "How's that feel?"

"Nice." She hummed, an angelic little sound. "Really nice."

"Outstanding. It's important that you're comfortable. You're the guest of honor, after all. At my circus," I elucidated after she quirked a confused frown. "You'll be here a while, missy. So many tricks to show you this evening." I winked again, rewarded by her giggle, along with the privilege of beholding her now, naked and ethereal, her hair spread out like a golden halo. This would be the image I used to get off for weeks, maybe months, to come, when I was back home and alone and yearning for her in my bed.

Disgusting thought for a much different time.

Right now, I'd make the most of what was right in front of me. The most gorgeous woman I'd beheld in quite some time. *Fuck, yes.* Taylor Mathews was a treasure I vowed to savor... and enjoy.

Starting right fucking now. In the best place I could imagine. With my mouth on her pert, perfect tits.

Her nipples were amazing. They pointed proudly toward the ceiling, her light-pink nipples nestling in areolae the shade of vanilla bean ice cream, and I needed a long, *long* taste. Licking around the first tight bud with the tip of my tongue, I then teased and nipped with my teeth before relieving the sting with my tongue. I moved to the other side when the first became angry and red and then switched back when I'd abused that one. The entire time, Taylor clawed at my scalp, begging for more but then panting at me to stop.

"Which is it, love? Stop or more?" I chuckled as I switched breasts again.

"Yes!"

I laughed again. She smacked the back of my head.

I went deadly still as she let out a high little yelp.

Our stares slammed into each other as we reached a mutual conclusion.

She was in big trouble.

"Did you just...smack me?" I said it slowly—so she'd hear every syllable of my menacing tone.

She huffed before whining, "Well, you're making me crazy with all that shit!"

"Shit?"

"You know what I mean, damn it." Her petulant pout was adorable, more befitting a five-year-old caught with her hand in the cookie jar. "I'm going to lose my shit already, and all you're doing is sucking on my—*oh!*"

The squeal popped out in the second I flipped her over. Clearly, she had no idea what had happened, and I liked it that way. A lot. My cock affirmed the point, surging in approval of the control I'd taken back. It jutted up as I relished the perfect sight of her with face crushed into the comforter and ass sticking into the air.

I swatted her three times, very lightly. The blows were more lenient than what I could dish out, and what I suspected she could endure, but nonetheless, I turned her back over to sit up in my lap. Her light weight made physically positioning her so easy—and fucking fun.

We sat nose-to-nose. Her eyes were so wide and glassy she looked like a cartoon character. I slid my hand up to the back of her neck, gripping deep to keep her firmly in place, suspecting what she was likely about to spurt out at me.

"You—you spanked me!"

"And you knew it was coming." I answered her cute glower with a Zen master stare. "I've warned you plenty of times now."

"*Warned* me?"

"And that was nothing compared to what you deserve—and probably crave."

She sputtered, seeming to battle rage and arousal at once. "Okay, whoa. Back the wagon up. My *cravings* have never gone—"

"Never?" I stretched my fingertips into her hair, tugging enough to keep her head raised and her eyes in my sights. "You sure about that, because I'd happily do it again. Answer me, Taylor. Do. You. Want. More?"

Her throat worked hard at a swallow. Just one, but it was a hard and heavy doozie. "I-I-I don't think I do," she finally mumbled. "At least not right now?"

"That sounds more like a question than an answer."

"Then no." This time she was more positive about the assertion—attractive but perfectly setting me up for the next prompt.

"No, thank you."

"No, thank you."

"Much better." A blush chased my fingers out of her hairline down to the base of her throat. "Good manners make my cock hard."

Her eyebrows leapt a little. "Uhhh...glad to know it."

"'I'm glad I pleased you, Sir.'"

"I'm—" Her gaze fell, once more following the path of my touch...to the valley between her breasts. "I'm glad I pleased you, Sir."

"Fucking beautiful." I circled a thumb around one of her nipples. "Did you like having your tits sucked on, Taylor?"

"Yes. Very much," she answered without hesitation.

"And do you like having your pussy eaten?"

"Yes." Again, not a moment of hesitation.

"Yes, please?"

"Yes, please."

"Good. Now lie back, girl."

A new gulp. Her teeth turned her bottom lip into hamburger. "My bottom hurts."

"No, it doesn't."

"It *does*." Her mewl, a little petulant and a lot bratty, made my dick even harder than her etiquette—probably because I saw the behavior for the act that it was. The barrier to which I'd gotten too close again. The bedroom she wouldn't let me breach. *Her truth.* "That was nothing," I gritted. "A few harmless swats. Suck it up, buttercup."

She swung her head back and forth. "No. It really *does* hurt."

Resigned sigh. "Then let me take your mind off it. Turn over. Lie on your belly."

I gave her a nudge to get her moving. With a heavy sigh, she crawled off and assumed the position I'd ordered—though she squirmed a little when all I did was gawk for the better part of a minute. Good God, how could I not? My big handprint was a dark-pink bloom on her almost fluorescent skin, like a brand I'd seared there, denoting her as mine. Even in the dim light, I could see it perfectly. *Mine.*

She shivered slightly, jolting me back into motion—though for the first time tonight, I didn't want to end this with a Mach Five fuckfest. I needed to savor this—enjoy *her*—for as long as my lust-ridden body would allow me.

I started by crawling over her body, though not making direct physical contact. I hovered just a few inches above, letting her feel my heat without crushing her with my weight. I shifted to one side, brushing her hair over one shoulder so I could get in to kiss—and then lightly bite—the sensitive skin behind her ear.

When she began shifting with more fluid movements, her lithe limbs tightening and then releasing with lusty languor, I knew it was time to continue. I kissed down the back of her neck to the valley between her shoulder blades, using my tongue and teeth to change the sensations she was feeling. At the same time, I rubbed her back and ass with my palm. Her body started to tremble as I overwhelmed her senses with mounting pleasure.

"Mac. *Damn.*"

"Sssshhh. Just enjoy."

And she did.

Her hips began swiveling in sync with my palm, which ground her pussy into the blankets. Soon, I leaned over and traced my handprint with my tongue, which made her moan into the pillows. Over and over I taunted her, knowing her skin was extra sensitive and the hot prickles of my touch would start spreading through her sex.

With her wanton gasps now filling the air, I shifted to slide my touch between her legs. Her pussy was tight, wet, creamy... *paradise.*

"My God, sassy. Your cunt..."

She replied with a high little keen, her thighs falling open as I added a second finger to my first. With steady rhythm, I fucked her like that while continuing to press the flesh of her butt with the flat of my tongue. She moaned deeper and writhed harder, her pleasure bringing more hot liquid to the tip of my dick too.

"Taylor?"

"Huh? Whaaaat?"

"Do you want to come for me?"

"Yes. God, yes!"

"Yes, please?"

"Yes, please. God on high. Ruler of my universe. Just... don't stop. *Please*...don't stop..."

I almost did, just to hear her call me ruler of the universe once more—but her joy was too contagious, her arousal too addictive. "That's it, girl. Take what you need. Do what feels good."

She raised her ass higher in the air, all but demanding I insert another finger. I did with ease, sitting up to get more leverage for pumping into her. She groaned, shuddering from the force of the new depths my fingers achieved in her hot little pussy. At the same time, I started flicking my thumb over her clit, making her moan louder. It was then that I knew what else she needed. With my free hand, I smacked her ass, aiming directly for the mark from earlier.

Screw the moans. My sweet sassy started to scream.

"Fuck!"

I released a gloating growl. "Somebody likes a little sting."

"Yes. *No.* Mac. Damn!" She shrieked louder as I spanked harder. "Oh...*gah.* Please, please, yes—*noooooo.*" Feels so good! Yes! God! Oh, my God! Please! Please! Noooooo!"

I spanked a few more times, amused at the babbling that tumbled from her addled brain. Luckily, I knew to pay more attention to the tone of the begging than to the words—if that was what they could be called. Right now, I didn't care if she was spouting a mix of Pig Latin, Swahili, and Klingon. My victorious grin had nothing to do with her syntax and everything to do with her soaked, shivering cunt. I knew she'd love a good spanking.

It wasn't long before she flew apart for me, her pussy gushing around my fingers as her lips spewed an incoherent mix of pleas and filthy cuss words. Briefly, I wondered how all that sass would sound when muffled by a ball gag—before reminding myself we'd likely not get to the part where she trusted me that much.

Gently, I pulled my fingers from her heat—and then lifted my hand to my face and inhaled. Her scent was unforgettable, a nectar so sweet that I fought the urge to suck my fingertips with the will of a thousand men. No way. I needed that nirvana straight from the Garden of Eden itself. I was going to lick her creamy slit from bottom to top and make sure her huge blue gaze took in every delicious second of the act.

"Flip over, love."

"Hmmm?" She moaned like I'd just given her a four a.m. wake up call. "No. Why?"

"I need to taste you. And I will. Turn over."

"Oh, God. Mac...not now. I'm about to die over here."

"No, you're not. And even if you are, I'm a doctor. I'll bring you back to life. Then I'll eat your pussy."

"Oh, points for the romance, clown." Her face was still crushed into the blankets, muffling her voice.

"Not my concern right now. My face needs to be buried in you, sass. If I don't get to taste what is coating my fingers, my balls are going to blow into a million little pieces. Now flip the fuck over."

I brought the point home by biting into her ass. She jumped and groaned but complied with my wishes—though I sensed it wasn't the horrid sacrifice she painted. Her pussy gleamed with new arousal, and her face, surrounded by a cute rat's nest of freshly fucked hair, was bright with a foolish grin.

"You're so fucking gorgeous." And I sounded like a pussy-whipped idiot. And I hadn't even had my fill of said miracle pussy. And I didn't care one damn bit.

"*Psssshhh*." She flung her face to the side, emphasizing the twenty different directions of her hair. "I look frightening, and you're too scared to admit it."

"You look stunning," I snarled. "And sated."

"And *you* look mighty pleased with yourself."

"Shouldn't I be?"

She waved a hand with flighty dismissal. "I suppose."

"*You suppose?*"

"You have something better?"

"How about 'thank you, amazing Mac'? Or maybe 'you're a fucking god in bed, Mac'? No, no. I got it. Wasn't there something about being the ruler of your universe..."

She giggled. Then snorted—which made her giggle harder.

"You're such a dickhead."

Immediately, she recognized exactly what that impudence would earn her—though I chose to go right for showing her the consequences instead of telling her. As soon as I'd positioned my face between her legs, my arms under her knees and my hands around her thighs, I pulled her down toward me. She easily slid in my direction, though the move dragged her off the pillow mound, making it impossible for our gazes to meet.

"Grab the pillows again, firecracker. I want your stare on me. Watching me pleasure you."

"Hmmph." She clearly knew she'd get away with the dainty snort, since she got busy accommodating my order at the same time. "What makes you think I want to watch? Maybe I want to close my eyes and pretend you're someone else, like Bruno Mars or—*ow*!" She reared up as I sank my teeth into the inside of her thigh. "Shit! Fuck. Okay! Not a Bruno fan? Christ. No *24K Magic* for you, then! Goddamn it, that hurt."

"Good." I smacked her hand away as she attempted to rub the mark. I had plans for that bruise, similar to the handprint on her gorgeous ass, but the queen had to trust her knight's strategy first.

"I don't think I like you very much, Mac Stone."

Yeah, even if she didn't like said knight.

"I think you probably do, Taylor Mathews." I sent her a wolfish smile. "You just don't know it yet."

"We'll see." She folded her arms over her breasts and pouted—a damn amazing pose for a girl about to be eaten out, but since it shoved her tits in all the right directions, I didn't complain.

As a matter of fact, the sight became my inspiration—to do away with any remaining preamble and give this woman one of the best erotic experiences of her life.

Without ceremony, I spread her thighs far apart, opening her pussy wide. Christ, she was stunning—so pink and juicy and inviting. I licked my lips before dipping in, lapping her from asshole to clit, pausing to savor the ambrosia I'd been waiting to finally experience. When I was finished, I did it again. And again. Was there anything more delicious than Taylor Mathew's come? At that moment, I'd say unequivocally no. She was heady and musky and sweet and tart all at the same time, an intoxicating nectar I could spend a lifetime trying to top but likely wouldn't. Gourmet cuisine might come close— and yeah, deep-dish pizza too—but no other pussy would ever compare.

I licked her slower this time, concentrating on the plumpness of her labia, sucking in the lower parts that protected the entrance of her channel. I savored the cream that coated my taste buds as I began fucking her with my tongue, imagining what it would be like when I finally sank balls-deep into her.

Heaven. That was what it would be. *Fucking heaven.*

I spread her wide again with my thumbs, looking up while I toyed my tongue along her clit. I stabbed at her tender bud with just the tip, flicking the bundle of nerves until she squirmed and her arms fell to her sides to grip at the blanket. When I bit her clit, she let her head loll back, giving in to the pleasure and pain I brought, moaning loud and long.

The sound continued pouring out of her as I licked along her thigh to the bite mark I'd just left. When I pressed into the welt with my tongue, she angled her head up to watch. I licked around the bruise, leaving a wet trail, before experimenting with a soft suck in the same spot, watching intently to see how much she could take. Taylor groaned and then shivered, and the tang of her lust thickened the air, giving me encouragement to increase the intensity of my suction. Every time I pulled in harder, I observed her more closely. I watched as her eyes glazed over, her breathing increased, and her chest began to rise and fall. Slowly and steadily, I sucked harder and harder, until the pitch of her moan rose with distress instead of pleasure. Obeying the cue, I moved my mouth back to her succulent pussy, repeating exactly what I'd just done from start to finish.

By the third or fourth time around the circuit, she was panting hard and bucking against my grip. If my tongue hit her clit again, she'd surely climax—so I made sure it was a damn good detonation by adding a couple of fingers to my effort, burying them deep in her pussy. For the third time today, I reveled in the screaming pleasure of this fascinating, captivating, passionate, powerful woman.

"Mac!" she shrieked.

"Hmmm?" I countered.

"Dear God, stop!"

"But why?"

"Because you're going to kill me. Seriously. Jesus Christ! Fuck." She gasped for breath as I slid back up and gathered her into my arms, a wide grin on my come-coated lips. I worked them together, savoring the last delicious drops of her incredible taste, before reassuring her. "You're not going to die, silly girl."

"Says Doctor Know-It-All?"

"Says the man who thinks I've never seen a woman look more vibrant or alive." I caressed some of the hair out of her eyes, "It feels good, right?"

"Yes. Yes," she panted. "It feels so good. I...I had no idea it could feel *this* good, which I'm going to regret admitting now. Just make sure your head still fits through the doorway later on, okay?"

I rumbled out a chuckle. "Sure. Okay." But yeah, the humble tone was a bit of an act. I'd made her nearly scream the roof off tonight, times three. Maybe I *was* the ruler of the fucking universe.

"Christ. This is ridiculous." She muttered it into my sternum. "I mean, you're inhuman."

"I'm *what*?"

"In the good ways, dork. But shit. *Shit.* Maybe in the crazy ways too."

"Wait. So there're levels of 'inhuman'?"

"You know what I mean," she scoffed. "And we haven't even hit home plate yet."

Oh, how I wanted to jump on that one—literally. But I forced myself to just hold her for a few long minutes, stroking her hair and enjoying the feel of her in my arms. This would likely be my only chance for all the mushy shit, which would've normally been fine, since mush was, by and large, a pretty huge waste of time for me. I mean, the end goal had already been reached, right?

But with this sassy girl...

I wanted goals.

At least more of them than the surety of getting kicked out of here in the morning, with my chances of a repeat slim to none. She had more defenses than a Scottish castle—and I'd purchased a round-trip ticket back to Chicago.

There'd be time to get morose about all of that tomorrow. Right now—make that about thirty minutes ago—my body needed to be deeply, tightly, inside hers. My cock's reminder of the fact didn't make it easy to lay her back on the blanket, but I managed to do so before rising and heading toward my pants, still in a heap against the couch.

"Mac? Where are you going?"

"Condom."

"Oh." She cleared her throat. "Right."

I paraded over to my pants, the aching erection bobbing in front of me, and grabbed my wallet out of my pocket. By the time I got back to Taylor, I had one of the packages ripped open and the rubber fitted over my length. My need for her was nearly at red-alert status, despite the tight latex. There wasn't a guy alive who'd say "gee, I love wearing a condom" but I'd never gone bareback a single time in my life, and I wasn't about to start now.

With a determined whoosh, I swept back down over the breathtaking lover waiting for me. We kissed but not for long. Like a kid in line at Disneyland, my cock knew the fun was about to get intense.

"All right," I murmured, my mouth a few inches above her. "First things first."

Taylor smirked. "You mean there are *more* first things?"

"One more." I planted a quick kiss on her. "What's your favorite position to get fucked in?"

She choked softly. Her full-moon eyes gobbled my attention up. "Uhhhh..."

"What?"

"*Why* are you so forward?"

"Why is that forward? I like knowing things about you. Things about how to please you." I cocked my head. "You like knowing the same about me, right? What makes me feel good? None of that has to be a secret, especially if it brings more pleasure."

"When you put it that way, it makes sense," she admitted. "It just seems like..."

"Like what?"

"Well...embarrassing stuff."

She made me chuckle. "Embarrassing? I just had my tongue in very intimate places, and now you're embarrassed by me asking about good positions in the traditional sense? That's a little backward, don't you think?"

She smacked my chest. "For the record, I think you can just stick your dick in me and wiggle around a little bit. You've proven that no matter what you do, it's amazing."

I narrowed my gaze. Asked with taunting softness, "Did you just smack me again?"

Her mouth popped open, and I almost expected a protest to fall out. Instead she blurted, "Yeah. Okay. I did, but no more crazy-kinky-amazing clown stuff tonight, okay? Damn it, Mac, you know you could tie your dong in a knot and my pussy would give you three *more* orgasms as a welcome party, but right now, I just need you to straight-up fuck me. Please, *please*, just fuck me."

It didn't take me long to decide on an answer to that. "Crazy-kinky-amazing, huh?" I drawled while sliding my cock through her slit a few times, getting my tip wet. "*How* amazing? Like, all four times?"

Her eyes rolled back in her head as I pushed in an inch or two. Nevertheless, she rebutted, "You mean three times?"

"I mean *four*. Earlier counts too. Say it." I pressed in farther, making her moan again.

"Yes. *Yes*, all right. Earlier counts too. Now move, goddamn it."

She dug her nails into my ass cheeks, making me hiss. I

loved feeling pain as much as causing it, but she didn't need to know that. Still, the tiny bite from her ruthless nails ignited a chain reaction through my body—a fucking good one. I started pounding her wildly, taking full advantage of her loosened hips, pliable pussy, and willing libido. She was flexible and flushed, spreading wider to get me deeper, until I began bottoming out against her ass on each downstroke. Her corresponding moans told me she liked receiving that brutality as much as I liked giving it, and I thanked every saint I knew in heaven for her open, generous passion.

I ground deeper. Harder.

She gasped faster. Heavier.

I succumbed to the fantasy being dictated to my brain, hiking one of her legs up to my shoulder. The other, I left flat on the floor, forming a capital L with her body—and a deeper junction of her pussy.

"Christ, you feel good. I'm so deep inside you. Can you feel me?"

"Yes. *Yes.* It feels...so damn good." Again, each word was practically a mindless pant, pushed out through the haze of passion that I saw blanketing her like enchanted mist.

"You going to come again?"

Despite how her nipples sharpened into erect points, she nervously wet her lips. "I'm—I'm not—not sure..."

"Wrong answer." I gave the raised half of her ass a fast swat from underneath. "You're going to come again, sassy. Just for me. Put your fingers on your clit and rub. Let me watch you get off while my dick fucks you."

She reached between her stretched legs and fingered her swollen nub. "God, it's so sensitive."

"Yeah, it is." I murmured the words as praise. "That's my

good girl." I turned my head, kissing the inside of her knee. At the same time, I slid my hand down her thigh, once more working my thumb into the darkest part of the bruise from my love bite there.

"Oh, my *God*." As she stroked herself faster, a look of abject confusion possessed her face. "What the *hell*? How do you *do* that to me?"

"Don't fight it, love." I pressed in over her, damn near giving it as command. "If it feels good, embrace it. Let me push you, Taylor. Let me take you to new places—and then let me watch you ride those highs." I lay over her and kissed up her neck, alternating kisses and bites, more careful now not to mark her where it would be seen above clothing lines. When I got to her ear, I whispered, "Ride it out, sass—and then come all over my cock. This time, I'm coming with you. Let's do it together, love. Feel me explode deep inside you."

She detonated again, at the moment I sank my teeth into her earlobe. She climaxed hard, squeezing my cock so tightly my own orgasm was launched into motion too. Spasms pulsed through my balls and up my shaft. *Heaven. Dear fuck...*

The same words tumbled off my lips as I jerked and twitched before going completely still, enjoying the feeling of my body emptying into hers—in theory, at least. The condom held steady while I enjoyed the final tremors of my release and our breathing evened out. A minute or two passed, and I couldn't hold my weight off her any longer, so I slid out and rolled to the side, reaching down to remove the condom and tie it off. I'd get rid of it later, when I wasn't completely spent—and damn, after this long and insane day, I was *spent*. The only concept even half-tempting my dregs of energy would be if Miss Sass wanted a fifth climax. Saying no just wouldn't be an option.

If the woman asked for an exact count on the sand grains in Mission Beach, *no* wouldn't be an option.

But she didn't have to know that.

At least not right now.

She scooted back against me, not asking for the fifth screamer or the sand count, thank God, simply sighing with contentment as I wrapped one of the blankets over us. I grabbed the throw and spread it out too, not knowing how cold she got overnight. The woman's body fat was probably in the negatives, meaning she had zero insulation. I would happily do my best to keep her warm through the night tonight.

And any other night she would allow me to.

A thought that should have had me running for the hills. Quickly.

Instead, I pulled her closer, burying my nose in her sweet blond hair and falling asleep with the dumbest grin on my face—and the warmest feeling in my heart.

Yeah, goddamn it, my *heart.*

A feeling I hadn't had in a very long time. Not since the day I'd saved my first patient in residency.

In short, a moment I wouldn't soon forget.

And a woman I'd always remember.

CHAPTER EIGHT

Mac

"Flight 1713 with nonstop service to Chicago is now boarding through gate C-16. We invite our first-class passengers, any Elite Gold Reward members, and any active duty military passengers to please make your way to gate C-16."

The flight attendant's saccharine-sweet voice traveled around the seating area of the terminal. People started gathering the things they had taken out while waiting for our plane to board.

The last fucking thing I wanted to do was make my way to gate C-16.

I wanted to still be in Taylor Mathews' bed—or rather, on her goddamn living room floor, even with its warped floorboards that caused the worst muscle spasm my lower back had ever known, and its weird smells that had backed up my sinuses like the Hoover Dam, and—

Christ.

Even the laundry list of low-rent craptastic wasn't going to help. I'd take the three-ring germ circus again in half a heartbeat if it meant spending one more night there. Even one more *hour* with her all to myself, filling my hands with her china-doll skin, lashing my mind with her nonstop word whips, making every minute better than the one that came before it, with her verve and force and life...

Life.

That fucker was *not* my friend right now. He—she?—was a sadist, and not in any good ways. What the *hell* had I done to deserve the punishment? Finally, someone as perfect as that woman had stumbled into my life, and I'd had to leave her in a rumpled mess on that eighties shag floor, after every effort to rouse her for one last fuck had been made in vain. I smirked at the memory, knowing damn well she'd just been playing me, but that hour of "adamant persuasion" had been just as much fun as if she'd actually given in...

Okay, maybe not as fun.

Around two o'clock this morning, while watching her sleep in my arms—because again with the weird mush affliction—I'd decided I would accept the job at Scripps. Not *just* because of the moonlight on her skin and the night breeze in her hair—though those didn't suck—but because of the "life picture" thing as a whole. Chicago just didn't hold the appeal it once had and I was ready to make a fresh start. The Scripps position also held new challenges. The Neurology Department head was looking to retire early, meaning the promise of advancement shone on the near horizon.

And yeah...

Mother was a major factor too.

I'd had some time to mull about the conversation I'd overheard between Claire and Killian. The more I did, the deeper I realized how often my mother had interfered with my life—and how many times I'd let her. That truth wasn't comfortable to face. At all.

It was time to cut those strings. Emotionally *and*

physically. All right, so they weren't whopping *Oedipus*-style ropes, but strings were still strings, boundaries were boundaries, and it seemed my mom wasn't humanly capable of respecting the guidelines on both that I'd tried setting between us. Now, maybe putting *miles* between us was a better idea. A clearer shot across her proverbial bow.

My stepfather was a nonissue in the decision-making process. Mother had remarried three times in my life so far, and I wasn't convinced this one would stick either. Constance Stone was a difficult woman to live with, and I'd never blamed any of my "daddies" when they'd eventually tapped out.

And what about my biological father? He'd been smart and opted out very early, sometime between my second and third birthdays. My mother only ever had negative things to say about him, which hadn't deterred my quest to reach out to him right after I turned eighteen, craving a relationship with him on my own. Nothing had ever reached relationship status, though, resulting in a few years of mutually lame attempts to make something out of nothing. We'd had a few forced outings, with awkward conversations about things neither of us was interested in. Finally, we'd both stopped calling, probably coming to the same conclusion. Just because we shared DNA didn't mean we had to be pals. Once in a while, I still received an email or card from him, but I knew his health was flagging so it wouldn't be much longer before I heard of his passing.

I resigned myself to boarding the damn plane. I got to my seat and didn't bother taking out a book or my smart pad to keep me busy, hoping I'd fall asleep after we took off. I'd gotten less than an hour overnight, having deemed it impossible to indulge in sleep when watching over Taylor.

Memorizing Taylor...

It'd be a while—perhaps longer—until I saw her again. I shoved aside the pang of the thought through my system, plugging my logic into a potential exit plan from Memorial. Of course, I'd await the offer from Scripps before submitting my resignation in Chicago but imagined the process would be straightforward. Nobody at Memorial would be ordering cake and streamers for my last day, unless they all couldn't contain their excitement about the asshole finally getting out of Dodge. I'd also need to put the condo up for sale, pack the place up, and decide what to do with my cars. Fortunately, it wouldn't all have to be handled before I moved, which was once more a cart-before-the-horse situation. But I'd sent my letter of interest to Scripps from the airport, and hopefully their offer letter wouldn't be long in return. My terms had been fair, and their need was fairly urgent. Luck—which was really only opportunity meeting preparedness—was on my side.

And that was the moment Lady Luck made me eat my words.

Right before she abandoned me, to the seat mate who dropped her oversize bag into the empty middle seat between us while struggling to wrestle her enormous carry-on into the overhead bin. How the woman had wheeled the huge thing past the gate agent was the morning's biggest mystery, but I started running a secret odds pool with myself about whether she'd fit it or not. Hey, it killed time—and kept my mind away from the ping-pong game...

Or not.

Most standard overhead compartment bins accommodated bags no more than forty-five combined linear inches. That was about as big as the "foyer" in Taylor's apartment. So technically, if one took out the dividers between a bunch of those bins, I could stretch out up there, next to my firecracker, and we could spend the flight—

Holy fuck.

The ping-pongs had turned into grenades.

And she's not your *goddamn firecracker, asshole.*

Completing the buzz kill was elephant-bag woman, who miraculously won the struggle with the bin though screwed anyone else who planned on using those forty-five linear inches for themselves. When she was done, she looked down at me and wheezed, "I'm actually the middle seat, but maybe no one will come and we can spread out a bit." She finished with a smile, ensuring that the only thing I'd notice about her now was the red lipstick clinging to her teeth.

Hopefully, whatever she said didn't need a response beyond my cordial nod. I let my eyelids slide closed, hinting how I planned on spending the flight asleep, not becoming her new best friend.

But the ping-pong grenades were fucking merciless.

They exploded in the depths of my exhausted sleep, filling my imagination with vivid dreams of the woman I was obsessed with. Jesus, maybe even more than that. I didn't know yet, but in sleep, I was relieved of the burden of caring. In my dreams, we could just...be. She came to me, all gorgeous blond hair and pearlescent skin, her ocean-blue eyes so wide they looked like a child's drawing. She gazed up at me with the full power of those eyes as she begged me to fuck her more. *Harder, Mac—* and I obliged without asking questions—*deeper, Mac*—until the familiar weight gathered in my balls, and I pumped faster and faster and faster until she screamed my name over and over, even calling me Sir by the end. *Yes, Sir. Hurt me, Sir. Fuck me, Sir. Please, Sir...*

"Sir!"

"Wha? What?" I jumped a bit as reality crashed in. Consciousness followed fast as the woman leaned across the empty space between us, shaking my arm. The second I focused, I yanked out of her grasp.

"So sorry, hon. I didn't mean to startle you. We've landed and are getting off. You've slept like the dead." She smiled at me, kindness crinkling the corners of her eyes, causing a hint of guilt for the way I'd treated her earlier. *But just a hint.*

"Thank you. I appreciate you waking me. I had a long night." My voice was dry from the processed plane air.

"Sure." She patted my arm. "Take care of yourself, hon."

"You too...hon." But she was long past hearing me, having bustled off with all her bags and extraneous shit. I was left inside the big tin can with just the cleaning crew as witnesses to my scowl of puzzled introspection. *Since when do I give a weirdo like that lady anything other than my disdain, let alone a chuckle and a nicety?* Granted, it'd been *secret* politeness, but still...what the hell?

My physical state didn't help worth shit. As I stood and stretched, rearranging my crotch quickly became a practice of discretion. I was damn sure I'd been on my way to a sleeping hard-on, and even now, the downstairs junk was registering at the high end of a semi. Everything was bunched up.

And to be honest, I liked it.

Bunched up because of a woman, even hours after I'd left her side.

When was the last time that had happened?

Never. *That* was when.

I should have been terrified. Instead, I wore a fat grin as I left the plane, pulling out my phone during the walk. I'd had the wherewithal to text myself from Taylor's phone as she'd slept, realizing she might not have supplied it had I asked. Wasn't as if I was committing a high crime. The woman's device wasn't password protected, so it served her right for not being more careful with her personal security. Maybe there would have to be discipline about that. My smirk widened at the possibility.

No. Not *possibility*. Somehow, in some way, I had to make it a reality. *Had* to see that girl again. To be uncomfortable because of her again.

Might as well start now.

I stopped, leaning against a wall to let an airport passenger cart roll by—Lipstick Lady rode shotgun, waving cheerfully as they passed—weirdly making it possible for my thumb to stop shaking as I tapped out a text, testing the waters.

> *Good morning, sass. Hope you slept well*
> *after I wore you out so thoroughly.*

I thought better of adding an emoji to emphasize my macho gloat—though the punctuation would've been justified. I didn't know a man alive not inclined to preen after making his woman scream down the neighborhood. And fuck the semantics. Last night, Taylor Mathews *had* been mine.

A few minutes passed as I made my way to baggage claim and waited for my luggage. By the time I got my bag and headed to the parking structure, still without a return text, I figured the cold shoulder *would* be my response.

At least the welcome wagon softened the blow a little.

My daily ride was a mineral white BMW m235i. Like all of my cars, I loved this little beauty. She was fun to drive, and this particular one was perfect for city commuting. I hated leaving any of my cars at the airport while I went out of town, but sometimes it couldn't be avoided. Hopefully traffic would be light, since it was still during midweek work hours, and it wouldn't take me long to get home.

Just before I started the car, my phone chirped with a new text message. My idiot grin reactivated when I saw Taylor's name on the screen.

Clown. How did you get my number?

I quickly tapped back a reply.

Good morning, sunshine.

Seriously. How?

*You should password protect
your phone, love.*

STOP calling me that.

Trust you slept well?

*How I slept isn't really
your concern, is it?*

Just asking on behalf of my cock—

since your sweet ass kept IT
up most of the night...

There was a long delay, but the little balls kept dancing on her end, betraying her dilemma about how to come back to that one. I chuffed, betraying my fresh gloat. I'd thrown the sass off-balance—fitting retaliation for what she'd done to me.

Finally, her answer sprang to the screen.

Where are you?

Oh, yeah. She *was* off-keel—though my victory was toothless at softening the sting of giving my reply.

Chicago.

Good.

Took her only five seconds to fling that one.

Good?

Yeah. Good.

Now I was the one with nothing to give, except a scowl of butt-hurt and an ego with a black eye. And my ego did *not* like bruises.

Have to drive. We'll talk soon.

No. Let's not.

For some reason, I chuckled again. She was still plenty pissy, which meant, whether she liked it or not, she was still in the game. I could work with that.

I could work plenty with that.

I sent her a winking emoji—sometimes they *did* come in handy—and let our exchange end at that. For now. She could interpret it however she wanted, or maybe she wouldn't take it as anything at all. I even shrugged off the little blow she'd gotten in, remembering what she'd revealed to me yesterday. If she'd spent her whole life cleaning up after an addict parent, she only knew one way to react to fear. Punch back first.

Which meant she *was* afraid.

As afraid as I was?

Deeper thoughts for a different time. Right now, I pulled in a long breath and reassured myself that every syllable of her reaction, especially after what had happened between us last night, made perfect sense. It was time to weigh expectations against reality. I mean, come on. I made my living throwing expectations against the walls of reality and could usually knock those fuckers right out of the ballpark, but that didn't mean I ignored the wall.

So now, it was time to study Taylor Mathews' walls.

I couldn't kid myself. I was good in bed, but I wasn't a goddamn sorcerer. Breaking down this woman's walls in one take—or even four orgasms—wasn't realistic. She was going to take some full bombardments, set on repeat.

I was more than up for the challenge.

But first, I had to get my own shit in order.

A good drive into the city would help.

I shifted my little rocket into first gear, let out the clutch, and took a right out of the O'Hare parking garage. A drive, a shower, and some food were on the schedule, and then, if I had enough stamina, maybe a visit with Mother, to let her know my plans in person. No way would a phone call suffice. If I tried news of this magnitude over the phone, she'd do one of three things. Option one—screaming. A lot of it. Option two and most preferable—a bald hang-up. Option three and most torturous—talking at me in circles until I was worn down enough to change my mind. None of those outcomes were acceptable. My best chance of keeping the upper hand was to deal with her face-to-face.

In the end, the Scripps Green Neurology Department saved my bacon on having to deal with my mom that day. Their formal offer letter didn't arrive for a few more days and, as expected, the initial salary wasn't what I'd hoped for. I countered at once and was waiting to hear their response but was confident the position would be mine. I went ahead and clicked Send on my resignation letter at Memorial, so James McCafferey's phone call didn't come as a huge surprise. I'd been friends with Jim since our residency days, so it also wasn't shocking that he dove right into the subject as soon as I opened the line.

"Mac. What do we need to do to keep you on? Is it the money? The hours? Rescheduling that asshole resident in Trauma you've been butting heads with?"

I laughed. "Jim, I butt heads with everyone." If they got rid of all the staff I didn't get along with, HR would be handing out a hundred pink slips today.

"Yeah, but that Brooks kid is a king-size cocksucker."

"And a brilliant doctor."

"Semantics."

"Sorry, man," I said after another snicker. "I can't help you. I'm not content here, you know that." He also knew I enjoyed putting shits like Brooks in their place eventually. "It's Chicago in general. The city, the crowds. The *winters*."

"Really?" Jim was thoughtfully quiet for a minute. "But that kind of makes sense, with the racing and all. It's become a real passion, eh?"

"Yeah." I toyed with a little steel balancing doo-hickey on my desk, debating whether to confess that wasn't the only passion pushing me toward the West Coast. While Jim wasn't my fucking therapist, nor did I expect him to be, he might be a good sounding board about this kind of shit. He had a sweet wife and a kid. Or three. Or maybe it was just a dog.

The bouncing ball on the curved steel rod began swinging back and forth, as if telling me no. I heeded the ball. The thing had served me well over the years. It had been a gift from my secretary a few Christmases ago, long before those spinning things were declared the be-all-and-end-all for ping-pong brains.

"So you have to put all that on hold over the winter months, huh?"

"Yeah," I said again. "Either that or head to the circuit down south."

"Which isn't realistic with your schedule," he filled in. "So where are you headed?"

"West," I supplied. "Scripps. In San Diego."

"Well, anyone will be lucky to have you. I'm sorry it comes at the price of us losing you. You're an excellent surgeon, Mac. You'll be missed around here."

We exchanged pleasantries and hung up. Jim was a good man, a very fine doctor, and an even better administrator. Most hospitals would give anything to have a man like him running their show.

My realtor agreed to sublet my condo for the first six months in case things didn't work out in San Diego. If I decided to stay in California, I would have the option to sell or continue to rent at that point. I could sublet the unit furnished, to make the move easier. I could just take personal items and find a furnished place in San Diego. I claimed no emotional attachment to furniture—except maybe Taylor Mathews' bed, the beacon of my new Holy Grail. Now that this change was going to be a sure thing, I vowed my ass would finally make it to that bed—right before I fucked *her* into its mattress.

The thought made me smile as I enjoyed a bottle of Flywheel in my living room the next night. Everything was coming together nicely. Maybe too nicely. I started waiting for the other shoe to drop—suspecting that thud would come when I broke the news to my mother.

But tonight wasn't the time for facing the dragon. I'd been on my feet for ten hours and then completing dictations for another two, and all I wanted to do was enjoy my view, my beer, and the sassy center of my spirit.

I'd been dropping her texts here and there, cautious about wearing out the scant welcome she allowed me to have. Sometimes she replied, though others—more than I cared to count—she ignored altogether. But today marked three weeks since I'd ravished her on her living room floor, and the memories could only take me through so many more hand jobs. Sure, I was officially free to dial up a number of willing booty call participants from all corners of this city, but what would that bring me? Flimsy stand-ins for the woman I'd be fantasizing about in their place. The pussy I yearned to be buried in, instead of theirs. The lips I craved around my dick, milking me of every drop of my orgasm...

I dragged on my beer, shifting in discomfort, and contemplated unzipping my fly and just dealing with this fucking ache...*again*. But goddamn it, I was tired of jacking off. I needed to touch her flesh again. Fuck it. I needed *her* again, in any way I could get.

I called up her number on my phone and tapped out a swift, frantic note.

Taylor. Please. Talk to me.

The dancing dots appeared at once from her end. Thank fuck.

I'm still at work.

I smiled. *There* was my sassy.

No, you're not.

Hello? Two-hour time difference?

Oh yeah.

You're not very bright for a "brain surgeon."

Let's FaceTime. I want

to see your beautiful face.

You have to stop this. We aren't bf/gf.

Bf/gf?

Boyfriend/girlfriend.

Oh. I think I'd be a good bf.

LOL.

Why is that funny?

No, you're funny.

Call me tonight when you get home.

No.

Yes.

The next few hours were torture. I really wanted to hear her voice. No. *Needed* to. God, her giggle. Her snark. Her sass. Just thinking of all of it was a complete reaffirmation of my decision about the job, the move, the massive life change. Hearing her would make things even better. Just a few minutes of her unmistakable, irreplaceable fire, even from thousands of miles away, would be the best thing for my spirit—not to mention my throbbing cock.

More minutes inched by like hours.

I even started rehearsing what I'd say—and maybe what I wouldn't. I'd held off on telling her about the move to San Diego. A deep instinct said she'd try to talk me out of it and then spook herself away as soon as she suspected she was the reason for it. And fine, maybe she *was* one of the reasons—maybe even a major one—but I'd agreed to the interview at Scripps weeks before she became a huge pixel in the picture, and my increased hours at the track were a direct result of feeling restless with Chicago as a whole. I'd known I needed this change long before Taylor Mathews became one of its catalysts.

Around eight thirty, my phone rang with the very special ring tone I'd chosen for her profile—*I Feel It Coming* by The Weeknd.

"Sassy."

"Well, if it isn't Doc Clown himself."

"I've missed your voice." I sounded like a mooning teenager and didn't care.

"Mac." Her tone was thick with resignation. And I hated it.

"There's nothing wrong with me saying that. It's the truth, damn it."

"But really, what's the point?" She was frustrated, that much was clear—though I couldn't pinpoint if it was with me or herself.

"Of what?" Playing dumb wasn't my specialty, but I thought I'd try it out.

"Of what we're doing here."

"Taylor. We're two grown adults, just talking to one another. We're friends. Sometimes we text. Why are you making such a big deal out of it?" Perhaps because she sensed it was "big deal" territory for me? But I'd been careful about the messaging. Casual about the approach. At least I thought. At least I hoped.

"I just don't want to be giving you the wrong idea."

Her voice edged on whiny. When the tone came from other women, I started searching for excuses for the End Call button. From her, the sound was like my fucking catnip. It made me even more restless. More desperate. Christ, were my palms sweating?

"And what 'wrong idea' would that be?"

Her huff roughened the line. "Don't be obtuse."

"Obtuse? I think I've been pretty straightforward with you, Miss Mathews." I dropped my voice in volume and tone.

"And *don't* use that voice with me," she retorted.

"Why not?" I dipped my octave again.

"Because I know what comes next."

"You, hopefully."

Ahhh, now we're getting somewhere.

"See? This is what I'm talking about. We're not doing this again!"

"I'm open to hearing your supporting argument on that, sassy—because the screaming opera you gave your neighbors and me last time is a glaring barometer otherwise."

"Barometer?" But she laughed out the end of it. "What, am I your damn dew point report now?"

I growled, filling the sound with dark pleasure. "You're gorgeous when you're dewy."

"Oh, my God." Another laugh, longer this time. "You're such an ass."

"The ass who can make you scream again like that," I promised. "Even, I'd wager, from all the way over here."

Her breath snagged. She probably thought I didn't hear it, but I was listening so hard to her end of the call, I'd have heard her stomach growl.

"You are so full of shit, clown."

"Place your bets, sassy."

Fuck, yes. I had her, hook, line, and sinker now. Her accelerated breathing, audible over the line, already gave her away—and swirled its way straight to the space between my thighs.

"Well? What's it going to be, Taylor? Name it, and it's yours if I personally can't deliver." But I was damn confident I could—because now, I was so fucking sure of what she needed.

"Think you're that good?" she blurted.

I hissed, letting her hear every note of my brazen confidence. "Yeah. I do."

"Okay, so let's do this."

"What do you have in mind?" I growled it with gravelly seduction.

"Whoever gets off first loses. And no lying or faking. Deal?"

"No."

"Huh?"

"No deal *yet*." I let my wolfish smile permeate my tone. "Any smart betting man knows the stakes first."

"Hmmm. Maybe you *are* sharp enough to be a brain surgeon."

"Sassy?" I prodded, hearing her coy attempt at the stall. "The stakes?"

"Okay." Her confidence came roaring back, erasing my smirk for a second, until she answered, "If you lose, I get a ride, on a real racetrack, with you at the wheel."

I almost expected her to finish with electronic trumpets or something. Her voice was such a flourish she obviously thought she had a deal breaker. Sweet, clueless woman. She had no idea I'd love nothing more than to show her what it was like to test the limits of a vehicle built for speed...to defy the laws of physics...

"A hot lap?" I drawled. "Done."

"Wait. Huh? What's a hot lap? I just want a ride. I said a *ride.*"

I gave her a thick thunder-bank laugh. "Adrenaline is the body's finest natural aphrodisiac, love." I leaned forward, again knowing she'd sense my advance more than see it. "And I guarantee you'll want to fuck me even more afterward."

I listened to her swallow. "But...but only if you lose."

"Sure," I returned, without a shred of sincerity. "Whatever you say, missy."

"So...uhhhh...what if you win?" Her voice had started to roughen as well. The sensual stakes weren't lost on her, and I sure as fuck wasn't complaining. Between her sexy breaks in breathing and the mention of high-performance racing vehicles, my body was like an engine getting warmed at the starting line. All I needed now was the green flag...

"If I win, I want a date to Oktoberfest. Three hours minimum. Skirt required. Panties prohibited."

"Done." She chuckled with smug delight, as if she thought she had this shit in the bag.

"Wait!" I blurted back.

"What?" She acted impatient, as if my interrupting was an annoyance.

"I have one more condition."

"Dear God." I could practically see her eye roll from here.

"We do this on FaceTime."

"*What?*"

"We do this on FaceTime," I repeated. "Give me a second to go get my laptop, and then call me on FaceTime."

I was curious about her brazen boldness now.

To my pleasant shock, she responded with a hearty giggle. "Such a kinky clown."

"You know it."

"Fine," she acquiesced, her tone turning silky. "FaceTime."

I couldn't set up my machine fast enough.

The whole time, blood raced through my veins and pooled in my dick. It throbbed and swelled and pounded at the zipper of my jeans, screaming to be let loose.

Easy boy. We have a bet to win.

And damn it, I wanted to win. I mean, either way this thing fell, I'd won—she was getting that hot lap no matter what—but it was the whole principle of this. *Her* challenge, *my* victory. The mind-fuck of it was epic. More than that, I hated losing—at anything. It was a personality defect. I just had to remember that no matter what happened, I came out of this a winner.

My screen came to life. My very own goddess filled the rectangle from one edge to the other. She was so close to the camera, all I could see was her face, but that was enough for the moment. Christ, she was...breathtaking. She was still dressed in some sort of blouse, probably her outfit from work, but I could barely make out the color because the lights were so dim in her apartment.

"Fuck...you're stunning. As usual." My voice was unintentionally soft. Or maybe intentionally. It wasn't as though anyone else was around. Something about her made me want to be gentle and careful, until the point that she made me mindless with lust. This female had me chasing my own tail, and I was gladly dizzy from it.

"I'll bet you say that to all the girls you have phone sex with."

She issued that with a shy smile, but I wasn't buying the bashfulness.

"Is that what you call this?" Or maybe I could believe her new timidity. Crazily, I was stricken with it too. Strange. *Really* strange.

"Do you have a better name for it?"

"Guess not." I laughed, a hoarse sound because my throat was so dry from need. I was in deep shit here. Deep, inescapable shit. I could still remember the taste of her pussy on my tongue, the smell of her come in my nose. I wanted to be buried in her heat more than anything right now. "And for the record, I've never done something like this with anyone else."

Her face became an adorable quirk. "Weirdly, I believe you."

"Oddly, I'm glad." After we relieved the tension by a notch with mutual laughs, I continued, "But now you know why I was being the cavalier clown with my wager."

"Uh-oh. Is the master doubting himself?" She leaned back a little and began unbuttoning her blouse. Very slowly, one small button at a time.

My mouth turned the texture of the California desert.

"The master, huh?" My words felt like fire—appropriate,

since she'd stoked exactly that inside me.

"Don't let it go to your head." She parted the material at her bra, letting me have a glimpse of the white lace cups that had the very enviable job of holding her breasts.

"Fuck," I rasped, now sounding like I'd come down with strep.

"See something you like, Doctor?"

"Pull your shirt down over your shoulders, love."

She did what I asked but gave me hell while doing so. "I told you to stop calling me that." Did she know how her impertinence turned me on? She had to. I was gaping now. Fixated on every one of her seductress moves, on every teasing breath from her pouting lips...on the telltale undulations of her body, betraying how she ached to get relief too...

"I'll worry about it more when you're in a position to do something about it. How does that sound?"

"Depends on how you define *doing something*."

She flushed while saying it, giving up a bit of the lead to me—and she knew it too. Her mouth trembled.

The edges of mine curved up. "Do you remember where I bit you?"

No more shaking lips. She pressed those plush surfaces together, jogging out a little nod. "Yes," she whispered.

"Touch it now, Taylor," I growled. "Show me the spot."

Her fingers went right to the spot as though it were tattooed atop her shoulder. At the same time, she looked directly into the camera and then slowly closed her eyes. She opened her mouth just a bit as she inhaled through her parted lips.

"Mac." Her voice was nothing but a feather. A moistened, needy wisp.

"I know, baby," I encouraged in a soft snarl. "You need new marks. And I need to give them to you."

She didn't respond in words. Just let me see her small nod. *Sweet little doll. Southern little lady.* She still wasn't ready to admit how much she'd enjoyed the pain I'd given...but one day, *fuck me*, we would get there.

"Pull your bra down now, Taylor. All the way, so I can see your gorgeous tits...your incredible, hard nipples. *Good girl,*" I praised when she pinched her nipples without my suggestion. The points stood on end, pushing up so red and taut. She ran her fingers over the tips, her breaths getting faster with every repeat.

"Does that feel good?"

"Yes," she husked. "But it feels better when you do it. Even better when it's your mouth." She was preparing to say something else when her eyes popped open, something taking her attention away from her arousal. "Hey!"

"What?" I queried.

"You're not playing fair."

"Why do you say that?" I was truly confused.

"You're not touching yourself, clown. You still have all your clothes on. You're just telling *me* to do stuff." She raised one perfect eyebrow in speculation. "I'm on to you now, Stone."

I whipped my dark-green T-shirt over my head and then threw it over my shoulder. "Better?"

She leaned in, inadvertently showing off the deeper valley of her cleavage. "God, yes. You are so gorgeous, Mac."

I let out a pleased hum. "I like it when you say my name. My *actual* name."

"Yeah? Well, don't get too used to it." She flashed her sassiest grin, the one that frustrated me more than the words themselves, because now I saw right through her game.

"I know. I know." I scrubbed my hand through my hair. She was always so worried about re-erecting her walls...about protecting herself. "I'm not going to hurt you, Taylor."

She paused for a second, gave her head a barely visible shake, and then easily—too easily—slid her sarcastic mask back into place. "So...I was about to see your amazing dick, was I not?"

I sighed, using it as a mask of my own. On the outside, it was an aroused growl-huff thing. On the inside, it was concern about her continued façade—even what she chose to show me. Even *after* I'd told her, time and time again, that in the space of *us*, she was safe. But she still didn't get it, making it necessary for me to play along for now. Eventually, I'd have her where I needed her. Where *she* needed to be. In a place where she could trust me with her emotional wellbeing as well as her sexual satisfaction. It was just going to take a while. The more fragile the glass, the tougher it was to move a vase.

"Your wish is *very* much my command, m'lady."

"Oooo la la," she teased while I stood and opened the button on my jeans. Without hesitation, I slid the zipper down and then spread the material open for her to see the deep muscled vee of my lower abdomen.

"Ohhhh...my," she sighed, giving me a perfect soundtrack for reaching into my boxers and coming back out with my erect cock in hand. I stroked it, reveling in the heavy flesh in my fist, letting my balls surge out on their own, weighing down the material of my underwear.

"Jesus...Christ."

"He's got nothing on me, baby." Two could play at the swagger game.

"That's what all the boys say."

"I'm not a boy, Taylor. I think I've proved that. A few times, actually." I fisted myself tighter, a blatant reminder of the pleasure I'd given her the night we were together. The best night of my goddamn life.

Her sharp exhale sounded over her computer microphone. "Yes, Sir," she cheeped out, her voice quivering.

"Do you still have your panties on? And if so, why?" I sat back down so I could watch her undress—and enjoy the hell out of it.

"I was just wondering the same thing, actually."

It was her turn to stand up. All I could see on her cam now was the area from just below her tits to just below her pussy, which sadly was still covered by a gray pencil skirt. But not for long, thank God. I watched, licking my lips and working my dick, as she reached back and unzipped the skirt. She wiggled her hips in order to peel the garment away, and then everything in my view was her silky skin, glowing with translucent splendor in the dim light of her living room.

"My God, woman. Your skin..." She was responsible for permanently smashing *incredible* with *epidermis* in my figurative book. She was so pale as to be transparent, the veneer like nothing more than haze and, in the right light, I could trace the map of her veins and arteries right through it. The tracing paper fascinated me as a surgeon *and* as a man. That was her *life*, thriving just beneath the surface...

My cock jerked in my hand. A drop of come leaked from the tip. I spread the milky liquid down the shaft and closed my eyes for a second, battling for fresh control—but when I looked at her again, she'd slid her hand beneath the waistband of her panties. Had reached inside the chaste covering to rub herself in the sexiest way...

I was mesmerized. How she made that damn dowdy undergarment so fucking sexy, I couldn't figure out, but I never wanted her to stop wearing them. Plain white little Jockey for Her had become the latest search on Amazon on my computer. Did that make me a freak? Maybe. Did I care? Not even a little.

"Taylor?" Now my voice was a straight-up growl.

"Hmmm?" Hers was a sexy moan.

"Is your cunt wet?"

"Oh, yeah."

"Show me."

She reached farther into her panties, gliding her fingers into her folds. When she held them up to the camera, they were glistening with her arousal. A frantic moan spilled from me.

"How you doing there, big guy?"

"Jesus." I slicked my hand along my swollen cock, the friction made better by more drops of white-hot arousal from the slit at my tip. "*Taylor.*"

Her laugh was breathless...and beautiful. "Th-That good, huh?"

"I love those fucking panties. Do they come in other colors besides white?" How *that* was the question of the moment was beyond me. Chalk it up to lack of blood supply.

"I think so. Maybe pink? Would you like that?" She beamed a devilish grin.

"Yeah. *Yeah*, I would. But pull those white ones down a little. But not all the way. Like you're sneaking in dirty thoughts of me at work."

"Mac." It hardly had any volume. In the cam, her middle finger disappeared into the rosy lips of her perfect pussy. Drops of arousal gleamed on the trimmed hair protecting her intimate entrance.

"Good. *Shit*. Really good. Finger yourself...harder." I loved telling her what to do and the way she so easily obeyed.

"Ohhhh." She pumped her finger in and out, in and out. *So naughty. My goddamn dream girl.*

I stroked myself faster. I was hanging on by a thread. "I'm not going to last, baby. I don't even care about the stupid bet. Losing will feel so fucking good."

"Do it." Her guttural tone goaded me on. "*Do it*, Mac. Come for me. Show me how much you want me. Show me that I turn you on. Do you want to fuck me again? Eat my pussy until I come on your face?"

"No fair, sassy."

"Fuck fair."

"I'd rather fuck you." I let my head fall back as my orgasm built. It was coming on fast. So fast. Too fast...

"Show me. Do it. Show me the come you want to spill inside me."

"*Fuck.*" So close. So damned close. Intense sensation racing up my shaft, stripping the oxygen from everywhere else in my body. Knowing I would be inside her again was the last thing I thought before I blew my load into the shirt I had taken off and dropped on the floor minutes before. "Fuck," I repeated. "Taylor. *Woman.* Fuck. So good." I kept pumping my shaft until the very last drop seeped from the tip, sweat dripping from my brow, down my nose and onto the keyboard of my laptop.

When I looked at the screen of my laptop, Taylor's blue eyes were glued to the monitor, fascination and awe painted across her face. A slow, sexy grin spread across her pouty lips when our eyes met.

"Winner, winner, chicken dinner," she whispered.

"I'd say I pretty much won that round, girl." I slid out an exhausted smirk. "And I got a victory circle bonus. I still get to see you again for our track date. Hello? Ding ding. Double win."

Her grin fell when she realized I totally had a point—though she still also looked a little sexually frustrated. Perhaps more than a little.

"Sassy, don't get uptight," I assuaged. "Let's handle this. I'd never leave you hanging." And I meant every word. I never left a woman unsatisfied. Especially not *this* woman.

Sincere or not, they were the wrong words at the wrong time—or maybe the all-too-accurate arrows, fired into the weakest spots of her ramparts. At this point, the trigger didn't matter. It had definitely been pulled.

"You kidding me?" she snapped. "You think I'm 'hanging,' clown, because you seriously think I can't masturbate without your help? Trust me, mister, I've got this. I've had years of practice."

"Wait. Whoa. That's not how this was supposed to go down."

"Well, guess what, mister? It's not the first time, and probably won't be the *last* time, that a man's grabbed the fast-pass on me in this department." Her expression twisted a little, as if she alone knew the punchline to a hidden joke. "But hey, thanks for the entertainment for the past, what was that? Ten minutes? Nice."

Only now, the joke wasn't so private.

Or so funny.

A point she refused to let me make, as she gave a sassy shrug and then disconnected our FaceTime.

Hanging up.

On me.

Leaving me in the middle of my living room, my dick in my hand, naked as the day I was born.

What. The. Living. Fuck?

The girl was trying on every level, but this was a new one altogether. I immediately tried to reconnect the call, but she didn't pick up. I tried her cell phone, and it went to voice mail. If I didn't have a procedure scheduled for seven tomorrow morning, I would've been on a damn plane for San Diego inside the hour. Once there, that woman's tiny ass would *not* be safe.

But her ass would have to wait.

Only two more weeks.

Because that was when I drove there on a one-way trip.

After that, there'd be no more running for Miss Taylor Mathews—from a lot of things in her life that clearly needed addressing.

First on the list? Her commitment to me.

CHAPTER NINE

Taylor

"Our massages aren't for two hours, so we have some time to enjoy the pool and have some lunch. Are you ladies hungry?"

Talia snapped her phone cover closed and looked around our little group.

"I'm always hungry!" Claire was the first to answer, though it was in a stage whisper. Since we were at the spa, we had to make a conscious effort for quiet in the common areas—not always successfully achieved with our bunch.

Luckily, it was a weekday, making it easy to find four lounge chairs in a row next to the outdoor pool. The weather was perfect, though the calendar had registered winter. These were the days Southern California real estate prices seemed completely logical.

"Add me to the starving list," Margaux added as we settled in. "I had no idea breastfeeding a child would burn so many calories. I haven't even been working out, and I swear I'm eating like a cow. I'm seriously fucked when Iris stops nursing."

"Language!" Claire's chastisement was as on-cue as Margaux's transgression.

"Christ, will you stop? My kid's not even in the same town right now. Caroline has her today. And are you seriously telling me my bossy pants brother doesn't let an F-bomb drop every now and then around Regan? Really?"

Talia and I joined in a grin as Margaux and Claire bantered over our reclined torsos about child-rearing practices. It was almost a word-for-word repeat of the conversation they'd had in the ladies' room at Talia's wedding, meaning they'd be at it for at least a few minutes longer—leaving me a perfect opportunity to turn to the still-glowing bride, lowering my sunglasses by half an inch.

"Soooo...inquiring minds want to know. How is married life treating you, Mrs. Ford-Newland?"

Talia smiled, her happiness all but gushing out of every pore, mixing with the tan I'd always been hideously jealous of. "It's still Perizkova," she explained. "And will probably stay that way, regrettably. The guys and I had a long talk and figured it'd just be easier. Avoid any questions from outsiders as well as hurt feelings from insiders, you know?"

I nodded. "Makes perfect sense. It's a great solution." We joined in a chuckle as Margaux and Claire moved on to debating diaper brands, giving me one more pause to consider my next question. "Can I ask you something personal, T?"

Talia scooted her own sunglasses lower, regarding me with open shock. "Oh my God, are *you* asking permission now, Taylor Mathews?" She finished with an elbow nudge, ensuring me she was teasing, though her astonishment was justified. Normally, I was the girl who barreled ahead of everyone, figuring forgiveness was easier to ask for than permission, bull-in-a-china-shop style.

"You can ask me anything, *chica*. You know that. We don't have secrets here, do we?" Her smile was so genuine I knew she meant every word she said.

"Are you guys going to have kids?"

There. I'd gone ahead and let the hog run wild in the yard—though she hardly seemed surprised, which was no shocker to *me*.

"I hope so," she answered at once. "We've certainly been practicing." She grinned and then added, "A lot." Then burst into a full giggle, her perfect tan even more resplendent.

"But..."

"But what?"

"Do you think Drake and Fletch will care who the real father is?"

It was my true curiosity anyway, so I pushed on with it. Once more, Talia responded as if she'd been asked the question a thousand times.

"No. I don't think they will. As a matter of fact, I know it." Her gaze stretched across the sparkling azure of the pool. "It's hard to explain how things are between the three of us. It's..." She still stared off, as if wanting to find the perfect words for expressing herself. Finally, after a sigh of exasperation, she said, "It's just special. I know that sounds lame, but it's true. Never, in my whole life, would I have believed a marriage like this could be possible, let alone for someone like me. If someone had tried explaining it to me, I'm sure I would have been as judgmental as the rest of the world—then would've arrived at the same conclusions about imbalance and jealousy in a triad relationship.

"But honestly, there's none of that with us. Maybe less than none. We support one another so much and build one another up, but not in a patronizing way. And I think because there are three of us, we always have a nifty checks-and-balance system."

"Nifty?" I interjected. "And did you really just compare

your marriage to online banking?"

She giggled. "I guess I did—but who the hell doesn't think online banking's the best thing since streaming TV? We use the balance every single day. We can each look at one another and with one look we're saying, 'is he bullshitting me right now?' And the other one usually says, 'no way, it's totally true, you look amazing.' And you feel ten feet tall. God, does that sound crazy?"

"That sounds amazing." My reply was just as adamant. "Not crazy."

Her shoulders visibly slackened, as if she'd expected me to protest. "Well, to get back to your original question, I don't think it will matter who the baby's father is at all. He or she is simply going to be so loved, it won't even matter."

"That's a good thing," I remarked. "Because you *know* once you drop that critter, the world will know, one way or the other, whose swimmer paddled the farthest upstream."

Margaux, in the middle of telling Claire about an article she'd read on homemade baby food versus jarred food, interrupted herself midsentence. "*What* did you just say, Miss Mathews?"

Talia, already in the middle of joining me for a hard giggle, answered to all of us. "All three of us are aware that once the baby's here, the paternity will be obvious. The boys do look so different..."

"Whoa," Margaux blurted. "Are you already knocked up, Tolly Pie?"

"No. *No*," Talia protested, laughing again. "But once I am, and things move along, none of us see it as an issue. Our hearts are full right now, and they'll be even fuller once our family expands."

"So you guys *are* trying?" The question came from Claire, who looked amazing in a black bikini with a patterned sarong to match.

"Well, let's just say we aren't trying to stop it from happening anymore. I stopped taking the pill after the wedding, and that was the only birth control we'd been using for some time, so we'll see, I guess." She shrugged, giving me the impression aliens could've done a water landing in the pool and not ruined her sunny mood. "What about you two?" she asked, looking between Margaux to Claire.

"Whoa, missy." Margaux stretched both arms out in time to her drawn-out words. "Just slow your roll right there. I have all I can handle with my little hellraiser already. Iris still gets up in the middle of the night and still only wants Mama to hold her, unless Grammy Caroline is around. And my mom is happy to help out, but poor Michael feels so helpless. I'm not sure why Iris is so obsessed with me, but I wish she'd warm up to him a little bit. He feels like he's doing something wrong, and I don't know how to make it better. I've tried finding books and support online because I really don't know what to do about it."

I grimaced for a second. "Yikes."

"Right? And the more he worries about it, the more she doesn't want to be around him. Diana said he was the same way when he was a baby, but that doesn't make him feel any better. And when I'm exhausted and she's fussy and he can't help, it just sucks."

We gave Margaux a round of sympathetic nods, but no one had a suggestion to offer. Before we could brainstorm any suggestions, Claire inserted one sad comment.

"Well...Regan loves Kil." She seemed to blink rapidly

behind her shades, and her voice wobbled while adding, "Sometimes a little too much."

"What do you mean, sweetie?" I asked.

She sucked in a weighted sigh. "I mean that I get jealous," she snapped, her lips a thin line. "And I hate myself, but I can't help it. The minute he enters the room, she wants nothing to do with me. It's all Daddy, all the time."

"Claire Bear." Margaux got up, pushed onto her sister's chaise, and then scooped up Claire's hand with forceful comfort. "My brother has that effect on most of the females he meets, remember? Why should Regan be any different?"

Talia and I nodded with vigor. Margaux spoke the truth, however painful it could be for Claire.

"You have a point," Claire mumbled. "But it still sucks. All I'm good for is boobie juice and diaper changes."

"Wait until she gets a little older," Talia inserted. "I remember my sister always complaining that her husband was the playmate and she was the drill instructor. But I think that's how it usually goes. Someone has to rule the roost, and it's usually the momma."

My hearty snicker came out louder than I expected, though that didn't dilute its obnoxious "yeah right" subtext. As soon I finished it up, the three others riveted their stares on me, obviously expecting an explanation.

Damn it.

"Well," I said without a note of apology, "it wasn't that way when I was growing up. Not even close."

"Your mom was the pushover?"

Talia's query was innocent enough. Unfortunately, there was no matching answer—but if I'd learned anything from the sexual game-changer who'd been Mac Stone, it was that honesty sometimes didn't have to be painful. The truth, given to friends who cared in small and controllable doses, really could set someone free. At least a little.

"My mom was the over-doser, sugar." I smiled as openly as I could about it. I wasn't walking around morose because of this shit, and I didn't want them to, either. "Or the over-drinker. Or the over-sleeper, so she would lose whatever dead-end job she'd been holding down at the moment."

"Honey." Claire kept up with the musical chaises, stepping over to pat my hand. "I'm so sorry."

Obeying pure instinct, I yanked away from her. "Sorry," I mumbled. "I didn't mean that as shitty as it looked."

"You have nothing to apologize for," Margaux chastised. "We don't get to pick out parents, Tay. Look at the piece of shit adoptive maternal unit I got stuck with for my formative years. Now she's a fucking criminal. And look at Claire. She had a great one, but she died when Claire was just a girl. We all got the fuck stick, just different ends. But now all we can try to do is break the cycle, you know? We have babies of our own, we can do our best to be better at it than they were." She followed Claire over, bringing me a glass of iced tea from a tray the waiter had brought. I accepted it with a watery smile. *Damn.* I had the best girlfriends in the world.

"I don't want to be the downer on our day." The regret in my voice was sincere. "It's gorgeous out here, and wasting it in wallowing is pointless. My mom is a piece of work. She always has been and still is. She's an addict, and she basically has been my whole life. And I've spent more money bailing her out and plumping my therapist's kids' college funds than I care to think about."

I drank from my tea, wishing it were something stronger to dull the ache at the middle of my chest—though wouldn't that make me just like Mom? Sucking down a cocktail at noon just to make the demons go away?

"Okay, she's right." Margaux clapped her hands like a freaking basketball coach. "I hereby declare babies, boobs, and booze as off-limits subjects. What else is going on in our lives? There has to be something, right?" She pivoted toward me with gusto. "Tag. You're it. What's new? Seen any good movies? Getting any hot cock?"

"Margaux!"

Thank God for Claire, the captain of the Profanity Police. Her outburst was perfectly timed to my choke on the tea—not that Margaux let it slip by for more than two seconds.

"The girls are practically in another fucking county," Margaux snapped at her sister. Then, with her gaze glittering back in my direction: "Besides, Tay has promising news." She sat forward, rubbing her hands together. "*Very* promising, if that blush in full sun is any indication—and we'll take it as one."

"Stop." I held my hands up, laughing. "Just *stop*, girl, before you even get started."

But the woman was like a dog with a bone. "Hmmm. Well. Keep your secrets, then. I'm a little bummed to even have a hint of a new guy, actually...because Killian told Claire and me last night that his cousin Mac is back in town."

A fucking sneaky dog.

I bit the inside of my cheek to keep my jaw from plummeting. That didn't stop the blood from draining from my face. Sweat broke out on my forehead, despite the shade in which we were lying.

Bastard.

The sneaky, smug, God-I've-missed-you-FaceTime-sex-me bastard.

He'd never said one word about coming back to San Diego. Not. One. Single. Word.

I bolted off my chaise, needing to know I wouldn't be numb forever—also needing to remind myself this wasn't the damned Apocalypse. And in all fairness, *I'd* left *him* hanging— pretty literally—the last we'd spoken. And since then, I'd ignored every attempt he'd made at contact.

Attempts most normal guys wouldn't have even bothered with.

But Maclain Stone wasn't normal. In any realistic sense of the word.

"Well, that got someone's attention." There was an ear-to-ear grin in Margaux's voice.

"Whose?" I bit it back quickly. Too quickly.

"Ohhh, ba ha ha." Margaux repeated her hand smacks, this time in applause. "Nice try, Tay baby. Now you've got to spill it, sister."

"I thought we'd established the whole abolishment of the sister thing," I retorted. "At the wedding, remember? Where you sold me out to the devil himself?"

She just laughed, much like she did on that day as well. "You mean the devil who now has you pacing this pool deck like a virgin on prom night?"

"You're terrible." Claire playfully smacked Margaux's arm. "Stop." She looked back up at me. "So for argument's sake, Miss Mathews, let's just say you were a little interested in the good doctor..." She paused, waiting for any sign from me to go on. I twitched slightly, apparently giving enough of a green light for her comfort. "Kil said Mac took a job at Scripps Green in La Jolla. He's moving here permanently. I guess he's looking for a place to live and called to ask if Kil had any recommendations.

Of course, I insisted he stay in our gatehouse until he finds a place of his own. My husband wasn't thrilled with the idea, but I can be, how do you say? Very persuasive." She grinned just before digging in to the newly delivered salad. "God, this is divine. Did you get the same thing?" She pointed at Talia's dish with her fork.

"So spill it, girl." Margaux took over on the interrogation—not that she'd ever really walked away. "What made you go ghost white—well, more than your usual Casper—when Bear said Mac was in town?"

I folded my arms.

Margaux folded hers.

I wrinkled my nose.

She did the same.

Damn it.

We were both two moves shy of sticking out our tongues at each other, and I reflected on how much she really had become like a sister to me. Because of that, I went pure crass on her, hoping it might shock them all into silence.

"I fucked him."

Claire and Talia dropped their heavy forks in unison, metal clattering against the fine china their salads were on. A few of the spa goers stopped their conversations because of the din, but life continued as normal for them, while my three friends gaped as if the world had halted on our side of the pool.

"What?" I bounced my stare between all three of them. "You can't really be surprised. I mean, *look* at him."

Claire recovered first. "Do I want to hear this? I mean, he is family."

"Barely. I don't think he and Kil spoke between their childhood and Fletcher's accident."

"Did he say why? Killian still won't open up about that fully." Claire looked hopeful.

"Sorry, Bear. Wasn't the first thing on my mind. I was too busy coming. Repeatedly."

Margaux jumped up and bounced on her toes. "Repeatedly, huh?" How the wench loved the dirty minutiae.

I nodded my head and rolled my eyes for extra affect. "Ridiculous."

"Details. I need details."

"What?" I bantered. "Why? Why do *you* need details?"

"Oh, my God," Talia giggled out.

"Do they have popcorn on this health freak menu?" Claire muttered. "Because this is getting goooood."

"You've got your own sexy freak at home," I reminded Margaux. "Right? Or have things settled down now that you're an old married couple with a baby? Ohhhh, shit. You don't let that poop bomb sleep in your bed between you and Michael every night, do you? Talk about a sex-life killer."

Margaux laughed so hard, she snorted. "No, we don't. And don't call my precious angel a poop bomb, though at times it's very fitting." She thought for a second and laughed again. "That's funny, actually. I may reuse that. But no. That child sleeps in her own damn bed. I'm just a nosy bitch, you know that. I want to know everything."

"Me too!" Claire and Talia chimed together.

"So when did this epic come fest happen?" Margaux inquired.

I shrugged. "I don't know."

"You *don't know*?"

Of course I knew. The date would be etched on my memory for a good long time to come—along with *that* horrific pun—

but the girls didn't need to know that, just like they didn't need to know about the filthy Mac dreams I'd had before *and* that too. "A few days after the wedding," I finally offered, managing to convince them of my nonchalance. "So, what was that? First week in September? I went to give blood like I always do, and he fucking showed up in front of the Blood Mobile. But now that I think back on it, I think he said something about a job interview. It didn't sink in because he had me all flustered and then lightheaded—"

"You were flustered?" Talia gasped.

"And lightheaded?" Claire sighed.

"Because I'd just let them drain a pint of my blood?" I rebutted.

"Uh-huh." Clearly, Margaux was buying a truth somewhere between the girls' swoons and my acerbity, likely the wisest choice.

"Anyhow," I went on, stabbing at the word, "I had to take a second to lie down, and he turned all growly caveman and jealous of John—"

"Who's John?" Once again, the Claire and Talia choir sang out.

"Did you fuck him too?" And once again, so did the Margaux jukebox.

I shook my head at all of them, focusing on my recount. "Mac bullied me into letting him drive back to my place."

"Because he'd made you faint." Talia dropped her fork again, in order to clutch both hands to her breast. "How romantic!"

"No." I spread out both hands, erasing her conviction. "*Not* romantic. Just fun, sweetie. That's all. He drove me home. One thing led to another. We fucked. It was nice."

It was beyond nice...

But they weren't going to know that. I enforced the point with a casual shrug, like it was an everyday occurrence to screw guys who drove me home. It was better that they thought that. *Much* better, if Maclain fucking Stone was going to be a Southern California resident now.

"He left early the next morning and flew home to Chicago," I went on. "We talked and texted a few times over the next couple of weeks, but he's never said anything about moving out here." As the admission came out, so did my completely perturbed glower. "I wonder why he didn't tell me. He's such a dick."

Talia, with hands still clasped like a damn movie princess, piped in, "Maybe he wanted to surprise you?"

"Surprise me?" I snorted "Isn't that a pretty big assumption? Moving halfway across the country is kind of a big 'something' to conveniently leave out of a conversation." Or a text message. Or a round of FaceTime sex, in which the parties discussed having a hot track date. *Oh, my God.* No wonder he sounded so sure about delivering on that shit with me...

"Well, maybe it wasn't all because of you." Despite the pretty princess pose, Talia was faithful to her textbook logic. She'd always been the most reasonable one in our group, grounded and sure, another contributing factor to people's shock when they learned about her unconventional marriage. "It sounds like there was a lot of career motivation there too," she suggested. "Maybe he didn't want you to feel pressured into thinking it was all about you."

"When exactly was the last time you spoke to him?" Claire's questions, on the other hand, carried the professional curiosity of a crime scene investigator.

"Hmmm," I teased back. "I'm not sure, Officer Stone. We had video sex about two weeks ago, before I hung up on him. We haven't talked since."

"Wait. You did *what*? After *what*?" Now even Margaux was stunned. Maybe that was a good thing. I'd started off with the cavalier attitude about all this but shown more of my hand than I wanted when going butt-hurt about Mac's cute "surprise." This new revelation could help me save face.

"You want that exact date too?" I taunted them, reveling in my fine, fine smartass skills. "I could check my FaceTime log..."

"Yes. Check!" Margaux nearly shouted.

"Gawd." Claire grabbed at Margaux's arm, visibly prompting her sister to dial shit back. "We don't need the call log, Tay—although shit, to have been a fly on your wall..." She fanned herself with the dessert menu.

"I have no idea what the two of you are carrying on about." I turned up my Southern drawl and batted my lashes a bunch of times. "Though I do swear, ladies, if you are telling me hot sex dries up just because you've had babies, I will never ever have a boob gobbler. *Evah*. I love sex too much to give it up for a little snot factory."

"Hmmm." Margaux cocked her head, contemplating that. "I think it's been quite the opposite, actually. I'm afraid I'm going to get knocked up again. My hormones are on overdrive all the time, and Michael doesn't seem to mind coming up with new and more devious ways of making me suffer. So no, babies don't necessarily mean sex dries up. At least not in my house." She sat down and took a big bite of her sandwich, looking to Claire for support. "And yours? Though I dread asking, because...my brother, and...*ew*."

"Mine, neither." Claire's expressive eyes twinkled with mischief. "There are times you have to be quieter, but that just means getting creative." She high-fived her sister. She and Margaux were adorable to watch, which made thinking backward, to the start of their relationship, that much more amazing. They'd come a long way in a short time. Healed a lot in each other...

I wondered if that would ever be possible for Mom and me. Could we ever mend stuff enough to have a loving, positive bond? It was so hard to imagine that ever happening, considering all the pain of our past and the resentment I harbored because of it. Because of her. *Toward* her. Even with years of therapy under my belt, there were issues tough to let go of. In addition, because so many of the triggers continued to happen, it seemed like I took one step forward and two steps back. Regularly.

The girls started talking about a new project for which the Stone Global R&D team was accepting ideas. I listened with only half an ear because strange dots were beginning to connect in my psyche. I thought more about Mom. A lot more. Turned over all the issues I had with her and how deeply they affected my ability to trust anyone's word in general. It was different with the girls because they accepted me at face value, even knowing so many parts of my heart remained walled off. But Mac...

Had been different.

Demanded more.

He'd wanted to see everything...

And for a few insane moments, when I'd been falling apart in those orgasms for him, he'd gotten exactly what he'd demanded.

But people who saw everything turned into people who could hurt me. Deeply.

Was that why I was so hesitant to trust anything about his move here? Especially because he'd kept it from me until now?

My stomach suddenly felt like it was choreographing a strip tease to *Versace on the Floor*, though I still tried to cram my veggie sandwich down. But by the time Bruno was singing "let's just kiss till we're naked," the squaw bread the chef had so artfully trimmed into tiny triangles threatened a repeat performance at the lunch table.

Damn it.

My mom's history would haunt me for the rest of my life if I didn't get a grip on myself. I knew, in all practicality, that her choices had been, and still were, hers alone. They didn't dictate that I would make the same mistakes—but my own life had started to show the same stupid patterns, and that terrified me. I seemed to have a loser magnet buried somewhere deep within myself, and a guy who seemed perfectly normal at the onset of a relationship ended up being a useless, jobless leech within months of me making a commitment to him.

Okay, but Mac Stone was far from a loser.

But there was baggage there, nonetheless. Freight I couldn't ignore. The mother that Claire had mentioned was a major red flag. Second, he'd just waved goodbye to a lucrative career in Chicago—because of what? Did he want to work on his tan driving a convertible up and down PCH on a regular basis? Not exactly a picture of stability, and the dude was still decades away from a significant midlife crisis.

But as long as I was on the subject of his cars...what about the whole racing thing? While that scene seemed thrilling and sexy, it was also dangerous and possibly irresponsible—at the very least, reckless. What kind of husband and eventual father would he make if he didn't respect his own safety?

Whoa. Hello.

Cart before the horse, anyone?

"Are you even listening?" Margaux looked at me, frustration and a hint of amusement on her face.

"What?" I barked.

"Yep. Just what I thought. Not listening."

"I am now." Impatient scowl. "What is it?" Though if she asked me one more time if the spa sandals made her legs look doughy, I was going to cut the wench.

"I was asking if you just want to make up a reason to go back to Claire's with her," Margaux expounded. "Then, maybe you can happen to mosey on by the gatehouse...maybe in your cutest bikini or dress and sexy heels?" She giggled.

I slammed my head down on the table. "Stop!"

"Why? You haven't heard a single word any of us just said. And we were talking about *your* account. For *five* minutes."

"I'm sorry, you guys." Great. Now I was whining.

"Don't be ridiculous, honey. We've all been right where you are." Claire stood up and tightened the belt on her robe. "But come on. Our massages are in ten minutes. We need to shower and be in the quiet room when they come for us. We can go back to the house from here." She winked my way. "And maybe you *will* find a good excuse to wander out to the gatehouse."

"Uh-uh." I pouted petulantly. "There's no way I'm going to your house. Ever again."

We all started laughing as we walked arm in arm in arm into the locker room of the spa to enjoy a little pampering and relaxation. Maybe this was exactly what I needed. The massage could bring some much-needed clarity—and right now, I'd take every drop of the stuff I could get. I was in deep where Mac Stone was concerned, and seeing him—by accident or otherwise—was the last thing I needed.

CHAPTER TEN

Mac

"Can I get you anything from the cafeteria? I'm going to scoot down for a cup of coffee."

My new nurse, Devon, popped her head into my office without knocking—a habit we'd need to break her of, but not today. I was in such a great mood, it could wait.

"Is it worth it?" I replied with a grin, hanging my stethoscope around my neck. "Or should I wait until someone makes a run to the shop on the corner?"

Devon, a curvy brunette with a killer smile and sparkling eyes, returned my smile before turning to go back out to her station. "It can get pretty busy once the clinic starts up. If you need caffeine, you may as well get used to the cafeteria. It's not too bad. How do you take it?"

"Triple espresso. I'll go easy since it's right before lunch."

"Christ. That's going easy?" She winced at my caffeine tolerance. *Med school conditions a guy pretty well.*

"Rookie," I teased as she left for the coffees.

I looked out of the window of my office, at the Pacific Ocean crashing on the shore below. The waves sent glistening sprays into the air, catching the sunlight like stars.

It was a fucking postcard.

And if it was a dream, I didn't want to wake up.

Never again would I start my day to wind howling off Lake Michigan, to be sucked to screaming velocity between the city's skyscrapers. I'd never listen with dread to the morning weather report, holding my breath as they spoke of the snow that had accumulated while I slept. I'd never rush into work to be debriefed on the casualties awaiting my attention, brought in from the numerous pileups on the tollway because assholes couldn't handle the road conditions.

"Fucking paradise," I muttered, adding a happy sigh to appease karma, just before my cell chirped with an incoming text. "The hell?" No add-on sigh this time. My cousin was the summoning party. And yeah, I'd used the verb on purpose. When Killian Stone summoned, he *summoned*.

Can you meet for lunch?

> *Clinic today. On call tomorrow.*
> *Wednesday?*

He responded quickly. *Board meeting.*

> *Thursday?*

Yes. My office. Noon.

> *See you then.*

Yep. Summoned.

He didn't reply after that, so I figured we were on. It had shocked the hell out of me when his wife invited me to stay on their property, easing the initial chaos of the transition. I didn't kid myself into thinking Kil and I would spend weekends barbecuing by the pool after that, but now I'd gotten a summons to the top of the golden boy's kingdom, and maybe that meant he wanted to play nice. Maybe—gasp of gasps—the guy would even offer to introduce me around town. He seemed to know everyone between here and Santa Barbara. Maybe, like me, he'd also started to see that most of our bad blood was between our parents, not us. Maybe adulthood would bring the two of us a different energy. We could set aside the bullshit—quite possibly another by-product of my narcissistic mother—and try a relationship of our own.

Relationships felt like a good thing to be working for right now.

Wonder what Taylor's doing.

It wasn't a leap to connect those two thoughts—though the woman was no more than two links away from *any* of my thoughts these days. Just being here brought her closer to my psyche. The very air seeming to bring hints of her delicious scent. I saw her eyes in the vast blue sky and heard her laughter in the music of the sea.

She was in my fucking blood...

But she still wouldn't answer my text messages or phone calls.

A few more ignored attempts, and I resolved to plant myself on her damned doorstep. I wasn't above doing it. Hell, Claire had come home from a spa day with a few of her girlfriends the other day, and I'd peered at them from my window like a first-rate stalker, sure I'd heard Taylor's voice among them. But then they'd disappeared into the main house, vanishing too quickly to give me certain confirmation. For the next twenty minutes, I'd racked my brain for a viable reason to go to the main house but had ended up hiding in the dark like a pussy—and then fantasizing about *hers* while jacking off under a cold shower.

Loser.

Wait. Make that *obsessed* loser.

It was official. I hadn't felt this ass-over-teakettle about a girl since grade school. Maybe not even then.

"Here's your rocket fuel."

I jumped about a foot out of my chair when Devon barged into my office with my espresso. *How long was I out in the land of Taylor Mathews daydreams this time?*

"Annnd maybe you don't need the nuclear juice after all."

I shook my head, managing to blurt, "Huh?"

"Gosh. Sorry, dude." She slid over one of my leather BMW coasters and set the coffee on it. "Guess I should've knocked." At least she had the decency to look embarrassed now.

"Yes, please. I'd appreciate if you would get in the habit of it. Even if my door is open slightly. I tend to get lost in thought." I barked more than I meant to, but the request would stick at least—and to be honest, it was best she knew this shit about me upfront. When the ping-pong balls were set free, God knew where my mind could bounce.

"I see that. Sorry, really. I didn't mean to startle you or to be rude."

"You weren't. Neither of those." I didn't really mean it, and she was smart enough to know that, but *something* had to be said, because now she was nervous to the point of blotchy, and I felt like the dick I was known for being. Only why did that idea suddenly chafe in a dozen ways? I was used to the arrogant asshole shoes. I'd proudly, painstakingly worn them in and had even been comfortable in them, all too okay with letting people worry about their own damn insecurities if they couldn't keep up with me.

But now, somebody *could* keep up with me. Was even besting me. Or at least she *had*...

"It's fine," I followed up in a rush to Devon. "Everything's fine. Don't stress. That's my job today, right?"

"Oh, stawwwp." Her blotches faded, becoming a pretty enough blush. Nothing like the roses that could tint Taylor's incredible skin, but I was glad she no longer looked ready to plunge into the waves outside and never come back.

"Well, thank you for the—errr—rocket fuel." I glanced at my watch. Clinic started in fifteen minutes. I grabbed my white coat and espresso and motioned for her to lead the way. "So shall we? After you, please."

"Of course," she replied. "And don't be nervous. You'll be great."

I indulged a laugh. "I can do this shit in my sleep. I just still have a lot of loose ends from the move."

"Hmmm. Anything I can help you with?" She glanced back over her shoulder while we walked. I couldn't tell if she was genuinely nice or pushing the edge of personal boundaries.

"Nope, it's all stuff I need to handle on my own. Thanks, though."

"Well, just give a holler if you change your mind. Glad to be of service. I remember what it was like when I first moved here. Didn't really know anyone..." She sighed. "It was a bit lonely."

She didn't add any more glances to that one, which

enforced my impression. *Yep. Pushing the edge.*

"Soooo...this'll be your clinic office. You can use that computer and log in to the hospital's system with the login and password HR gave you. The patient roster for the day will be loaded in the menu screen that comes up after you log in. If you need help, just find me. I'll do the vitals and the intake, and then patients will be ready for you. Pretty basic stuff."

"Yep." I made it noncommittal. "Basic drill." *In my sleep, remember?*

"I'll go bring the first one back." She lingered in the doorway, not-so-subtly taking me in, clearly trying to decide if I'd be captivated more by professional crispness or a friendly, flirty edge. I pretended to check something on my phone, hoping she'd understand the answer was *neither.* "You all ready?"

"Let's do it."

She left the small office, leaving me with a few empty minutes with my phone still in hand. Like the smitten sap I was, I decided there was no better time to attempt texting with Taylor one last time before the day's rat race began. On the other hand, was there ever a *wrong* time to keep trying?

I'd never stop trying.

Thinking of you, I tapped in but then hesitated, my thumb hovering over the keypad. And then I added to it and hit Send.

> *Thinking of you. In fact,*
> *all I do is think about you.*

What the fuck—wasn't like I'd have time to wallow in regrets about it.

> *Please answer me, sassy.*

"Well, that makes it official," I muttered while switching the device to vibrate and sliding it into the big pocket of my white coat. "You're officially whipped cream, asshole."

On that uplifting benediction, I concentrated on work.

I had a few minutes to kill before Devon triaged the first patient, so I used the time to log into the hospital's system. I had twelve patients to see over the course of the day. Not a punishing schedule. I expelled a breath of relief—

Only to have it stolen from my lungs as the phone vibrated in my coat pocket.

I grabbed in for the thing so fast, my stethoscope and fingers twined and then caught on a thread in the bottom of the new coat, punching the phone into the air and crashing onto the tile floor.

"Fuck," I snarled. "Jesus *fuck*. Don't break. Don't break!"

I dropped to my knees so fast I heard one of my caps pop. I was going to fucking debilitate myself over a text message from a girl I wasn't even dating. Yeah, I was Taylor Mathews' fucking puppet. Pathetic.

Upside? The screen was still intact. I grinned like a drunk rat at seeing the message was from her. If I was going to limp through the rest of my day, at least the pain was worth it. She'd responded. *She knows I'm still alive*—despite the brutality of how she communicated it.

Why didn't you tell me?

Her fury seemed to seep from every word.

My smile only widened—despite her demand bringing on true confusion. What the hell was she...

Shit. Killian and Claire must have told her I was back in

town. I hadn't asked them to keep it a secret or anything, and if she *had* been in that giggling group up at the main house, then the subject had probably come up. It just seemed my little sassy wasn't too keen on surprises.

Guess the cat's out of the bag?

I added the little face that looked like a guy feigning innocence after a murder.

I'm allergic to cats.

So much for innocence. At once, my cock twitched in my scrubs, making me reach down and adjust. *Damn.* This was no time to sport a woody. The thin material did nothing to conceal an erection, but her adorably impertinent answers always shot straight to my dick.

Have dinner with me.

As long as we were stabbing straight for the important points...

No.

I chuckled. Sort of. She didn't think I'd let this opportunity sift away like beach sand, did she?

Why not?

I don't appreciate being lied to.

Puzzlement returned. A hefty, straight-up version of the stuff.

I've never lied to you, Taylor. Ever.

Lying by omission is still lying, clown.

Okay, so she *really* hated surprises.

I'll explain when I see you.
Pick you up at 8.

Won't be there.

Please.

Well, you can't come to my place.

Why not?

Because we both know what will happen.

Isn't that the idea?

The idea is dinner. Period.
I'll meet you somewhere at 7.

*I have clinic until 6. I won't be
able to make it somewhere by 7.*

Guess you'll have to try really hard, then.

I knew better than to send another message—and almost didn't want to. Christ, what this anticipation already did to my dick. It was torture. It was heaven. No matter what, one thing was clear. The negotiation round was over. She'd agreed to see me, but thoroughly on her terms. I could do that. Her terms. Maybe just this once.

Later, I'd check in with a restaurant choice—maybe even go to if-you-need-anything-just-ask Devon for a suggestion or two. If I could lure Taylor closer to La Jolla so I didn't have to deal with the traffic between here and Mission Valley, her dinner call time could be juuuust this side of workable.

There was a soft knock on the door. A second later, Devon tucked her head in—and scowled at seeing me on the floor, gawking at my phone. "You're on deck, Dr. Stone. Room one. Chart's on the door." Clearly—and thankfully—she thought better of asking any questions.

"On my way." I hurried to my feet, plunked my phone back into my pocket, and then took off down the hall.

It was effortless to fall back into the routine of seeing patients, making notes in charts and consulting with Devon when I needed extra tests, labs, and films ordered. Before I knew it, the end of the day had already sneaked up—and I was damn glad of it. Not that the day had been banal. Just the opposite. The expectation of what awaited at the end of my work made every second of it that much more rewarding... and meaningful. For the first time in a long time, patients were people to me, not just conditions or diagnoses or insurance approval codes. Yeah, even little Lois Wilkes, who'd recounted the highlights of her life for me three times.

Around lunch, I'd checked my phone quickly, only to see Taylor still hadn't read my suggestion of the Crab Catcher for dinner. When I checked around four, she'd finally read it and sent back a simple thumbs-up. The confirmation was enough to get me through the ninety minutes with Mrs. Wilkes.

Ultimately, emerging from the room with an exhausted scowl, I bellowed down the hall, "Devon!"

"No need to shout." She proved the point by emerging from the triage and charting station, four feet away. "I'm right here."

I bristled at her reprimand. She and I were going to need to lay some ground rules sooner rather than later.

"Can you please refer Mrs. Wilkes to whoever handles the dementia cases here? She'll likely need her residence moved, services updated, the usual. Thank you. I'm going upstairs to my office to finish charting from my computer up there."

"Got it." She was brisk to the point of brusqueness. I'd probably ticked her off—again—but had little time to care.

But the thing was...I did.

Goddamn it.

I halted, one arm still sheathed in my white coat and one arm already freed, and pivoted back toward the nursing station. "Hey."

"Yes?" Devon was still all business. And yep, still pretty pissed.

"I...uh...really appreciate your help today. Thanks." Whoa, this was weird—but kind of nice—to watch how I brightened her features just a little. "I'm sure we'll find our groove in no time."

"Sure," Devon murmured and then smiled. "See you tomorrow."

"Good night." I shed the rest of the coat as I walked, also unbuttoning the top button of my shirt from beneath my tie.

Screw the remaining charting. I only had one goal on my mind now.

Meaning I skipped steps on the stairs back to my office, disrobing further as I bounded up. Once inside, I made sure to lock the door behind me before getting in a quick shower in the small bathroom connected to the office space. I already had a change of clothes stashed in the closet and threw those on after hastily drying off.

While attempting to tame my hair into some sort of style— the shit was curling around my ears and seriously needed a trim—I checked my phone to make sure the reservation was locked down at Crab Catcher. It seemed to be a popular place, and I'd asked for a prime table with a great view. Nothing like a little oceanic ambience to help smooth my way back into a certain firecracker's good graces.

The restaurant hadn't called.

But Taylor had.

And before I jabbed the Play arrow on her message, my gut clenched.

"Hey...Mac."

Mac. Not Clown or Dork or Ass Monkey.

Shit.

"It's...uhhh...me. Taylor. But I guess you know that, caller ID and all. Hey, I'm—well shit, I'm really sorry, but I have to cancel. Please don't be mad. Something came up. Oh, my God, that sounds lame, but...well...I just can't do it tonight, okay? I have to...it's just that...well...yeah. Okay, I'm really sorry. I guess

I'll see you around." Her voice wobbled on that, despite how she inhaled sharply to even out that betraying keel. "Okay," she rushed out. "Bye."

Click.

Then the dial tone filled the quiet air of my small office.

And pierced at the target all but painted on the center of my chest.

And tugged at the curiosity in my brain. Relentlessly.

Something wasn't right.

As in, *really* not right.

After thinking a minute, I picked up my phone and tried to call her—or whatever strange alien had replaced her in that message. I'd never heard the woman sound so small and unsure, not even when she was seconds from passing out in front of the Blood Mobile, in the parking lot outside.

Three rings. Four. Five.

"Hey there!"

"*Sassy.* Thank fuck. What—"

"You've reached Taylor Mathews with Stone Global Corporation. Please leave a message, including your number, and I will return your call at my earliest convenience. Thank you."

Well, there was the Taylor I knew, at least. Confident, sharp, and sure of herself—not the stammering stranger who'd called no more than five minutes ago.

This wasn't just strange anymore.

It was way off-kilter.

The hairs on my neck stood up. I didn't get the vibe that she was physically in peril, but she hadn't just voice mailed from poolside at the spa, either. Something was out of whack, and I wasn't about to just go on my merry way with the awareness tearing at me worse than Mrs. Wilkes's third retelling of her wild night in Vegas with Mr. Wilkes, three decades ago.

I turned into a human ping-pong ball, pacing zigzags across the office a few times, before deciding to suck it up and text my cousin.

> *Don't take this the wrong way, Kil Joy.*
> *I need to talk to Claire. Have her call me.*
> *I'm worried about Taylor.*

If she ended up angry with me, I would deal with it then.

In a few minutes, my cell rang, displaying Killian's information, though I picked up to hear Claire's level but urgent tone. "Mac? What's going on?"

"I'm not sure," I replied tightly. "And maybe I'm totally out of line here—"

"That's stopped you before?" Kil's interjection told me I was on speaker with the two of them. An infant's gurgle rapidly corrected me. The *three* of them.

Normally, I'd be gunning to return that shot right back over his bow, but there was shit bigger than that at the moment. Who the hell cared that he'd had a couple of extra polo ponies and a bunk bed nearly twenty years ago? I gave voice to what was much more important, right here in front of me.

No. Not in front of me. And that was the terrifying point.

"Taylor and I were supposed to have dinner tonight."

"Yay!" Claire exclaimed.

"Shock of shocks," Kil drawled, droll as fuck.

"Well, she just left me a voice mail, calling it off." Relieved my cousin held back on twisting his knife deeper because of the tension in my voice, I went on, "And something's...not right. At all."

"What do you mean?" Claire's voice was closer now, as if she had leaned in toward the phone.

"Her voice," I stammered. "It...just wasn't right. You know how she's normally so..."

"Spunky?" Claire filled in.

I laughed, "Yeah. That's it." And it was, describing my girl with freakish accuracy. "Only this time, she wasn't. Not by a fucking long shot."

A new rustling. Claire hauled in a deep breath. "Oh dear."

I started pacing again. "Have you talked to her today?"

"No. We don't always see each other at work, since we're both so busy."

"*I* saw her," Killian offered. At once, there was a delighted baby's coo. That little girl was pretty smitten with her daddy.

"Really, baby?" Claire's reply was tender. *Honestly, the pair of them must be bathing in sugar water every morning.* "Oh yeah, that's right...the meeting for Kim's new Asia launch thing..."

"What time was that?" I fought to keep my asshole tone out of it.

"And was she okay?" Claire added. "Her usual spicy self?"

"It was near the end of the day." Kil finished addressing my query with a soft coo to his daughter. "Right after four our time, I think, since Beijing is fifteen hours ahead. And no, Fairy, I didn't notice anything off. What's going on?"

"Probably not anything." His curiosity was oddly grating, perhaps because he enjoyed the freedom to be openly concerned about Taylor—a privilege I coveted. "I didn't mean to get anyone worried," I stressed. "Just thought I'd check. Thanks again. I"—was going to choke on this, but I vowed to get it out—"I appreciate it."

"Hey," Claire spoke up. "Why don't I try to give her a call, Mac? If I get through or find anything out, I'll let you know."

"I'd appreciate that too." That one didn't feel as rough to spew. Maybe, with practice, I could manage this "manners" nonsense from time to time—especially when the payback came in the form of a text from Claire just before I got into my car for the drive back to their gatehouse for the night.

Found her. She's at her mom's place.

The joy of reading the first sentence was clobbered by the ire of taking in the second. "What the hell?" I grumbled, texting back an abbreviated version of the same.

T just got done posting bail.
Janet got into some sort of trouble
with the police again.

Again???

I didn't take time out to verbalize it this time. Claire's reply was equally fast in coming.

It happens from time to time.
Not my story to tell, though.

Thank you. Sincerely.

Anytime. Sincerely.

I believed her. "Keep that woman happy, Killian," I murmured while watching Claire sign off. "You don't deserve her, motherfucker."

But now, the motherfucker's cousin was in a real dilemma. Go home and worry about my sassy girl all night, or follow my gut and take a different route, through Mission Valley instead? Texting her to come to me would be useless. She'd ignore the message, just like all the others I'd sent since listening to her voice mail. Then I'd sit at the gatehouse and worry about her all night long.

Damn. I'd had no idea Taylor was still dealing with her mother's shitty lifestyle choices, even now—but the revelation filled in a lot of blank spaces about why the woman was so skittish when conversations turned halfway serious about even going on a regular date, let alone attempting any kind of a monogamous choice with each other. No wonder she'd been furious with me for not being more forthcoming about the move, as well. Her entire life, men had brought only misery, mayhem, and "surprises" she'd rather forget, not cherish. Even the males with whom she worked, strictly platonic in nature, probably felt the fallout from Janet Mathews' crappy decisions.

That was all going to change.

At least if I could do anything about it.

New plan. Finding ways to show her men could be worth believing in. That *I* was worth believing in. That I could be stable and true, a safe bet for the long haul. For *her* long haul.

Whoa. Hold the fucking phone.

When had the body snatchers come by and replaced my usual douchebag self with this guy talking in my head right now?

Stable?

Safe bet?

Motherfucking long haul?

"Paging Dr. Clown," I muttered, almost sealing it off with a laugh. But I couldn't laugh, because every fiber in my being confirmed the conviction as my truth. I was in deep, disgusting adoration and veneration of this woman—a devotion plunging even deeper now that I'd been handed the key that unlocked her darker truths.

Worth it.

Her light was worth every fucking step of that darkness already.

I couldn't stop thinking about her. Her porcelain skin. Her quirky smiles. Her gigantic blue eyes, fringed with those thick, beautiful lashes and shining with the constant workings of her incredible mind. I could close my own eyes and recall every inch of her perfection in my memory.

Well, that sure as hell did it. "Fuck this," I growled in agreement, right before gunning the engine in order to veer onto the 52 freeway, heading east toward Mission Valley. According to the car's nav, a few more interchanges would land me on the freeway passing nearest to her apartment complex. San Diego had a pretty involved freeway system, but I was getting used to the lay of the land very quickly.

Not more than a half hour later, I pulled into her complex and took a loop through the parking lot. Her 240sx was there, parked in space seventeen. I really doubted Claire would've lied to me on her behalf, so I assumed she'd gotten her mom situated and then come home. I found a visitor's parking spot with ease and then jogged up to her door and knocked.

It took a second knock before the porch light came on.

She opened the door but then just stared at me with dull eyes. She looked exhausted, small and frail.

Without waiting for an invitation, I stepped inside her apartment and wrapped her tightly in my arms. Wonder of wonders, she let me—though at first my embrace went unrequited. Her posture was like her gaze, limp and lifeless, her skinny arms just hanging at her sides. But she didn't push me away, either, nor did a single syllable of sarcasm tumble off her lips. She just seemed to...exist.

I'd never been more freaked out in my life.

So I squeezed her tighter, pressing my lips to the top of her head. The poor thing smelled of smoke and stale air, much like the corner seat in a bar or a cheap hotel room. This was nothing like her beloved Allure...now my beloved Allure too. The scent of *my* beloved woman. No wonder she was as limp and defeated as a stray cat who'd been kicked into the gutter. She was covered in the rot of her mother's world.

"You okay?" I murmured into her hair. When she nodded, I fought the urge to turn her over my knee and swat her for lying. Right now, that would accomplish nothing. *Stability. Safe bet. Long haul.*

So instead, I pulled back far enough to push the hair from her eyes, making her look at me. And *see* me.

"What can I do for you, love?"

"Stop calling me that, for starters."

"Tell me and it's yours," I persisted, barely skipping a beat. "Why don't you come back to my place? Well, what's sufficing for it right now. I'll give you a hot bath. It's a Roman tub. That gatehouse is like the Four Seasons."

"I know." She sounded as if I'd just confirmed bears shit in the woods.

"So throw together a bag. Put some work clothes in too. I can take you to the office in the morning, and then on your lunch—"

"*Stop.*" She pushed a hand over my mouth, just to make sure I got that one. "I don't need anything, okay? Not from you. Not from anyone else, for that matter." As she lowered her hand, she narrowed her glare. "Why are you even here? Didn't you get my message?"

"Of course I did."

"Then why—"

"Because I wanted to see you." I reached in, twining my fingers with hers. "But more than that, I wanted to help you."

"No."

"Damn it, Taylor."

"Don't 'damn it' me."

"Then don't push me away."

"I said I don't need your damn help."

"I *know* what you said." *For the love of fuck.* Where I drew the patience of a saint to deal with this girl was beyond my understanding—but maybe those saints were on to something with the whole divine strength line and I'd never understood it before now. I'd stand here all night and let her tear me apart in twelve *more* ways, if that was what she really needed...

But I knew it wasn't.

Now, she just needed to realize it too.

"Then why are you still standing there?" she snipped.

"Because I care about you. And whether you need me or not, *I* need to know you're going to be okay. Don't you get that?"

"No." She yanked out of my arms, circling toward her Barbie doll-sized kitchen. "And stop with the *caring* shit too.

And now you can see I'm fine, so we're dandy, yeah?"

I gave in to a heavy sigh. This bullshit was in the express lane to nowhere. Maybe I needed to change tactics. "Have you eaten dinner?" I made it a demand. "Can I at least make you something?"

"Clowns don't cook." She turned around to challenge me.

"Of course they do. Where do you think all those cream pies come from?"

That scored me the smallest trace of a smile. *Yesssss.*

"Here's an idea." I approached her again, wrapping my arms around her. When she started to protest, I pressed an index finger on her lips. "Let me finish. You go shower, or take a bath, or whatever you do in there." I thumbed over my shoulder toward her bedroom. "While you do that, I'll make you something to eat."

She closed her eyes. The fight drained out of her frame. I moved in, kissing her forehead, but refrained from whooping in any further victory. Without further argument or discussion, she trudged past me and across the living room, closing the bedroom door quietly behind her. I heard the water running soon after, so I set to work in the small kitchen. Her refrigerator was basically bare and the pantry wasn't much better, but there was a plastic zip-top bag full of white powder. In hot-pink marker on the bag's label, it read *Pancake Mix.* Okay, I could work with that.

Back to the refrigerator. *Score.* I found butter and syrup. A brief dig through her cabinets turned up a waffle iron. Yuri, my college roommate, and I had lived on waffles in college. We had at least thirty different ways to make them and often joked that if we didn't get into med school, we'd open an all-waffle restaurant and make a killing. There was a package of sausage links in her freezer that looked like they had been in there a few months too long, but I defrosted them in the microwave and then tucked them under the broiler, hoping for the best.

I heard her getting out of the shower as I poured batter into the hot waffle iron and turned the sausages. I found clean, matched plates and silverware and set her little café table for two. All she had in her refrigerator were beer and water, so I made two cups of coffee in her Keurig and set those on the table with two glasses of water. By the time she came out of her room in a sexy black cotton robe, I was piling the third waffle onto the serving plate to bring to the table.

"Breakfast for dinner?" I winked. "I hear it's the new rage...somewhere."

"Oh, my God. Waffles."

"Do you like them?"

"No. I love them." She beelined for the table, betraying how hungry she truly was. "Shit. It smells delicious, Mac. You really didn't have to go to all this trouble."

"It was no trouble at all. But do enjoy it now, because this is literally the one thing I know how to cook." It gave me a strange amount of joy to see how excited she was about the food. The meal I'd prepared for her—with a hell of a lot of happiness.

She sat down on the chair, one leg tucked under her bottom, hair still wrapped up in a towel. Her gaze was more brilliant, her skin rosy and fresh once more. She smelled like Chanel Allure again.

She was the most beautiful woman I'd ever laid eyes upon.

I served her a waffle and passed her the butter. "For your arteries, my lady."

She looked up at me, mischief dancing anew in her incredible, saucer-wide eyes. She remembered that first altercation just as clearly as I did.

"Thank you, kind sir."

"Do you want a separate plate for your sausage?" I had a small plate in my hand.

"What?" Her confused look was more adorable than her pissed look.

"Some people don't like when the syrup gets on their sausage."

"Clown." She snorted. "I'm from *Georgia*. A little syrup on a piece of greasy pork just makes it that much better."

"Point taken." I put the plate back in the cupboard.

"You hang around with too many pansies," she said around a mouthful of food.

I almost choked on the water I had just sipped. "I'll keep that in mind the next time I'm at the gym and the guys are benching over three hundred pounds."

"Nobody really does that."

"The hell they don't."

Her features crunched in. "That's, like, three of me."

I shrugged and dug into my own food. I didn't really want to debate her weight because I had a hard time believing she came in close to a hundred pounds, but she'd had enough crap already today. And of course, I'd already learned the ins and outs of the word "like" in Cali-lingo. It was a power lifter in these parts, giving people a very generous margin around facts and figures.

"My God, these are delicious. How did you learn to cook?" She shoved another big forkful into her mouth.

"Clown school."

She grinned over her next bite but didn't say anything more. We finished our food in silence, and it was...nice. Damn nice. For a few quiet moments, we were just two people at the end of their work days, filling their bellies with comfort food.

I stood to clear the plates at the same time Taylor did.

"I'm cleaning up." She smacked at my hand as I reached over for her plate. "It's the least I can do since you cooked."

"Uh-uh. You've had a rougher day than me." I tossed over a mock scowl. "And haven't you learned your lesson about hitting me?"

"Hmmm." She glossed over my challenge. "Debatable about who had the worst day. Wasn't today your first day at the hospital?"

"In clinic," I clarified. "I've had a few meetings and surgical consults, but today was full of seeing actual patients."

"First days always suck."

"It was okay." I shrugged. "Certainly not my first rodeo. Same problems, different city. Please. Let me clean up. Go lie down, or sit down, or whatever. Relax."

"Fine, fine." With a cute little smile, she took her coffee off the table and went to the sofa in the living room. I made short work of cleanup since I'd started washing the dishes as we bantered and there weren't any leftovers to store. After stowing the syrup and butter back in the fridge, I left the clean dishes to air dry in the dishrack on the counter. I was astonished her place didn't even have a dishwasher but didn't bring it up.

I flipped the light off in the kitchen and then stood in the doorway to the living room and watched the light from the TV flicker on Taylor's pale skin. I was captivated—but there wasn't much about her that didn't mesmerize me. Even her feet were beautiful.

"I...uh...guess I'll head out." I kicked lightly at the floor, grimacing from the acid that sprang to my mouth in revolt at the words.

"Do you want to stay?" Her voice was quiet and sexy.

"Yes. More than anything. But I know you've had a shitty night, and I'm not sure it's the best idea."

"I'm positive it's the worst idea. But I'm also positive I don't want to be alone. Especially not right now."

Damn. Her honesty, delivered on a serrated rasp, sliced through my heart like a hot knife. "Okay, love. I'll stay—but can we sleep in your bed? That floor fucked up my back for days."

"No. *No bed.* House rules."

Christ. "All right. Do you have an air mattress?"

"Aren't those for camping?"

"Okay, so I'm going to buy you one when I'm shopping for my new place. When I *find* a new place."

"Do you plan on sleeping over here a lot? Kind of presumptuous, don't you think? Especially from the clown that didn't bother mentioning he was moving across the country to the town I live in."

Ohhh, boy. So that was where we'd go with this—though I'd all but asked for it, insisting she rejuvenate with the shower, the food, and the caffeine. Now she was fired up and damn sexy, sitting on the edge of the sofa, spoiling for an argument. And if that was what she wanted...

"Because of exactly this," I stated, making a twirling motion above my head to signify the all-encompassing shit storm about to crash down. "I was *ready* for a career move, Taylor—and one presented itself in this town. Go ahead and shoot me for it if you want, but I'm not fucking leaving. Guess what? *I like it here.* It has complicated roads and boba everything and real fucking palm trees. Right now, the city I 'ruled,' as you have said, sucks big frozen hairy monkey balls.

If this is December, I can't wait to see January and February. Must be really brutal."

"Don't get too brazen. It does rain in February." She paused for a beat. "Sometimes."

I burst out laughing. These thin-blooded beachcombers had no idea how good they had it—and I couldn't wait to become one of them.

"Why the hell are you laughing?" She was getting more pissed by the minute.

I just shook my head. "Doesn't matter. Seriously, sass, let's just go to bed. I promise I'll be a gentleman this time. I'll even sleep above the covers. I just want to hold you. But I don't want to have to see a chiropractor every time we spend the night together."

"Then maybe we shouldn't spend the night together anymore." She stood up, folding her arms as she straightened. "I told you, we aren't sleeping in my bed together."

Well...fuck.

"What is this really all about, baby? Will you just explain *that* to me, so I understand?"

"No. It's my issue!" She was yelling now, but I didn't try to stop her. "You don't have to understand it!"

"Okay. Okay." I raised my hands in front of me in supplication. "I'm sorry."

"It's been a bad night." She dropped her head into her hands.

"Do you want to talk about it?" I walked toward her and reached out to stroke her shoulders with my hands. She jumped when I made contact. "Hey," I whispered. "Did someone hurt you?"

"No, no. No one did anything to me. Maybe you should

just go. This will never work between us. I'm so fucked up. Don't you understand that? I'll never be what you want me to be."

"How do you know what I want? We barely have civilized conversation. All we do is bicker and exchange clever insults. You don't know anything about me, and I know even less about you. And now, the minute I try to reach out to you, you want me to leave. Why not just give talking to me a try? Tell me what happened tonight."

"You don't want to hear all my shit, Mac."

"How about I decide what I want to hear and don't want to hear?"

I took her hands in mine. They were ice cold and trembling. I gazed into her eyes, brimming with so much fear and dread I just wanted to fold her into my arms and hold her for the rest of the night. I sat down on the sofa, deep into the corner of the old piece of shit, and tugged her into my lap. Her black robe was thick and cozy—there was no reason her skin should be as cold as it was.

"Do you want me to turn the heat up? Why are you so cold?"

"I think I'm just tired."

"Is it because your hair is still wet?"

"It's not wet. I just piled it up in the towel in the shower to keep it from getting wet." She let the towel fall away, and her blonde hair tumbled loose. I wrapped my arms around her and held her tightly against me, trying to help her warm up.

"Do you want another cup of coffee? That might help." I was trying every home remedy I could think of.

"No, I'll be up all night."

We were so close, almost nose-to-nose, and I could smell

the maple syrup on her breath. I couldn't resist kissing her sweet lips. Just one innocent kiss, nothing too passionate, although my dick didn't take much to wake up and take notice of what was happening.

"I'm glad you came back to San Diego." She said it so quietly, I almost asked her to repeat it so I could be sure. I knew if I did, though, the magic would be spoiled with some smartass remark.

"I think *that* was the reaction I hoped for more than the original one." I said it just as quietly, hoping to give her the same shimmer of magic inside that she had just given me.

"Why did you cancel our dinner plans tonight?" I really wanted her to know she could confide in me, and I knew I was pushing her but figured she would feel better once she was able to get it off her chest.

"Janet. That's my mom. She was picked up down by Thirty-Second Street today."

I must have looked confused, because she elaborated.

"Thirty-Second Street is the navy base where a lot of the ships are docked. Apparently, she was soliciting. I assume for drug money. They've cracked down on that shit there big-time, so she should've known better. So, I had to go bail her out. Again."

"I'm sorry you had to go through that."

"Mac. Be serious." She looked at me like I was the biggest idiot on the planet.

"What do you mean, be serious? It sucks that you had to do that."

"I've had to 'do that' so many times in my life that they know me by first name at the station on B Street. *And* the one in North County. *And* the one in South Bay. It stopped being humiliating when I was around..." She made a stage face like she was really thinking. "Eighteen. Now it just pisses me off, because every time I've saved just enough money to do something for myself, like, say—I don't know—buy a fucking sofa I wouldn't be embarrassed to have someone sleep over on, I have to spend the money on bailing my degenerate loser mother out of jail. So, if you want to talk about things that suck? Let's talk about that."

"Taylor, I'd be happy to—"

She turned in my lap to face me so fast her robe bunched around her waist in her fury. "So help me, if you say you'll buy me a motherfucking sofa or anything even close to it, Mac Stone, I will castrate you and feed your balls to you one at a time, coated with maple syrup and butter. Then I'll make you write a five-star review in the fucking *Union Tribune* about the meal, like it was the best fucking thing you've ever eaten. Okay?" She didn't wait for me to answer. "Okay."

I stared blankly, afraid to so much as breathe. "Well, no sofa, then. Got it. I have to say, I'm not really sure why I have an erection after you threatened to cut my balls off, but I do. It may have everything to do with your current wardrobe malfunction." We both looked down at her exposed pussy and then back up into each other's eyes. "But I don't want to make light of the conversation we're having." I tried to pull her robe back together, and she slapped my hands away.

"Don't fucking touch me," she barked.

I pointedly pulled her robe closed anyway. "Hey, sassy girl. I'm trying to save you from me coming on to you during your time of need here. Help a guy out. And bring the attitude down a peg. I know it was a tough night, but I'm on your side, okay?"

She shocked the hell out of me by wrapping her arms around my neck and straddling my lap, robe opening completely now. Her mouth was on mine as I finished my diatribe, consuming, kissing, tongue thrusting, probing, pushing its way inside my mouth. I wouldn't have denied her in any circumstance. Ever. I spread my hands across her waist, easily covering the distance with my two palms.

"You're so tiny but so mighty. A warrior. You amaze me." I breathed my praise between her kisses.

"Stop." *Gasp.* "Talking."

"No. You should hear positive things about yourself, Taylor." I tried to hold her a few inches away.

"Dude." She leaned back on her own now. "I know I'm a badass. I would've never survived this fucked-up life if I wasn't. I just get pissed that I've had to be. Now get your dick out and fuck me. And make it good, mister."

I reached around to her ass and pinched her. Hard. She yelped, and I sat up and covered her mouth with mine, this time commanding the kiss, taking her the way I preferred. Stroking her tongue with mine, moving in and out the way I planned on stroking her clit next. I sucked in to take her breath away unexpectedly, sealing my lips tightly against hers, waiting to see if she would trust me or panic. She relaxed into my arms further.

I released her so she could breathe. "Such a good girl." It made my cock swell even more that she trusted me the way she did, even though she may not have even realized what she had done. She'd had to be a badass her whole life, but what she was subconsciously begging for was for someone to take care of her. Getting her to realize that, and admit that, was going to be the real challenge. Her body already knew it. However, her mind might not ever let her body have what it needed.

The robe fell from her shoulders and pooled around her waist. I skimmed my hands up and down her arms. Her skin was plenty warm now. She let her head fall back and gyrated on my hard cock with her bare pussy as I scraped my nails along her delicate skin.

"Take your clothes off, Mac. Please."

"No rush, sass. Let me make you feel good first. Although my cock likes when you beg so sweetly."

"I already feel good. I'd feel really good with your dick in me. And you owe me from that piss-poor showing on FaceTime."

I pinched her nipple. She moaned, jerking her head forward.

"That's your own damn fault," I growled. "I would've gotten you off that night, but you hung up on me like a brat. And, as I recall, you won a pretty sweet wager, so why the lady cock blocker?"

While I waited for her to answer, I kept torqueing on her nipple. She glared at me, seething and defiant, so I twisted the other side too. Why not? It'd be a great way to find out how much pain she could take—a mystery I was *really* interested in exploring. I just wished my jeans weren't still a barrier between us, so I could feel the wetness of her pussy too.

"Tell me, Taylor." I increased the pressure on her nipples a little more.

"Tell you *what*, clown?"

"You know what."

"You're—you're hurting me." She flared her nostrils and sucked air in through her nose.

"Why did you hang up on me?"

"Damn it—you're hurting me!"

"And you're liking it. Your eyes are as big as the moon. Your heart is racing. I can smell your pussy from here. Tell me to stop or tell me why you hung up on me that day."

She just stared at me, still such a sassy girl. My cock pounded at my zipper, begging for relief. I started counting in my head, trying to gauge how long until she tapped out.

"My cock is raging for you right now."

"Put it in me, Mac. Let's just do this."

I twisted just a little more.

"Because I liked watching you too much to stop. I didn't want you to stop! Fuck!" She finally smacked my hands away. "Fuck! Shit!" She covered her tits with her hands, rubbing at her bruised nipples.

"Put your hands down." My voice was lethally calm and level.

She glared at me again but slowly put her hands by her sides. I put my palms at the small of her back, yanked her body flush against my mouth, and licked her nipple, quickly switching back and forth to soothe the ache but build the sensations pooling in her pussy from the pain and pleasure combination.

"You're killing me. I'm dying. I'm going to die. Fuck, Mac, I don't even know what's happening." Her voice was high-pitched and whiny. I loved every bit of it.

She had the most adorable nonsense babble when she was aroused. I rammed a few fingers up into her creamy pussy, and she shrieked. I finger-fucked her relentlessly until she was moaning so loudly I pulled her head into my shoulder so she wouldn't be embarrassed to face her neighbors in the morning.

She leaned back to suck in a big breath of air just before

she cried out her orgasm. "Oh, God. Mac. Fuck, God. My God. Yes!"

I sucked her nipple, biting down into the abused bud, making her scream again as a second wave hit. She tried pushing me away, but I was much stronger than her. She relaxed against me, spent and completely satisfied.

"Why are you trying to kill me? You aren't supposed to kill people you have sex with. I would think they teach you that shit at doctor school. No?" She mumbled her comments into my neck.

"No. They don't really go into how to fuck in med school, love." I chuckled at her nonsense.

She sat up, hair crazy and sexy, eyes glassy from arousal. "Christ, I can't imagine how dangerous you'd be if you had schooling on top of your natural instinct, then."

"You're really good for my ego. You know that?" I kissed the tip of her nose.

"Time to lose the pants, clown. I can't take another cock-less minute. Seriously."

I burst out laughing. "Cock-less minute? I don't think I've ever heard that expression in my entire life." She scooted off my lap and slid to her knees on the floor in front of me. My dick throbbed in my pants just at the suggestive pose she took. I stood to my full height, crotch directly in front of her face. She looked up the length of my body, and I took a long few seconds to stare down at her. I wanted to memorize her oversize eyes looking up at me, her tousled hair going every which way, her perfect imperfection singing to my every manly need to please her as a woman.

She reached up to open my pants. Deft fingers undid the button, slid down the zipper, and pulled the material over my hips, freeing my erection in seconds. I stepped out of my shoes and jeans when she got them to my ankles and stood before my beautiful Taylor, waiting to see where we'd go from here. I didn't want her to feel obligated to suck me. Some women just weren't into it. I put my hand out to help her up, and I could sense her struggle with the decision. I took the decision out of her hands by taking my shirt off, laying it on the sofa, and sitting back down on it. I still had an issue with how many other bodily functions were probably completed on that fabric, but I wasn't about to ruin the moment with a repeat of that conversation.

"Come back to me here." I held my cock up for her to sit on, and she didn't disappoint. She actually threw me a curve ball, turned around at the last second, and sat on my cock facing away from me so her back was to my front. My legs were spread wide, so hers went between them, the perfect little heart of her ass in my palms as she lowered onto my shaft.

Fuck me, the heaven of her tight pussy made my eyes roll back in my head. I had to take a few seconds to collect myself when she slid all the way to the base, such a snug fit but so wet I went the full distance in one thrust.

"Goddamn it, girl, you feel good. So tight."

"Mmmmm. Right?"

"Move. Raise up. Slowly, though." I lifted up under her ass cheeks, sliding my long middle finger along the lips of her pussy from behind until I found her clit. "Christ, you're wet. Back down." I rubbed her clit while she slid up and down on my cock, instructing when she stopped moving.

"Why are you stopping?" I asked.

"It's hard. I'm doing all the work here." She glared at me over her shoulder.

"Put your legs on the outside of mine."

She flopped her legs as directed, and I sat up taller on the sofa and spread my legs as far as I could, in turn spreading hers as far as they could possibly go. Her reflection gleamed in the now darkened TV screen, and it was so fucking pornographic I almost blew my load on the spot.

"Look at yourself in the TV," I commanded.

"Oh, shit. God, that's hot," she moaned and laid her head back on my shoulder.

I reached around and rubbed her exposed clit, my hand so big compared to her body, I nearly covered her entire pussy. "How much of my hand do you think I can fit in your pussy?"

"Maaaaccc, stop. I'm going to come again."

"Isn't that the point? You like watching me fuck you?" I could feel the arousal dripping from her folds.

"Yes. It's so fucking hot."

"Can you see my cock going in and out of you?" I continued to antagonize her while I thrust in and out of her body.

"Yes." She reached down and spread her two fingers on either side of my cock as if spreading her pussy wider around me. She arched her back, forcing her tits out, and I slid my hands up her ribcage to pinch the nipples she offered.

"Fuck, God, they're so sore. It feels so good."

"Are you ready to come again?"

"Yes. Please. Yes."

"Look at yourself. Watch yourself come while I fuck you, Taylor. Then the next time I call you, you can think about this right here and pick up the fucking phone." I held her hips, digging my short nails into her bones, and pounded up into her, relentlessly chasing our mutual releases. Mine was boiling up my cock, seconds from blowing through the condom—

Holy.

Fuck.

I yanked Taylor off my dick just as I exploded, come spurting across her back and ass. By the way she was moaning and writhing, she was midorgasm as well. I would just play it off as wanting to mark her with my seed and all that happy horseshit. I grabbed my dick and stroked the rest of the orgasm through, panting like the animal I was, trying not to alarm her but internally berating myself for what had just happened.

Holy fuck. I'd never been so fucking stupid in my entire life.

She collapsed back against me, and I wrapped my arms around her. I wanted to fall asleep immediately, Taylor in my arms, and erase the last twenty seconds of the evening. Because the rest of it leading up to that shit storm had been amazing. This woman was quickly becoming everything I wanted in a woman. I wanted to keep her safe and be there for her when she needed someone to lean on.

But instead, I'd just fucked her bareback like yet another inconsiderate asshole.

Just what she needed in her life.

I'd just verified what she suspected about people in general. Everyone was out for number one and didn't care who they used on the way. I'd just fucked up royally, after I'd sworn to her she could count on me.

If she didn't speak to me after tonight, I wasn't sure I'd blame her. The only problem was, she was so far under my skin now I didn't think my life would be the same without her in it.

CHAPTER ELEVEN

Taylor

"I think I hate your husband a little bit for making us join this fucking gym. Can this even be considered a gym?" I scowled at the complicated obstacle course before me. *When did this become the vogue concept of working out?*

Talia laughed, but she had to know I was right. "I might hate him a little bit too." She smiled a very sly grin. "No, I don't. I can't even say it joking around." My dear friend was so head-over-heels in love it made my stomach hurt. The problem was, it was envy, not disgust, that churned in my belly. Not that I would ever admit that out loud.

"Oh yes! The honeymoon phase. Isn't love grand?" I made a vomiting sound off to the side as I tried another attempt at moving the tractor tire.

Literally. The tire of a mother-effing John Deere tractor.

"Who comes up with this stuff?" Talia's voice reached a new octave as she gave every effort to move the dense rubber off the ground. At least this time, she budged it an inch or two.

"And the better question—where did they find the tire from a *tractor* in Southern California? Bitch, please." I stepped up to give the challenge another go.

Bending deep with my knees, I thought about a worse kind of pain. Bailing my mom out of jail for the seventeenth time in my life. Yeah, that was the actual number. Some things one knew by rote, and unfortunately, this was one of those for me. I had come to her rescue that many times. My anger gave me enough strength to move the heavy obstacle a foot off the ground. A new personal best! If I added up the amount of money I'd spent on her legal aid, I could probably summon enough fury to throw the tire like a Frisbee.

"Wow, Tay—you go, girl!" Talia cheered from beside me.

One of the hunky trainers took notice and came over. "Great job, Taylor! Way to get after it. Great form too. Why don't you two move over to cardio next?" He pointed toward the treadmills and gave me a quick wink.

An actual wink.

I tried not to giggle while grabbing my water bottle and towel and walked toward the machines. Talia bugged her eyes out at me when she was sure he wasn't looking, and we both bumped into each other playfully. He was really good-looking and had a body that was seriously drool-worthy. I think his name was something exotic like Emilio, but I couldn't remember.

"What was that all about?" Talia dipped her head to say it as we set up the displays on our treadmills.

"I have no idea," I whispered. "Was I giving off the wrong vibe?"

"What would be the *wrong* vibe with a guy who looks like that?" We both started giggling again.

"You have a point there," I conceded. "But I'm not looking for anything right now."

"No? Someone else keeping your bed warm at night?"

"You know darn well no one keeps my bed warm."

"You know what I mean. And I hope one day you let go of that hang-up of yours."

"Don't you start on me too." Why didn't anyone understand?

She looked at me, puzzled, and I knew I'd already said too much.

"Explain?" She motioned at me to go on.

"I'd rather not." I pretended to be having a hard time with my machine.

"You seemed so distracted this morning at the sales meeting. Were you out late because of your mom?" She was not going to let this go.

"No. That was handled pretty early. It's pretty routine at this point." I added, "Sadly."

"Then what? Oh, does this have something to do with a certain brain surgeon?"

"Maybe." I still hadn't made eye contact with my bestie.

"Maybe? That's all you're going to say is *maybe*?" Her voice was gaining volume.

"God, Talia. You used to be the easy one to be around. You're as bad as Margaux these days. Is this what married life does to a girl?" We both laughed.

If I didn't give her the details, she was likely to implode on the spot. "I was supposed to have dinner with him last night and had to cancel when Janet got arrested. He ended up showing up at my apartment, and he made me waffles for dinner. It was adorable."

"Who would've guessed under all that smoldering sexy bastard he could be sweet?"

"Dude, you have no idea. He's very complex. Then he fucked my brains out, and we fell asleep on my sofa."

"Awwwww. See? You're capable of having a normal relationship, Tay."

"Oh. There is nothing normal about what we have going on. Trust me." I laughed, thinking of the bite marks and the peep show in my TV screen. "I sneaked out this morning and got ready in the locker room at work. I left him a note to see himself out. It's anything but normal, Talia. Far from normal over here." I realized how many times I repeated myself. Probably trying to convince myself along with her.

"What on earth made you do that?" she asked, as if I had just told her we held hands and watched an episode of *Game of* fucking *Thrones*.

"What?"

"Why did you sneak out this morning like that?" We were both walking at a pretty good clip, panting in between words.

"I don't know. I just couldn't handle the whole awkward morning-after thing. It gave me a low-key panic attack, and I freaked out and bolted. Then there was the whole bareback thing, and I didn't even want to address that because he thinks I missed his freak-out that he tried to play off. He's a terrible actor, FYI."

"Oh, my God. I don't know what to address first in that shit storm. You bolted from your own house?"

"Yes?" *Thank you, Jesus, for not going to the bareback comment first.*

"Taylor. Taylor. Taylor. Taylor."

"Stop looking at me like that, and why are you saying my name over and over like I'm five?" The pitch of my voice sounded like I was five too.

"Well, possibly because you're acting like it?"

"I'm not!" *Yep. Five alive.*

"You totally are." Now she was laughing too.

I cranked my treadmill's pace up faster. Suddenly I was

in the mood to run. Something I prided myself on *never* doing.

"You can't actually run away from me on a treadmill, hon. I'm still right here beside you," she shouted over the whine of the belt of the machine. "I mean, I get that running away has become your superpower and all, but we are on stationary pieces of gym equipment, so it kind of defeats the purpose." She burst out laughing again.

"Maybe you should concentrate on your form right now or something instead of your unsolicited advice. Hmmm?" I pumped my arms in time with my spindly legs. I looked like an ostrich when I ran.

She smiled broadly but stayed quiet. We both jogged side by side for about five minutes before I slowed my machine down again. What the hell had I been thinking? Running sucked, and people who did it for fun were just as crazy as they looked doing it.

I pressed the Stop button on the stupid thing, rode the belt to the end, and hopped to the floor. I braced myself on my hands and knees and took a few deep breaths, hoping the stars dancing in my vision would settle down if I got a little more oxygen. All I could hear was Mac's very bossy voice nagging me about the fact that I didn't eat enough. Normally my fast metabolism wasn't an issue, but clearly, if I was going to do any sort of exercising, more calories would be needed. They had a smoothie bar in this gym, so I suggested to Talia that we get something to drink before I hit the deck.

"My head is kind of swimming at the moment. I think I need some sugar."

"Let's go over there and see what they have." She tried to disguise her arm around me as a friendly gesture, but I knew she was making sure I made it to the smoothie bar without falling down.

We sat on the tall stools along the window and waited for the energy smoothies we ordered.

"I think you need to eat a little more in the day, sister." She rubbed my back while she spoke.

"Not you too."

"That's the second time you've said that to me in the past hour. Mac?"

"Yeah, he's a pain in my ass."

"I think it sounds like he cares about you too. Like I do."

The barista came over with our fruity concoctions just in time, saving me from having to address Talia's comment about Mac's feelings for me. Or so I thought it had.

"Are you falling for him, Tay?" She took a sip of her drink and grimaced.

"Are you kidding me? You know me, right? You know my history. I'm not the relationship type." I shook my head from left to right in disbelief.

"People change." She tilted her head to the side, and her long braid fell over her shoulder. "I thought the same thing about myself. It just took the right guy, or guys"—she laughed lightly—"to come along and show me that everything I thought I knew about myself was completely wrong. If I'd kept my head so buried in the sand, think of all the happiness I would've missed out on. And for what? A guy like Gavin?" She shuddered just thinking about the abusive asshole she'd been with before Drake and Fletcher had swept her off her feet.

"And you know better than anyone. There have been some hard times. Some really hard times. It wasn't all rainbows and unicorns getting to where we are today. And I don't kid myself into thinking we won't face crappy times in the future. But that's just life. And I believe that our love is what will see us through." She shrugged and took another sip of her drink. "Oh, Christ. This is disgusting. It tastes like grass."

I burst out laughing. "That's what you get for ordering something called the Green Goddess."

"I guess so. Yuck."

"Here, have some of mine." I pushed my drink toward her on the counter.

"No, you drink that. You need the calories. In fact, we aren't leaving until you finish every bit of that." She pushed the drink back in front of me.

I put my head down on the counter dramatically. "At least mine tastes good. Mango Mania was a much better choice, but we're going to be here awhile." It was a pretty big drink.

"I think I'm falling for him." I took a big sip from the straw, studying the contents of the glass like it was the most fascinating thing I'd ever seen so I didn't have to meet her wide-eyed reaction to my admission.

"I was kind of picking up on that. But honey, that's not a bad thing. You deserve someone special in your life. We all do."

"Something bad will happen to ruin it. Just like it always does when a good thing comes along in my life." I paused a second or two, continuing when I sensed she was going to ask me to elaborate. "When I was five, when we were still in Georgia, I found a kitten in our apartment complex. Janet said I could keep it if I took care of it. And for the four days she was with us, I loved her so much. I named her Barbie because she had blond hair and she was so pretty, like my Barbie doll. I took care of her like a good mama. I fed her and brushed her and cleaned her litter box. I was the best kitty mama ever. Then I broke out in hives and itchy watery eyes, and Janet took her away from me and said I could never have a cat again because

I was allergic. A part of me died that day. Honestly, I thought I would never get over that loss. I cried myself to sleep every night for a month. When Janet wasn't around, I would go outside and look for her where I found her in the first place, thinking maybe she was as sad without me as I was without her and she would be waiting for me to come find her again. It was my first time I think I felt devastating loss."

Talia looked like she was going to start crying, and I immediately wanted to take my story back. I hated when people pitied me more than anything else.

"I didn't tell you that so you'd pity me, Talia. I'm trying to make you understand that every time I have something good, something that I love and cherish, I have to give it up. It's been a pattern in my life. That was just the first memory I have of it. But then the shitty things in my life that I would gladly give up, the things that suck the life out of me, like, oh...say...my loser mother...that I can't seem to get away from no matter what I do? She just keeps turning back up like a bad fucking penny. Every time I think she's finally gone, nope, there she is again.

"So I've finally figured it's karma. In a past life, or maybe a combination of past lives, I must have been a really, really bad motherfucker. And now? I'm just paying my dues. I don't deserve happiness, and it's just something I have to deal with."

"I've never heard something so absurd in my life, Taylor Mathews." Talia shook her head like she wasn't buying my theory. But it didn't matter what she thought.

"Well, believe what you want. I'm the one who's been living with it, and it's the only thing that makes sense. Don't get me wrong. I like Mac. He's smart as hell, and he's one of the few guys I haven't scared off with my bad attitude. And holy shit, can we just talk about the sex for a minute? I think the guy went to the sex school of the devil himself. And that's absolutely fine by me, because, frankly, I am so tired of guys who treat me like a porcelain doll or some treasure or some stupid crap like that. But it will fade in time. It always does. But for now, we'll fuck and have fun, and when it's over"—I shrugged—"it will be over."

"That simple, huh? Boy, you have it all figured out. Must be nice." She rolled her eyes, patronizing me and pissing me off.

"I don't see the need to overcomplicate things, Talia. Life's just too short." I took another big gulp of my smoothie, tossing the straw to the side and just going for it straight from the glass. I regretted it about ten seconds later when the brain freeze struck like gangbusters and my head felt like it would shatter into a million tiny pieces like a broken windshield in a head-on collision.

"Hey, you okay?" My friend grabbed my arm.

"Yep. Brain freeze. It'll pass in a minute." I squeezed my temples with my palms.

"Maybe I should call Mac?"

"For a brain freeze? Are you serious?"

"I bet he'd rush right over here." She smiled as though she had come up with a pretty clever idea.

"And I would knock you out so he'd have to treat you instead."

We both laughed and talked a little bit about work while she tried to force down more of her Green Goddess before admitting she'd wasted seven dollars and ninety-five cents.

"I'll see you tomorrow at work." She slung her gym bag over her shoulder and tossed her nasty drink in the trash by the door.

"Maybe. I have a few calls to make in the field in the morning. Depending on how long they take and what your afternoon looks like."

"True. Okay, well call me at least after you get in. Maybe we can try to flip that tire over again or something." She motioned over to the corner of the gym where the tractor tire was resting in the up position. *Damn, someone actually stood that thing upright.*

"That is the stupidest workout I've ever done." I couldn't help but laugh after I said it.

"Right? But don't tell Drake." We hugged and walked out onto the street.

"Your secret's safe with me. Maybe we should try shaking the ropes next time?"

We both burst out laughing and went in separate directions toward our cars. When I got into mine and started the engine, I pulled out my phone to check my messages. Three were work-related, two confirming appointments for the morning and one checking the receipt of an emailed contract I had been waiting for. I could deal with that when I got home.

The other seven messages were from one very impatient Dr. Maclain Stone. Various demands, pleas, and suggestions on how I could or *should* be returning his calls in a timelier fashion, with more social grace and my favorite of all—with threats of sexual torture—if I didn't do his bidding immediately. I deleted each and every one after listening to them—twice— put my car into gear and left the downtown corridor toward Mission Valley.

Oh, silly boy. Doesn't he know not to poke at the girl with the bad attitude? It ruffled my pointy feathers more than if he'd just asked nicely. Eventually he'd catch on. Until then, it was a fun game to watch him flap in the breeze. I turned up the radio and sang out loud to Evanescence's "Bring Me to Life." That song could be my personal anthem.

That's right, Mac...*Save me from the nothing I've become.*

CHAPTER TWELVE

Mac

"I'm sorry for the things I said when it was winter."

When I was in my surgery residency, I found that quote somewhere. Through the years, it had really stuck with me—so much so, I had it painted on a plaque at some farmer's market in the Gold Coast district and then hung in my Chicago home office.

Winters in Chicago were physically *and* mentally brutal. I remember thinking, while packing everything before the move four months ago, that the plaque would be a nice decoration for the San Diego office and nothing more. That I'd never have to find those words meaningful again.

So, on that glorious sunny afternoon, as I dropped the plaque into the trash can in my Oceanside home office, it was cause for celebration.

"Babe!"

No answer. Then I remembered why. She was tied to a stool at my breakfast bar, makeshift gag made from her white Jockey panties stuffed in her smart little mouth. I strolled into the kitchen, hands in my cargo shorts, as though I didn't have a care in the world, evil grin on my face.

"Have you learned your lesson yet?" I bent forward at the waist to peer into her angry, denim-blue eyes.

The glare she shot me already said no, but I couldn't wait to hear the creative "clown" insults she'd devised while stewing there for the past twenty minutes. Before removing the gag, I leaned in and kissed down the slender column of her neck, ending at her shoulder—where I sank my teeth into her gorgeous white flesh.

Her moan escaped around the cotton filling her mouth, making my dick twitch in my shorts. I backed away from her, or we would never leave the house on time to make our appointment at the track.

I pulled her damp underwear from her mouth and tossed it on the countertop. Tilting my head to the side, I regarded her with playful eyes. "You better go get ready. We need to leave here in an hour if we want to be at the track on time." I started untying her hands that were held to the bar stool with some kitchen twine looped through the wrought-iron latticework of the back rest.

She took a deep breath, ready to lay into me, but then thought better of it. Maybe her twenty-minute kinky time out had taken the edge off her sour mood that morning.

We were headed to the Thermal Club, a private, members-only racetrack just outside of Palm Springs, for an amazing weekend at one of the villas situated on the course itself. Now that spring was upon us and the rainy season was gone, track conditions were perfect. And can I take a moment to laugh at the rainy season in California? Four inches total fell between December and March, and April here seemed much more like summer in every other part of the United States, so I wasn't holding my breath for additional precipitation.

There was a method to my madness, so to speak, besides spending more time with this woman. I was considering buying one of the villas on the track and also housing my car collection there. Translation? The sales staff smelled fresh blood in the water so had set up the weekend stay to let me "experience the lifestyle firsthand." Now, I had a friend along too and couldn't wait to get Taylor out on the track for a few laps. The club had loaner cars for members to put through their paces, so we were due for a really great weekend.

"I don't know what to wear." Seemed like a pretty typical girl response.

"Jeans will be fine. Jeans and a T-shirt. Something casual. And I plan on having you naked when we aren't on the track, so you won't have to worry about anything else."

"That's not much help, you realize." She stood there with her hands on her hips, trying to look frustrated but looking adorable and sexy instead.

I shrugged. "I was just being honest."

"What about dinner? Do you think we'll go out at all? Palm Springs has a pretty great foodie scene. Maybe we should hit Palm Canyon at least one night?"

"I'll check out Yelp while you pack. Deal?" Since I was so new to the area, I usually followed her lead on that sort of thing.

"Yes!" She gave me a high-five as she walked past me, and on the down swing, I smacked her ass super-hard.

"Dick!" she shouted without thinking.

I turned around and caught her wrist so fast she didn't expect it and couldn't evade my grasp.

"Do you need another time out, young lady?" I ground out very close to her lips.

"I think you're taking this new weird Daddy thing a little too far, don't you?" She tried to break the hold I had on her wrist while she spoke.

I took the wrist I still held and forced her hand to my steel-hard cock encased in my shorts. "Nah, I think it's working really well for us both."

Her eyes widened impossibly far, taking over the better part of the upper third of her face, entrancing me with the deep-blue color.

I mashed my lips against hers, kissing her so roughly I risked leaving a bruise. I said against her mouth when I was through, "I can't seem to get enough of you, Taylor Mathews. I don't know what you're doing to me, but it's like some sort of drug I can't—no, I don't *want* to stop. Now go get ready before I fuck you again, right here in my living room."

Insatiable clown. She mouthed the words, but I knew without a doubt what she'd said.

I bit her lip, softly at first, putting more pressure on until she squeaked.

When I released her, she hurried off down the hall. When she got to my room, where many of her things were collecting now too, she looked back over her shoulder and touched her lip, grinning, just before disappearing around the corner of the master suite.

Goddamn, I was in deep with this girl. Deep, dirty shit, and I didn't want out anytime soon. We'd been seeing each other at least once a week for the past four months, and I couldn't get enough of her smart, sassy, energetic, beautiful, giving, kind, adventurous spirit. She never passed up a chance to do something kind for someone else, which was brand-new territory for me.

Over the holidays she'd shown me a whole new definition of the giving spirit. Together, we'd volunteered at two homeless shelters, a food pantry, and an abused women's center. I'd had no idea of the amount of help that was needed right in my own backyard, and it made feel like a self-centered prick.

Taylor helped alleviate some of the guilt, though, by signing me up for some regularly scheduled volunteer hours at the shelter's free health clinic and wrapping the schedule I would be volunteering as one of my Christmas presents. I now did routine check-ups, gave flu shots, and did preliminary screenings for major illnesses that would need further care but, when detected early, stood a decent chance of being cured. Surprisingly, it gave me a great deal of satisfaction to help the underprivileged population, and that was something I would never have discovered without my amazing girlfriend's influence.

I still had to be very careful about referring to her as my girlfriend, however. Something about the term sent her into a version of a PTSD episode like I'd never seen. It definitely stemmed from something associated with Janet, her mother, but I couldn't put all the pieces together on my own, and when I asked her about it, she clammed up. When I suggested she introduce me to her mother, she all but went into the fetal position in the corner of her room, and I couldn't have a normal conversation with her for almost a week. Finally, a good fucking one night after dinner brought her out of her funk. Thank God for our low-key BDSM dynamic, because there were times it was the only way I could bring her back to me.

She had confided in me that she had seen a therapist several times throughout her life, but I suspected she still could benefit from one. But really, couldn't we all from time to time?

In about thirty minutes, we were heading north on the Fifteen toward a town called Temecula. Taylor insisted she knew a "back way" to Palm Springs that would thrill the driver in me, so I trusted her since she was a Southern California native. And boy did she deliver on her promise. We had the best time winding down into the Coachella Valley and really putting my m235i through its paces. Many car fans and motorcycle drivers took that road just for the passion of driving and really opened up around the hairpin turns and straightaways. That route would be a new favorite if I bought a villa at the Thermal Club and especially if I found a convertible I just couldn't say no to. Taylor pealed with laughter around the turns and looked a little pale a few times too when I drifted without the traction control feature engaged in my little rocket.

"But you trust me, right?" I really just wanted to hear her say it out loud. I already knew deep down that she did.

"Of course I do. I just didn't expect that to happen. Did you do that on purpose?"

"Yes. That's what your car can do. With very little effort. That's why it has that nickname."

"Can you show me how to do that?" she asked after thinking about it for a bit.

"If you want me to." I couldn't hold back my grin.

"Is it hard?"

"Kind of depends on how you want to make it happen."

She looked thoughtful, trying to figure out the physics of the drifting maneuver. It was adorable, and, frankly, erotic as hell to a gearhead like me.

"Are we almost there? I have to pee. Like really bad."

"Well, according to nav, we're in Palm Springs, but Thermal is still about thirty minutes. Why don't we stop in town here? I could fill up and maybe grab something cold to drink anyway. It's a lot hotter than I expected."

"Uh yeah...hello? Sonoran Desert?" She grinned, knowing she was being a smartass.

I reached over and pinched her inner thigh. "Are you always looking for trouble?"

"Are you always so uptight?" she volleyed right back.

"Me? Uptight? Please."

"You're joking, right?"

I got out of the car without answering and went through the process to start the gas pump. She got out of her side and came to stand beside me.

"I'm not uptight!" I insisted. "I have tons of fun, and you know it. Look at what we're about to do this weekend! Your mind is going to be blown." I held a hand on either side of my head and made an explosion motion. *Boom!* I mouthed.

She burst out laughing. "You're such a dork. Oh, my God. How do I even take you in public? Seriously. I'm going to the restroom."

"Do you want a drink?" I called after her as she headed into the store.

"Yes, please. Surprise me," she called over her shoulder.

I watched the sexy fucking sway of her barely there ass as she walked ahead, my mouth watering.

About thirty minutes later we pulled up to the clubhouse at the track's complex. A sales rep was scheduled to meet us and was waiting patiently to show us around the grounds and to the luxury rental we were staying in for the weekend. We had track time scheduled for later in the afternoon after we'd gotten settled and enjoyed a light lunch in the clubhouse. The place was extraordinary, and I was sold before we'd even arrived. I'd done a ton of research online, and thanks to my dead Uncle Josiah and the inheritance he'd left me, I had the kind of money it would take to own a piece of the paradise. In the meantime, however, I would let them wine and dine us and show us all the place had to offer.

We had the pleasure of driving the BMW M4 GTS on the track that day. Only seven hundred cars in that model were supposedly produced by the manufacturer originally, so getting behind the wheel of one, without actually being one of its rare owners, was a treat in itself. Pushing the machine to its limits on a track was even more enjoyable. Taylor squealed and giggled as I took the lefts and rights of the course and grabbed for anything to gain leverage on as we fought the centrifugal force of the carousel. The GTS had sweet racing-styled seats and Schroth harnesses, so she eventually learned to trust the apparatus and let it do what it was meant to.

By the time we pulled into the pit after the second lap of the North Palm Circuit, she looked like she was ready to puke.

"Okay, champ, let's get the helmet off. What's up? Too much?" I stooped down to be level with her eyes.

"How—how fast were you going?" She was weaving back and forth as she tried to walk to the bench.

"Not very fast. You okay? Let's get some water." I tried supporting her around the waist, but she pulled away from me.

"Mac, seriously, I'm fine. Stop, you're embarrassing me." She pushed my hands away again for extra good measure.

"What's going to really embarrass you is when you faceplant on the concrete. People get motion sick during hot laps all the time. It's not a big deal. It's the human body's natural reaction to the unusual physics."

We sat down on the benches under the observation tent alongside the track. A few other cars were still taking turns passing each other, playing a friendly game of lead and follow.

"Seriously, how fast were we going?" She wasn't going to let it go.

"Why is that so important? It's just going to freak you out more."

"I'm not freaked out. I thought it was fun. My head is just having a hard time getting the memo."

"The fastest we went today wasn't on that circuit. Too many curves. On the straightaway on the South Palm"—I pointed behind us to the first track we were on—"we hit one-sixty-seven."

"Shut the front door. Is that the fastest you've ever gone?"

"Nah." I sounded nonchalant.

"Seriously?" She did not, however.

"Babe, that car has a top speed of one-eighty-nine, I think. With the governor. Stock car racing, like Nascar? Those cars go over two hundred miles per hour on the regular."

"Okay, I don't think I want to hear any more for right now." She clutched at her stomach.

"Are you going to be sick?" I couldn't help but chuckle when I asked but looked around for a trash bin for safety's sake.

"No. I just don't want to think about it. I don't want to worry about you every time you get in a car."

"Why don't we go back to the villa? We have all day tomorrow to get on the track again. We can clean up, maybe rest a bit before our dinner reservations?" It had already been a pretty eventful day.

"That sounds like a good idea. I'd like to be on stationary ground for a while." She stopped abruptly and turned to me when I stopped to see what had suddenly snagged her attention.

"That was a very impressive circus today, clown. Thank

you for showing me that set of tricks." She hooked her arms around my neck and stood on her tippy toes to give me a sweet kiss.

My hands automatically traveled to her waist, and I pulled her against me. "I'm glad you enjoyed yourself."

The villas were situated along the track, allowing each owner to watch the racing action right from their back terrace. Every unit had been constructed with reinforced soundproof materials, allowing people to retreat inside if they'd had enough mach speed action for the day. Each home was built according to one of five master-planned templates, though owners had the option of designing their own home, as long as it stuck to the club's architectural guidelines.

Right now, I was leaning more toward buying a villa that was constructed, finished, furnished, and ready for move-in—much like the unit we were staying in. The place was immaculate, elegant, and very well-suited for my needs. Like most of the homes here, the place's first floor comprised a pristine, climate-controlled multi-car garage. The floor was epoxy-coated for easy cleaning, and there were roll-up doors on two sides. But the most impressive feature was the garage's ceiling, made completely of glass, so the resident could see through from the living space above down to their car collection at all hours of the day. In essence, it was a car enthusiast's dream. I could store the majority of my collection here, with room for eight cars in the villa and the availability for more storage in additional buildings on the property.

"What do you think of this place?" I asked Taylor as we walked through the gourmet kitchen.

"What's not to like? Everything looks brand-new, and it's clearly top of the line. Not that I would really know the difference, but it looks like a magazine picture. I'm assuming this is good stuff. I mean, if you want red knobs on your stove. Do people like that? I don't know." She shrugged, as if truly not caring.

I had to chuckle. I remembered my mother and her snooty Garden Club friends talking for hours about those very red knobs. I actually adored Taylor more for not knowing that they were a status symbol all on their own.

"What? Did I say something funny? I put my unsophisticated foot in my mouth again, didn't I?"

She plopped down on the white slip-covered sofa. I sat down beside her and grabbed her feet up into my lap, massaging the instep of her left foot and then the right. *Christ, even her feet are sexy.*

"I love these feet. In fact, I don't think there's an inch of this body I don't love." I squeezed her heel with my hand, knowing how good that felt. "Taylor...you don't have to feel self-conscious or inadequate around me, ever."

She huffed softly—though she didn't try to move her foot away. "Mac. Come on—"

"Stop. Don't bother arguing right now. Just listen to me. Humor a clown for a minute. Just let me say what I want to say. I think you're amazing, okay? Today was one of the best days of my life. From the minute I woke up this morning with you in my bed in Oceanside, to whipping around the track, to the amazing dinner we're going to have tonight, and the even more amazing sex we're going to have after that. Best. Day. Ever. And it's because of you. You've been the part that's been missing from my life for a really long time, and I hope I don't have to know what it would be like without you now that I know how awesome it is *with* you."

No more huffs. The woman just stared at me. No smile. No tears. No smart-mouth jokes. A simple stare.

"Was that too much? Did I freak you out?"

She shook her head a little, as though she had been daydreaming. I was bracing for a doozie of a comeback. I wasn't sure which way she was going to go with her response, but the way the air felt, I knew I wasn't going to like it.

But when she patted my hand like she was consoling a longtime friend, maybe an elderly neighbor whose beloved cat was flattened at the busy corner intersection, my spine stiffened.

"That's really nice." A thoughtful pause, then: "Yeah, that's nice, Mac." Even her pitch was fucked up.

"Taylor?"

"Hmmm?" Flat and lifeless tone, but she eventually made eye contact with me.

"Did you hear anything I just said?"

"Yes. I heard it all. I complete you. Best day ever. Blah blah blah. I said that it was really nice of you to say all of that." She patted my hand again, and I yanked it back like she'd burned me with a hot poker.

She actually stared like *my* reaction was out of line.

She took her feet off my lap and turned to face me. "Listen to me, Mac. You know I don't really open up to people. I find it...difficult." Another one of those damn pauses, followed by: "Yeah, I guess that works. I find it difficult. I've really been enjoying the time we've been spending together too. A lot. You've probably realized by now I try to live life one day at a time. If I've learned anything from the life I've had with Janet, it's that I pretty much can't count on anything or anyone but myself—so I don't expect anything from anyone, either. Not my girlfriends, my coworkers, and especially not a man. I mean, you're a great guy. You're amazing, actually. And as long as things are great between us, I'm happy to spend time with you. I will never expect a man to ride into my life like a white knight upon a strapping steed and rescue me from the cruel, cruel world. My mother did that my entire childhood, and I saw, time and time again, where that got her. I will never make that same mistake.

"So yeah, I'm glad you're happy. Because I'm happy too. Happy is a really great place to be. I'm going to go take a shower because I want to look extra-pretty for dinner tonight. I think the restaurant you made reservations at is pretty swanky, and I don't want to embarrass you any more than I already have today with all that woozy-head nonsense when we got back. Phew. I'm glad that passed, huh?"

She left the room so fast I couldn't get another word in on the ridiculous conversation we'd just had. It may have been for the best, anyway, because my temper was boiling under the surface, and I didn't want the memories of this weekend tarnished by an argument.

I was falling in love with Taylor Mathews.

Strike that.

I was already in love with Taylor Mathews. But I was not going to be able to battle the twenty-plus years of fucked-up self-esteem whittling done by her mother's unhealthy lifestyle choices and loser-magnet-man selection process.

I'd thought my own mother was going to be our biggest obstacle when she finally met Taylor. And that jury was still out, because up to this point, I had avoided the problem altogether. Eventually it would happen, but the longer I put it off, the better. The more time Taylor and I had under our belts as a couple before Constance met her, the more time I would have to build Taylor's confidence and self-esteem so my mother couldn't destroy her.

But this path of self-destruction she seemed hell-bent on taking—I didn't know how to begin to combat that. Honestly, I was frustrated that it was something I had to deal with at all. I was very motivated suddenly to have a heart-to-heart discussion with Janet and tell her to stay away from Taylor altogether. Even though I had absolutely no right to do so, it would be in Taylor's best interest. It had been several months since her last arrest, and according to Taylor, she was coming "due" for some sort of trouble. I was pretty certain the next time she called, she was going to answer to me instead of her codependent daughter.

★ ★ ★ ★

"They're racing tonight?" Taylor looked stunning in the moonlight as we climbed the stairs to the front door of the villa. Dinner had been amazing, and we'd both enjoyed our time downtown in Palm Springs.

"Yes. I guess once in a while they do a night race. We can watch from the balcony if you want."

"Oh, could we? I love the sound when they go by." At times like this she sounded so young and innocent and I wanted to show her the world.

"Score one for the lady." I smiled as I led the way through the kitchen and out onto the deck.

"What?"

"I love that too. It was one of the first things that got me into cars when I was a boy. The sound of the engines. We would try to guess the cars going by with our eyes covered."

"Who did you do that with?" She loved knowing things about my childhood. Probably because hers had been so fucked up.

"Killian and his brothers. Lance didn't like it as much as Trey, but he would play along anyway."

"Why did you all stop being friends?"

I knew she was close with Claire. I should probably watch where I stepped.

"My mom, mostly. She's a jealous lady. She just let it get the better of her. Over time it ruined her relationship with my Aunt Willa."

"That's too bad. I would've loved to have had cousins or siblings to grow up with. Built-in friends."

"They really were. But it got so ugly and at the wrong time—you know puberty and all—and I sided with my mom, like you do when you're that age." I just shrugged. Looking back at it now, it all seemed so silly.

"I'll light the fire pit." There was a modern blown-glass structure between two extra-large chaise-longues on the deck outside the kitchen. The view of the Santa Rosa Mountains was breathtaking, the racetrack in the immediate foreground, the purple mountains glowing with the moon's light from above. The fire gave off a bit of heat as well as serving as a natural bug deterrent.

Taylor still wore her dress and heels from dinner, so she crawled onto my chair with me for the extra warmth. Her burgundy knee-length dress had stolen my breath when she'd come out of the master suite before dinner and had had a similar effect on every man for the rest of the evening. And some of the women too. It was a mysterious creation of diaphanous fabric, crossing at her breast, wrapping over her right shoulder, and somehow swathing around her waist to become a skirt that was higher in the front than the back. Her bare midriff was as sexy and distracting as the flash of thigh where the material crossed and created the skirt. It was confusing and fantastic all at the same time. For most of our dinner, I'd imagined how on earth I would unravel it from her body.

Time to find out which way would work best.

I slid down the chair to unbuckle her matching shoes. "Do you mind if I help you out of these very sexy shoes, my lady?"

"Please do." She giggled and held her foot aloft for me to remove the shoe.

"How do you find shoes to match your dress exactly?" I was genuinely curious.

"Just another superpower I have." She grinned.

"I see." I finished with the left and started on the right.

"Now, let's watch this race." She held her arms out for me to join her back on the lounge chair. We snuggled for a while, watching the cars zoom past us. She asked various questions as they did, mostly about the different cars that were on the track. Since I was partial to BMWs, there were so many other cars for her to learn about.

I couldn't pay attention to the race with her so close to me. I wanted to get her out of that damn dress. I kissed the side of her neck as she ducked her head around me to watch the cars go by.

"Mac. I'm trying to see."

"I want to fuck you, though," I whispered against the shell of her ear, tracing it with my tongue.

"You always want to fuck me." Her voice was instantly husky.

"Is that a bad thing?"

"No." She breathed her answer when I got to the particularly sensitive area just under her ear and sucked harder. I grabbed a handful of her hair at the base of her neck, tilted her head to the side, and sank my teeth into her skin. "I love biting you. You taste like homemade vanilla ice cream."

"Really? That's pretty specific."

"Don't harsh my fantasy here, sassy. I say vanilla ice cream, it's vanilla ice cream," I teased back.

I felt her flesh pull tighter as she grinned. The cars sped by on the track again.

"Will you let me drive tomorrow?" she asked tentatively.

"Of course I will. You'll have to take a safety course first."

"I don't mind. Can I drive that car we were in today?"

"No. I think you might want to start with something—" *how do I say it without pissing her off?* "—a little less sensitive?"

"Oh, don't you think I can handle that car?"

"I think you can do whatever you set your mind to." *Perfectly safe answer.*

She rolled her eyes dramatically. "That's so PC and gross."

"It's not PC. That car is not for a first-time track goer. They will let you use the M3 probably. Or the M5. It's a little slower."

"And why do you always push the BMWs? I think I want one like that." She sat up out of my arms and pointed to a very sexy red Cayman GT4 that zipped by. When I laughed, she looked at me, frustrated.

"Why is that funny?" She pouted.

"That car is very fast too."

"Aren't all of these cars 'very fast'?" She mimicked my voice, and I narrowed my eyes at her, so she quickly added, "You know what I mean." This morning's panty-gag lesson must have done more good than I thought.

"The reason I 'push' BMW is two-fold. They are *my* maker of choice, but they also sponsor a driving school at this track so they have a fleet of cars on site that can be used by the members and their guests." I motioned back out onto the track in front of us. "That Porsche that you just pointed out is someone's private car—you can't just drive it."

"Unless I ask nicely and he says yes," she said in a very seductive, suggestive tone.

"You'll do no such thing." She'd just hit a very possessive nerve, and I wasn't even considering denying it.

"I'm not so sure, Mac. This dress might be pretty persuasive." She hiked the hem up her leg even higher while she said it.

"Don't test me, sassy. I'll tie you to the bed and leave you there all morning while I go out to the track. And when I come back in, I'll fuck you all the different ways I imagined while I was kicking that douchebag in the Porsche's ass on the track."

"Oooooo, caveman clown. I don't think I've seen this side of you yet."

I paused and raised my eyebrow. "Do you like it?"

She reached down between her legs and pulled her skimpy little thong panties to the side. "You tell me."

I wasted no time reaching up her skirt and thrusting my fingers into her very wet pussy. "That's a yes." I quickly pulled my belt from the loops of my pants and held one end in each hand.

"Show me your wrists," I ordered.

She held them out in front of her, and I slid the end of my belt through the buckle, binding her hands together. I kicked the stand that held the back of the chaise-longue up so the chair back fell flat. "Get up on your knees, sexy girl. Face the race track." I looked around for a few pillows and saw a couple on a chair over near the outdoor kitchen.

I caught Taylor still watching the cars tearing around the track when I turned and headed back to the lounge chair where she was kneeling.

"Can't take your eyes off the action tonight, hmmm?" I threw the pillows on the chaise-longue in front of where Taylor knelt.

She grinned, playing along, goading the caveman in me. I wasn't actually angry, but she had admitted that my being jealous of her and someone else excited her, so I'd go with it.

I knelt behind her on the chaise and reached up under her dress, slipping my hand into the waistband of her panties. I growled into her ear when I felt how much wetter she'd become in that short time. "Well. Isn't this interesting."

"I don't know what you mean." She tried to play innocent.

"Is all this for him?" I showed her my wet fingers, stickiness stretching between them.

She snapped her head back in my direction, acid voice answering, "Maybe. You'll never know."

I bit into her shoulder roughly. "But he's not here with you now, is he? It's just you. And me."

"I guess that will have to do. For now. God!" she yelled as I pushed two fingers back into her pussy.

"Does he finger you the way I do? Can he make you come with just his hand? Just his mouth? Does he make you scream the way I do? Does he, Taylor?"

She leaned back on my shoulder, smiling at our game, enjoying the pleasure I brought her. "You're so fucked up."

"I'm fucked up? That's kind of funny, don't you think?

Whose pussy is dripping right now?"

"Then stop fucking around and put your dick in me." Her voice was challenging and throaty.

"You're forgetting that you don't call the shots around here, do you?"

She grinned. "Not all the time."

"Ask me nicely."

"Fuck me, clown."

I reached around her front and pinched her nipple through the fabric of her dress. I knew she wasn't wearing a bra from some earlier exploration. "That's not what I consider nice."

"Oh, look, here comes that red car again." She turned her body to face completely forward to watch the cars passing the front of the villa.

I pushed her forward, and because her hands were bound, she fell into the pile of pillows, her ass presenting itself beautifully. I moved her dress up over her cheeks and tore the scrap of underwear out of the way.

"Hey! Those were brand-new!"

"Were they now? Pity," I answered with absolutely no remorse.

"You're totally replacing those." Her words were muffled by the pillows.

"Okay," I answered carelessly as I dropped my slacks around my thighs and stroked my cock a few times, preparing to slide on a condom. I'd never fucked up a second time after that night, and we'd never mentioned it again. After her bizarre reaction earlier to my profession of feelings for her, I didn't think we'd ever have a conversation about ditching the condoms, either.

Once I was sheathed in protection, I placed the head of

my cock at her entrance and waited. A few beats passed until she finally whined.

"Christ, Mac, what are you waiting for? A golden fucking ticket to enter?"

I smacked her ass and then grabbed a handful of her hair, cranking her entire body back up into a tall kneel again, her back flush against my front. I wrapped my large hand around her throat from behind.

I leaned in and growled into her ear, "Do I need to stuff something in that fucking sassy mouth of yours again to teach you some manners? Maybe my cock this time? You can give me one of those stellar blow jobs while your little boyfriend in the Porsche watches me fuck your face?" I felt her rough swallow against my hand and fought every single urge to put more pressure on her fragile neck. I knew she liked pain. I knew she loved dirty talk and rough handling, but we'd never touched on choking in any form, and I didn't want to go too far.

"I'll be good. Just fuck me, Mac. Please. Please fuck me."

"That's much better." I abruptly let her fall forward again onto the pillows so she wouldn't injure herself, since her hands were bound. I enjoyed being a dick, but I wasn't abusive. That wasn't my jam.

This time when I lined my cock up at her entrance, she patiently waited until I was ready to plunge forward, which I timed with the exact moment the Cayman GT4 passed in front of our balcony.

Taylor cried out at the sensation, and I encouraged her. "That's right, baby, let him know how good I fuck you."

"It's not that great. Not really," she had the nerve to answer back.

I smacked her ass repeatedly. "Stop lying to yourself, girl."

She had a big red handprint blooming on her ass cheek, and she would love it. After this many months of dating, I knew that when we parted ways for the work week, she loved having secret marks from our lovemaking. Her pale skin left a vast canvas for me to paint on.

"Come on, Taylor, come for me." I held on to her hips and drove into her, the movement from our bodies making the furniture skip across the deck a fraction of an inch with each thrust. We were almost up against the railing by the time she threw her head back and yelled my name. Any privacy that we might have had under the cover of the awning of the deck where we started was long gone when we finished.

And neither of us cared. I followed right behind her with my orgasm, shouting Taylor's name, several variations of the Lord's, and a few swear words in the mix too. I quickly released my belt from around her wrists and pulled her against my chest on the chaise-longue that was still over beside the fire pit in the shadows of the villa.

"You are one amazing woman." I kissed the top of her head and stroked my thumb up and down her arm. I was in love with her and I wanted to tell her so. But I knew she would literally run back to San Diego, on her own two feet, faster than that Porsche had just flown around the track in the desert night.

"You're not so bad yourself." She sighed into the crook of my neck.

All I could hope for was time. That in time she would see that I was worth taking a risk on. That I was the one worth handing her heart over to. That I was the one who truly was her white knight who would rescue her time and time again from any situation life threw at her.

CHAPTER THIRTEEN

Taylor

"Why don't I just Uber it home? I don't want to intrude on your visit." I was stalling while Mac held the passenger door open for me.

"Stop." He gave me a lingering kiss, and instantly I wanted more. "She wants to meet you. You're not intruding on anything. Get in, love. We're going to be late." He gave a gentle nudge with his hand to the small of my back.

"I just feel like an interloper. And I'm not dressed right for this restaurant. I looked at it again online. It's very upscale, Mac. I'm still in my work clothes." I looked down at the pinstriped blouse and pencil skirt I was wearing and cringed.

"Sass. You look amazing. Please, will you relax? And get in the car."

"I just would rather be at my best, you know? You've said some pretty intense things about your mom in the past. I'd rather be in peak form." I relented, slid into the front seat, and fastened my seat belt.

Mac hustled around the front end of his adorable little BMW, got behind the wheel, and started the engine. "Baby, please. You look amazing. She's going to love you. And I won't let her do anything out of line. I promise. One off-color remark, and we're out of there. Okay?"

"Who picked the restaurant?" I wished I wasn't already letting this woman get under my skin, but I was going to be such a fish out of water at Mr. A's. It was one of the fanciest, if not *the* fanciest, place in the city.

"She did. Why?" He was already getting defensive. *Uh-oh, closet mama's boy, perhaps?*

"I just didn't think it seemed like a place you would like. At least it's close by."

"So you *have* been there? I'm confused."

"No, I'd never go to Mr. A's. Not my style. Wait till you see this place. It's just a San Diego classic, like the Hotel Del."

"The hotel what?"

Sometimes it was easy for me to forget that Mac had just moved here in December. "Oh, my God, never mind. Thank you for picking me up, though. I hope my car gets stolen from the parking garage tonight so I can make an insurance claim and get a new one."

"Baby, I told you before. If you—"

"Do. Not. Mother. Fucking—"

"Sorry. Sorry. I forgot. But most normal people, by this stage in their relationship—"

"Oh, is that what this is now?" I was right back down his throat with my exception to the "r" word.

"Is that another taboo word? Christ. Okay, you know what? I don't want to fight with you on the way to dinner when you're meeting my mother for the first time. She's going to require the majority of my energy, I'm sure. She always does." The last sentence was said as he looked out of the driver's-side window. But I still heard him.

"What does that even mean, Mac? I mean you're a grown man, for fuck's sake. How needy can she be?"

"That depends on the day, I suppose."

"Take Fourth." I pointed toward the left. "We can either park at Horton Plaza or see if they have their own parking."

"Yelp said they have valet. And it's on Fifth."

"Never mind, then. I was just trying to help." We rarely ever argued, and this timing was the worst.

"I appreciate it."

His voice was so clipped and cold, I just glared at him before responding.

"I can tell."

We pulled into the valet line, and he turned his body to look at me fully. "Do you need a spanking before we go inside? I'm serious, Taylor. I can't battle you all night, so can you dial back the attitude? I'm already tense enough."

"I suggest you keep your hands to yourself, Dr. Stone. Let's just get this over with." I was pissed and didn't want to be there at all by that point. The lot attendant opened my door and helped me out, flirting when the hemline of my skirt rode up when I swung my legs out of the low-riding car.

"I'll take it from here, junior." Mac took my hand and placed it in the crook of his arm, his jealous streak flaring. He looked gorgeous in a full suit, something I rarely had the pleasure of seeing him in. Light gray over a crisp white shirt, lavender tie to finish it off. If I hadn't been so pissed at him, I'd have told him how yummy he looked.

"You're staring," he whispered in my ear.

"Because you're acting like a jackass," I whispered back. Then I smiled. "And you look good enough to eat."

"Later, baby. Later. Let's go make nice with the Wicked Witch of the Midwest."

"Boy, when you put it like that..." My palms were starting to sweat.

Mac's mother was already seated at the bar when we walked in, with what looked like a gin and tonic in front of her. Constance Stone was a very put-together woman in her midfifties. She must have been quite young when she gave birth to her only child. She stood when she saw us approaching, eyes twinkling in adoration of her son. Her tailored black slacks were paired with a pale blue cashmere sweater, accented by jewelry that was tasteful and refined. I was sure all of the stones were as real as could be. Teardrop-shaped diamonds hung from her ears, visible with her on-trend short hair style. Her makeup was neutral and appropriate for a woman her age. Basically, she looked flawless. Even her manicure was fresh and perfect.

"Mother, this is my girlfriend, Taylor Mathews. Taylor, my mother, Constance Stone."

I gritted my teeth when he called me his girlfriend, unknowingly dooming us to relationship hell, and offered my hand in greeting.

"Oh, now what's this?" The woman gawked at my hand. "Nonsense, dear. If my son loves you, then I already love you too." She pulled me in for a quick hug, stronger than I expected, bussing each of my cheeks with a sideways kiss. I felt like a rag doll in her grip. When she set me upright again, she looked me over from head to toe and then spoke to Mac as if I weren't standing right there.

"She needs to eat more, sweetie. She's a bit sickly looking, no?"

"She's beautiful and perfect the way she is, thank you, Mother." He snatched me back from her grasp with a gentle touch but a forced smile.

"She's also standing right here," I added, bugging my eyes out in Mac's direction.

The hostess picked the perfect moment to approach us and let us know our table was ready. Mac motioned to his mother to lead the way, and she did so with her head held high, like royalty walking among commoners. I followed directly behind her, taking note of her very expensive shoes and handbag, Mac bringing up the rear, strong hand on my lower back. If I could've made a run for it then and there, I would've. When the hostess pulled my chair out, Mac took over and insisted on seating me himself. He left his mother's wellbeing to the staff member, however. I was sure that pissed her off on some level. It certainly didn't go unnoticed.

The menu was very sophisticated, and the food was divine. I ordered a few things I didn't particularly care for, so when I picked at my food, it just brought more attention to the topic *du jour*.

"Aren't you hungry, Taylor?" his mother asked.

"No, I am. Or I was. These are very big portions." More than half my dinner remained on my plate.

"Do you have an eating disorder, dear?"

I nearly let my fork clatter to the plate. Instead, I placed it carefully on the edge.

At the same time, Mac plummeted his head into a hand. "Dear God, Mother."

"What? I don't think it's something to be ashamed of. You don't have to be uncomfortable around me, dear. I'm very easy to talk to. You'll see." She went to pat my hand, and I pulled it out of her reach.

"No. I don't have an eating disorder. Thank you for your concern, though. I just didn't care for the sauce on the shrimp I ordered. Mac, would you like this? I'd hate to see it go to waste."

"No, babe, I'm full. You weren't kidding. They really give you a lot of food here. There was enough food for three people on my plate."

"At least," I agreed with him, trying to steer the subject in a different direction.

"Or if you eat like a bird," Constance mumbled loud enough for us all to hear as she wiped the corner of her mouth.

"Mother. Enough."

"Well, I think you may want to take her to a doctor. Maybe one of your friends specializes in nutrition." She turned to me. "I know Mac said you had a rough childhood. Did you not have enough food when you were a child? I understand that can lead to eating problems as an adult."

I calmly placed my napkin on the table beside my uneaten food everyone seemed so concerned about. "Rough childhood?" I looked at Mac with a dangerously sweet smile on my face. "You tell me, dear. What problems could that lead to as an adult?"

"My mother is drawing conclusions that shouldn't be drawn and that certainly aren't her business." He swung his stare to Constance. "This is your last warning. You'll apologize to Taylor, or she and I are leaving."

"No, no need to apologize." I smiled at Constance. "I realize I'm on the thin side for a person of my height. It makes some people uncomfortable. But I assure you I eat plenty. I also assure you that my troubled upbringing has only made me a stronger adult, not weaker. If you will excuse me, I need to use the restroom. It will be to urinate and wash my hands. Not to purge my dinner. This food cost way too much of your son's hard-earned money to disrespect in that manner, not to mention I hate throwing up in general. If you feel like you need to escort me to the restroom in order to sleep better tonight, please feel free to do so. However, you will be missing a golden opportunity to talk about me behind my back while I'm gone."

I pushed my chair back quietly, got up, grabbed my purse off the back of the chair, and walked confidently to the restroom. When I made sure the woman hadn't followed me to the lounge, I collapsed onto the toilet, shaking like an addict needing a fix. I'd never been so fucking humiliated in my entire life. And my *boyfriend* had sat there at the same table and let it happen. If we were still dating by the end of this night, he definitely wouldn't be getting lucky. And that was for starters. I would think of better payback for this brand of torture as the night wore on.

And how dare he discuss my "rough" childhood with anyone, let alone her? And for what reason? So they could sit around and pity me? Judge me? Yeah, we were going to have a major fight tonight.

Major.

After I'd finished my business, I washed my hands and went back to the table. They both became noticeably quiet when I approached, solidifying the impression that they'd been talking about me while I'd been gone. Mac's face seemed particularly flushed, so he was either angry or aroused, and my bet was on the former. I held his gaze as he helped me with my chair, silently sending him death threats. If he were smart, he would let me take an Uber home.

"The waitress asked if we wanted dessert, but I figured you were probably too full." He went for small talk to gauge the temperature of my mood.

"Good call. I don't think I could eat another bite." I played along with the niceties.

"Do you want some coffee, dear?" Mac's mom asked.

"No, I have to work in the morning, and if I have caffeine after a certain hour, I don't sleep well."

"Oh, Mac knows you very well, then." She smiled at me, so fucking fake I wanted to puke.

"I told her the same thing," he explained off to the side. I wasn't impressed with the small detail he'd gotten right about me after the way he'd just let her speak to me for the better portion of the night.

As far as I was concerned, the check couldn't come soon enough.

"So, Taylor, where did you go to school?"

"I'm from Georgia, originally. I finished school here in San Diego, though." I knew she meant college, but I was trying to dodge the question. I only had an Associate's Degree in business, and it was always a sore subject for me.

"Did you go to a state school or one of the private schools? There are so many fine schools here in the area."

She wasn't going to stop until she got the down and dirty. I just needed to rip the Band-Aid clean off. "I went to San Diego City College, right in downtown San Diego. It's a junior college, where I got a two-year degree in business admin. It's all I could afford because my mother was in and out of jail a lot around that time and I had to work as well as go to school."

Oh. She was horrified, and it was priceless. "I see."

No, she really didn't, but it felt good to leave her speechless. *That's right, lady, no fucking debutante balls for this one.*

"I'd really like to go home now. If you aren't ready to leave, I'd be happy to call an Uber."

"No, I'll take you, babe. Let me just settle the check, okay?"

"I can handle the bill, Maclain."

"Don't be ridiculous. You're my guest, Mother."

"I'll go have your car brought around. Can you please give me the valet ticket?"

When I stood up, Mac and his mother did the same. "It was nice to meet you, Mrs. Stone. I hope you enjoy your visit to San Diego. There are so many great things to do and see in 'America's Finest City.'" I made air quotes around San Diego's nickname. When Constance went to hug me, I put out my hand to shake hers. I had no interest in pretending we were close enough to hug each other.

"Have a safe trip home tonight, dear."

"Thank you. Mac is an extraordinary driver. But I'm sure you know that. Good night."

My feet could not carry me fast enough to the valet stand, where I handed the young guy the ticket. He grinned and took off at a jog to fetch Mac's car. I hoped Mac was out here by the time he came around with it, because, I realized, I didn't have any money to tip him and I didn't know how to drive a manual transmission.

A few minutes later, Mac slid his warm hands around my waist, a feeling I would normally enjoy. Tonight, my instinct was to spin around and knee him in the balls. Lucky for him, the valet pulled up with his car at precisely the same time.

"Your car, ma'am." His young, boyish charm would've been adorable on any other evening.

"It's his." I motioned over my shoulder with my chin and then slid into the passenger seat and slammed the door shut before either he or Mac could do it for me. I was about to endure the longest fifteen-minute car ride home of my life. I would probably regret not calling a cab.

Mac got behind the wheel, put the car into gear, and slowly eased out of the driveway. We were on the road for several minutes before he finally broke the silence.

"I'm so sorry, baby. I'm sorry."

I wasn't even sure where to start. There was a part of me that wanted to just do my usual: sweep it all under the rug and walk away from it. Not deal with it. It certainly would be easier. That was how I got this far in my life. *Just don't deal with it.*

But that mountain of shit under the rug was getting bigger and bigger by the day. It was getting so big, as a matter of fact, I was going to have to start working it into my décor. It was starting to become part of me, to affect who I was and who I was becoming, and I didn't like it.

"What exactly are you sorry for, Mac?"

"All of it." He shrugged almost nonchalantly.

"No. That's a cop-out. Narrow it down for me. Start small if you have to. Just name one thing you feel remorseful about from tonight." I refused to let him off easy. I felt so angry and bad inside, there was no way he was walking away clean.

"I'm sorry she started in on you about your weight."

"There is nothing wrong with my weight." This was an easy one.

"I agree with you," he answered quickly.

"It used to bother you too, though," I challenged.

"That was before I got to know you better and saw how much you eat in a day. You just happen to have the metabolism of a hummingbird. You may find this hard to believe, Taylor, but *most* people are envious of that. *Most* people have to work really hard at keeping weight off, not on. So yeah, it worried me a little when I first met you. She just has a big mouth and doesn't have a filter."

"Do *not* stick up for her right now. She doesn't deserve that from you." I stared out of the window. The other cars seemed to stand still while we flew by. "And slow down, for Christ's sake. We're not in Thermal anymore, and I want to make it home to my shitty apartment and my shitty life that my rough childhood landed me in."

"Wow, you're really going for it here." He flicked a hard glare at me.

"For what, exactly?" I reared back, bracing against the door. "Did you really just go there? Because that's rich, Doc. Why the fuck would my childhood ever be a topic of discussion between you and *that* woman? How could that possibly be something you two needed to discuss?" I took the chance to level my own glare, though his stare remained solidly on the road—not that it mattered. "And I'm serious. Slow down. The speed limit is sixty-five here."

"Do you want to drive? I'm doing seventy. But I'll slow down to sixty-five if suddenly you need to control every single aspect of the evening." He was raising his voice louder and louder, surpassing normal conversational tones now.

"Do you hear yourself right now? Control every aspect of the evening? *That evening?*" I thumbed back over my shoulder. "That evening was one of the worst experiences of my life. And *you*? You!" I was shouting now. Jabbing my index finger into his shoulder while he drove. "You fucking sat there and let her take shot after shot at me like I was the fucking turkey plumped up for the Thanksgiving Day feast. You call yourself my boyfriend? You, Dr. Clown, suck dick as a boyfriend!"

We pulled into my apartment complex after a few minutes, and when he circled around to find a place to park as though he were coming in, I put my hand up in a stop motion.

"No, just drop me off here."

"No. Damn it, I don't want to end our night like this, Taylor."

I looked at him, and I couldn't be sure, but he might have had tears welling up in his eyes. I wasn't intimately familiar with crying, so I could've been mistaken.

"Oh, dude. We aren't just ending our *night* like this. We're ending *us* like this. I wasn't kidding when I said that was one of the worst experiences of my life. And trust me, I've had some pretty shitty things happen to me. But guess where we are right now? We're at that super-crappy part of the relationship you so desperately wanted to label us with, where I say, 'don't call me, I'll call you.' But the one thing I won't be saying...because it sure as hell is *not* the truth. It's not me—this was all you, buddy. Go home and tuck your mommy in. I hope she fucking sleeps well."

I got out of his sweet little white car for the last time, slammed the door shut as hard as my skinny body could muster, and didn't look back. I fumbled with the keys to my apartment, listening to the distinctive purr of the engine the entire time, wishing he would just drive away. When I got inside, I didn't turn on the lights, just flipped the deadbolt over to locked and slid down against the door until my ass hit the floor in the entrance way of my dumpy apartment.

Now, it officially wasn't *one* of the worst nights of my life.

It topped the whole damn list.

CHAPTER FOURTEEN

Mac

"Because I'm in love with her, Mother."

Why isn't she listening to me? Oh, wait. I already knew the answer to this one.

Because Constance Stone was incapable of listening to anything other than what she wanted to hear.

"Maclain, just hear me out. She's not the right girl for you, all right? Onward. Upward. Dear God, *please*, upward."

I locked my teeth. Let my breath leave me through nostrils as wide as a bull's—with a red flag waved in its face. "Don't go there," I warned. "Not right now."

"And why not right now? You're better off starting fresh, darling. Fresh city, fresh girl. Listen to your mother. I know what's best for you."

"You're the last person on this planet I'm going to take relationship advice from. I'm not sure why I'm even sitting here right now." I glared around the restaurant of the overly priced hotel at which she was staying downtown. The US Grant reeked of tradition and money—right up the woman's narrow cultural alley. It would've been convenient for her to stay in my home in Oceanside, but honestly, I'd rather have lost an eye than shared living space with the woman.

"I should be at her apartment right now, apologizing for

not standing up to *you*. I can't believe you asked her if she had a fucking eating disorder."

"Would you keep your voice down? People are staring." Her exaggerated whisper just fueled my rage more.

"Let them fucking stare. You aren't the Queen of England. No one gives two shits who you are in this town. Or Chicago, for that matter. Contrary to what you think."

"My heavens, you're being rude this morning. This is that gutter trash's influence on you. She has such a foul mouth for a young lady. You've been sounding like a sailor recently too. Now I see why." She concentrated deeply on putting jam on every millimeter of her scone.

I stood up so abruptly the padded seat I was sitting in fell backward and smacked the floor. "What did you just call her?" My voice echoed off the très ceiling.

"I beg your pardon?"

"What did you just say? What did you call my girlfriend?" I slammed both hands onto the table so hard the silverware and stemware hopped an inch to the right.

"Sit down. This instant. You're acting like a spoiled child. And I thought you said she broke up with you? So, in theory, that would make her your ex-girlfriend. Would it not?" My mother's voice shifted slightly. An outsider wouldn't recognize the change, but as someone who had been on the receiving end of her destructive comments his whole life, I braced myself for pain about to be handed down, just by hearing her voice change. Pain I shouldn't have been afraid of anymore but that had been ingrained by years of conditioning, courtesy of the tunnel vision she'd always kept on her world view and the psychological warfare she'd perfected to an art, thanks to the people who fell into her beautiful but shallow trap. But they did keep tumbling, didn't they? Because of it, she'd spent years—practically my entire lifetime—being validated for her vapidity and rewarded for her snobbery.

But now, the emptiness even I had enabled was here to inflict its worst damage on my life. It was no longer just the slow IV drip of poison on my relationship with my mother but a haunting dagger into the very depths of my heart.

My shattering heart.

In that moment, having to stand there and listen to this woman speak ill of the woman in my life—the goddess with whom I had fallen in love—made me see blood red. No, worse. My hands balled into fists, fighting the urge to topple the table over and rush at Constance Stone with my bare hands. To maul her haughty neck like a rabid, insane bear.

"You know what, Mother? Go fuck yourself."

Her mouth dropped open. Disbelief flooded her stare.

"Oh, you heard me right. Take your stuck-up ass and go back to Chicago. Tell all your friends how awful your son is, how awful he treated you. You can rewrite history like you always do, make yourself out to be the innocent one. You're an expert at it by now. I've seen you do it a million times. Hell, the more I think about it, the more I'm sure that's exactly what you did with Uncle Josiah and Aunt Willa. All these years of bad blood were really just you rewriting history. And you dragged me into the thick of it as collateral damage. Well, those days are done."

"Be careful what you say right now, Mac. You make a decision here, and it's done. You're either with me or you're against me. You know that."

"You make it pretty easy, Mother. I'm with everyone else *but* you. At this point, it doesn't even matter who it is. I'd be on their side." My voice was quiet but held the quality of a viper's hiss.

"You're going to be sorry. You will be written out of my will." This had always been the ace up her sleeve—or so she thought.

"Because that matters to me, madam? You need psychological help, lady. I really hope you find it one day, but don't call me when you do. Don't call me—ever again." I stood taller and folded my napkin on the table in finality.

"Not to worry, Mac." She paused just one small beat. "You're already dead to me."

As I walked out of the hotel, my stride was strong, despite expecting to feel—

What?

Nothing?

Maybe that was what I hoped. Instead, I had the strangest sense of relief. It seemed odd to feel that way after my mother had just announced I was dead to her, but I felt like a weight had been lifted off my shoulders.

Maybe that realization was what had brought on the faint sadness. Relationships weren't supposed to feel like burdens. They were meant to be living things. Gardens. We planted them, fed them, nurtured them, and when we needed to, we harvested from them. They weren't supposed to feel like parasites that fed from us and drained us and left us barren.

A big inhalation of fresh ocean air cleansed my soul, and I felt a new plan coalesce.

Since I was already downtown, I threw caution to the wind and headed toward the Stone Global offices. Taylor would not return my calls, texts, or emails since we'd had dinner with my mother two nights prior. How could we solve the problems between us if we couldn't talk? I knew she had a sales department meeting every Thursday morning, so she would definitely be in the office. After several minutes of navigating city traffic, I pulled into the parking structure and circled around the five levels until I spotted her car to verify she hadn't called in sick. I had no game plan, nothing organized to say or do, but I couldn't keep letting the hours pass by without trying to save us. She meant too much to me, whether she wanted to even acknowledge there was an us or not. The past few months had been the best of my life, and it was because of her. I was not about to let my fucking mother ruin another relationship of mine.

My car fit nicely into a corner spot on the same level hers was parked. Sitting there for a couple minutes, I ran through a few scenarios in my head. One—she freaked out and had security throw me out. I could handle that. I still wouldn't give up, because I was determined to work this out with her. Eventually, she would have to talk to me, but maybe I should find a florist and come bearing gifts? Women loved flowers, right? But what womanly stereotype did Taylor Mathews fit into otherwise? That might not be the best plan.

The second scenario was less likely to happen but would be the better option of the two. Taylor had had some time to cool down and think about dinner the other night and realized that my mother's behavior was exactly that, my *mother's*.

As in—not mine.

The only problem that remained was that my behavior had been less than desirable in Taylor's opinion too. And she was right. But she wasn't being fair in not giving me a chance to apologize. She was right. I should have put a stop to my mother's deplorable actions sooner that evening. But I was human and in the same uncharted water as she was when it came to relationships at this point. If we were going to survive the storms of life's seas together, we were going to have to promise to do just that, stick together. Not tuck tail and run every time the tide rose and the waves crashed over the bow. I needed my first mate back, and damn it, I was willing to battle whatever sea creature got in my way to do just that.

CHAPTER FIFTEEN

Taylor

The yawn I tried to hide behind my palm made a strange noise from the back of my throat, causing the two interns next to me to throw over furtive looks. All too quickly, they refocused on the PowerPoint Margaux was presenting to SGC's Marketing and Operations Departments.

"Ms. Mathews, am I keeping you awake this morning?" she said smoothly, never missing a beat from her talking points.

"My apologies, Ms. Asher." I was going to kill her the minute we got out of the fucking meeting. *What's the point of calling me out like that in front of everyone?* She'd have a good case of the guilts when she found out why I'd been up half the night.

Someone flipped the lights on as she wrapped up her goals for the next quarter, and everyone started talking among themselves.

The team filed out of the conference room soon after. I hung back, wanting to have a few words with my friend about embarrassing me in front of my peers.

"What was the point of that?" I hissed.

"Settle down, Godzilla." She was unmoved by my acid attack. "I was teasing."

"Well, everyone else doesn't understand your brand of

teasing. They still think you're the devil wearing Prada. So, thanks but no thanks."

"But don't you remember, honey? I *am* the devil." She folded her arms across her chest, eyeing me intensely. "What the hell crawled up your skinny ass?"

Tears filled my eyes.

Actual. Fucking. Tears.

"Oh, no. Oh, shit. No. No. No. Honey. I'm sorry. I'm sorry. And...I'm stunned, I think. I've never ever seen actual tears in your eyes. This is bad. Fuck. This has to do with Mac, doesn't it? What did that motherfucker do? I'll cut his dick off and stuff it in his jacket like a pocket square. Did he cheat on you? Bastard. I knew he was a bastard." She drifted off, likely thinking of other ways to use his dick as an accessory.

"No. Stop. And I didn't cry. They didn't actually come out. So my record is still clean." I took a deep, cleansing breath, pushing under my eyes with the heels of my hands.

"Stop that!" She smacked my hands down from my face. "Do you know how sensitive and thin that skin is under your eyes? You'll break those tiny capillaries without even knowing it, and there is no coming back from that shit. Don't ever push like that on that area again. Promise you won't!" She was like an epidermis-guarding maniac suddenly.

"Okay. Okay! Shit."

"Seriously, Tay. That's like a beauty felony. God. You almost gave me a heart attack, seeing you do that. Tell me what's going on, though." She pulled a chair out from under the conference room table, still shaking her head in disbelief, and then pulled a second one out and sat in it herself. When I just stood there, she pointed aggressively at the empty one for me to sit.

"I really don't want to get all into this," I blurted.

"Too bad," Margaux retorted. "Spill, sister."

Ugh. I hated this but knew there was no escape from my friend. In this kind of a mood, Margaux Asher wasn't a dog with a bone. She was a lioness with an entire carcass. "We had an ugly, *ugly* incident and broke up," I muttered. "It's not that big of a deal. It's not like we were really a thing anyway." I shrugged, trying to make light of the mess—if that were even possible.

"Oh yeah, I can see it's not a big deal." She rolled her eyes, all kohled-out in the season's on-trend colors. "And why do you do that?"

"What?" I slumped, feeling utterly exhausted. Last night's restless sleep was taking its toll in bigger chunks by the minute.

"Why do you minimize everything?" Margaux explained.

"I—I don't know what—"

"Yes, you do, damn it. Why is it such a bad thing to admit you were into him? It's not bad to say you were in love with him." She covered her mouth dramatically, like she'd just said a bad word.

I pressed my own mouth into a stubborn line. "I was not in love with him."

"Taylor."

"What?" I answered back just as dryly.

She just shook her head. "It takes one to know one."

"What?" Now I was confused.

"Remember when you were a kid and you'd get in a fight and you'd say 'takes one to know one'?"

"What does that have to do with anything? I think you're officially the sleep-deprived and crazy-talking one now."

"Just play along," she said. "I promise, there's a point to

this." She sat up taller, excited to explain her point.

"Oooohhh kaayyy. Yes, I remember doing that."

"So, do you remember thinking when I was going through all my issues with Michael, and Andrea, and hell, Caroline too, that I was so fucked up in the head, but of course I thought I had it all figured out and everyone else could see how far from the truth that was but me?"

"Boy, do I ever. And it was really hard to watch it go on, because we wanted to help you, but you wouldn't let us."

"Exactly. So, when I say it takes one to know one, why do you think that is, Taylor?"

I thought about what she was saying, and all the pieces fell into place. I had my head so far up my ass and my friends recognized it and I just kept pushing them away instead of letting them help me.

"Denial is the place I'm most comfortable, Mare. You know that."

"I know, honey." She covered my hand with hers. "But nothing ever gets fixed there. Sometimes you have to do some hard work if you want true happiness. You deserve it, baby. We all do. And Mac does seem like a good man who really cares about you."

"You really would think that, wouldn't you?" Before I could help it, a bitter laugh escaped. "But then he let his mother wipe her feet on me like the welcome mat outside the front door. And I don't think I can let myself be treated that way by anyone anymore."

Margaux let loose with a heavy sigh. "All right. I can see that point. But let's just back up and look at things from a different angle real quick."

My chuckle died out. My gaze narrowed. "Excuse me—

but who are you and what did you do with my friend Margaux? You know, the one all but allergic to phrases like 'back up' and 'different angle'?"

She accepted the allegation with grace, and was about to answer to it, when a commotion in the hallway made linear thinking impossible. Scratch that. Thinking at *all* was suddenly impossible. From in here, it sounded like two mail carts had been overturned and twice that many women had had their skirts flipped up, making Margaux and me trade baffled glances. It was impossible to discern anything about what was really happening, though, due to the frosted glass of the conference room door as well as the windows with closed blinds for our meeting.

Our confusion wasn't drawn out long.

I knew exactly what was going on from the moment I heard him speak.

"Taylor! Taylor Mathews?"

All right, *speak* might have been an understatement.

He was yelling. Bellowing. All but nuclear bombing the place with his voice.

"Is she here? Has anyone seen Taylor Mathews?"

And still, even at the height of his urgent and demanding loudest, turning my nerves into complete applesauce.

"Sir. *Sir.*" The interjection belonged to Britta, Killian Stone's executive assistant. Though her desk was situated where it should be, in front of Killian's office on the *opposite* side of the floor, I was certain the woman had come running as soon as she'd felt the Disturbance in the Force. Yes, she was *that* good. "You cannot just come barging—"

"Hi, Britta. It's just me."

"Good to see you again, Dr. Stone. But you still can't just storm in here and—"

"I'm not storming."

"Dr. Stone, I don't care if you're unicycling. We are conducting business here."

"And I'll let you get on with it, as soon as you tell Taylor Mathews that I'm here and need to speak with her. *Right now.* It's important."

"If it is, then I'm sure you can wait down near *her* office—"

"But she's not *in* her office. She's up here, or so they told me, and now I'll just find her and talk to her, if you don't mind."

"Dr. Stone. I *do* mind."

"Oh, my God." Margaux was on her feet right behind me, peeking out of the blinds on the conference room window. "Your man is taking on Killian's Britta. Is he drunk?"

"Holy shit," I mumbled. "What the hell is he thinking? I-Is Killian even here? In the building, I mean?"

Margaux rolled her shoulders in a grim shrug. "The BOD meeting is in two days, so I'm pretty sure he is."

"Oh, my God." I dropped my head into my hands as Mac, looking luscious as hell in black fitted pants and a French-blue dress shirt, timpani-drummed his way on the doors up the opposite side of the hallway. "He's going to get me fired."

Margaux pushed me toward the door. "Just get your ass out there and get him to be quiet before Britta enlists Kil with her crusade."

"Jesus Christ, this day just keeps getting worse." I finger-combed through my hair for whatever reason and opened the door to the hallway.

The second he saw me, Mac ceased the pounds and the yells. "Hey," he blurted instead.

"Hey," I muttered back.

"You look stunning."

He took a step toward me. I held my hand up, making him stop. "Shut the fuck up," I gritted through my teeth. People were looking out into the hall to see what the commotion was about. "What the hell are you doing here?"

"We need to talk." He looked like he hadn't slept, or maybe showered, since I'd seen him last.

"Well, I'm at work. You need to leave. I'll call you later."

"No, you won't. I know you won't return my calls. Can we go somewhere and talk now?"

"No, this is my office, Mac. Have you been drinking?" He came another step closer, hands stretched out in front of him. "No! Don't touch me."

"Taylor." His voice was so raspy he sounded like a lung patient. "Please."

I wanted to blast out a huge yell at him now too. Yearned to tell him how begging didn't suit him and this was ridiculous and he needed to hop back into his snazzy car—well, *any* of them—and take his gorgeous ass home. But, damn it, if he didn't melt me a few degrees more with every second that passed with him standing there, humble and open and willingly breaking himself for me...and asking me to do the same. Asking me to meet him on the middle ground where we could work on fixing this shit between us.

In short, what nearly every asshole had ever done to my mom. Had said to her. Had promised her...

"What's going on here?" a distinct voice asked.

"Oh, fuck. Perfect," I mumbled.

Killian's voice came from behind me while security appeared in the hall on the other side of Mac, adding the finishing garnishes to this perfect sandwich of discomfort.

"Nothing to see here, folks. Everyone can just go back to

their jobs." I turned around to Killian. "I'm really sorry for the disruption, Mr. Stone. *Dr.* Stone was just leaving."

"I'm not leaving until you agree to speak to me." His defiance was going to get him arrested.

"You are *not* helping right now," I gritted through my teeth again. "Just leave before he has you arrested."

Killian stepped forward by another step. "You heard the lady, cousin."

"I'm not leaving," Mac spat.

"Stop it!" I retaliated.

"Is he bothering you, Taylor?" my daunting boss asked.

"I'm *not* bothering her," his cousin answered for me.

"Not necessarily. We're just having a little mix-up here. Nothing I can't handle. I'm really sorry to have troubled you," I continued to try to defuse the situation.

"Mac, why don't you run along and see Miss Mathews on her personal time, then?" Killian egged Mac on.

"Why don't I let Miss Mathews tell me when she wants to see me and not see me?" Of course Mac rose to the bait.

"Damn it, Mac!" I snarled.

"Well, she's told you several times to leave and you're still standing here. So, either you have a hearing problem, or you're looking for trouble. In which case, I'd be happy to show you to our front door personally." Killian wasn't one to be the first to walk away from a situation.

"Please, can we just stop this?" Claire came waltzing in on her fantastic high heels at the perfect time. "Can I be of assistance to anyone? Hello, gorgeous husband." She kissed Killian square on the lips, always making it clear who she aligned herself with.

"Fairy." He gripped her hips and held her for a second

kiss. They were sickeningly adorable and exactly what I didn't want or *need* to see at the moment.

"Nope." I issued it so breezily I could've been a dryer sheet commercial. Whipping my glare back around, I concluded, "Mac was just leaving."

He gave as good as he got, stabbing a determined stare right back into me—a corner of his mouth lifting, as if knowing exactly how his dominance shredded me from the inside out. "Actually, Taylor and I were just going to step out for lunch."

"Over my dead body." At this rate, that might just be the case too.

"And *that* says it all." With the same edge of severe decision, Killian suddenly surged forward. His rush was so textbook Killian Stone, a mix of grace and power, that I hardly realized he'd hooked Mac by the elbow at the same time. Only when Mac wrenched against his cousin, baring his teeth in an expression tempting to go supernova with profanity, did anyone else realize it, either. "Time for the locker room, cuz," Killian uttered.

"Like hell it is!" Mac seethed back.

"It is because I say it is. And because we've all had enough of your shit for the day."

I didn't hear what Mac had for a comeback to that. Nobody did because Killian didn't stop with his forward momentum until they were out of sight completely.

In the strange aftermath of silence, I just stood there, dumbfounded, not sure what to do or say now myself.

Claire came to stand beside me, and Margaux appeared from the conference room doorway too.

"Shit," I finally stammered.

"It's okay." Margaux joined Claire in embracing me.

"What my Mary said," Claire said softly. "It's going to be okay, Tay. We promise."

"Shit." I couldn't help but repeat it. "God. Do you think—I mean...I hope Killian won't—"

"Of course he won't hurt him," Claire assured. "He'll probably just talk some sense into him. It was foolish for him to come storming in here like that."

"Although kind of adorable too. *Adrian! Adrian!*" Margaux did her best Rocky impression when he was searching the crowd for his wife. Claire and I burst out laughing.

"All right, let's get back to work. I'll let you know what happened between my husband and his cousin later, okay?" She gave me a quick squeeze of the shoulder.

"Yeah, thanks. You too, crazy." I motioned with my chin toward Margaux. "I love you guys. So much."

We went our separate directions to finish our workdays. I could only speak for myself, but I got nothing productive done for the rest of the day. I couldn't concentrate, and I kept wondering if Killian had had Mac arrested or if they'd ended up in a fist fight. As upset with him as I was, I didn't wish him physical harm.

When I went out to my car to leave for the day, I saw there was something on my windshield as I approached. It was a handwritten letter from Mac. Although I was tempted to tear it into a million pieces and throw it away in the trash bin in the parking garage, I slipped it into my purse and waited until I got home to read it.

Claire texted me to let me know that Killian had told Mac that he understood what it was like to have to fight for the woman he loved, but he couldn't disrupt my place of employment again or he would have him arrested. They'd spoken about their family issues a bit and agreed to let bygones be bygones. I was happy for Mac on that front because I knew that feud between Killian and him was a sore spot for him, because he felt like it had been contrived by his mother more than anything. It was good to hear they were putting it behind them.

I didn't mention the letter he'd left on my windshield. I wanted to read it first in case it was something I didn't want to rehash with my girlfriends. The paper sat on my small coffee table, half-unfolded by the breeze of my air-conditioning vent, and his chicken-scratch writing took up most of the page.

Might as well pull off the Band-Aid.

Taylor,

The past months we've spent together have been the best of my life. I've told you that, time and time again, but you minimize my feelings when I open up to you. I thought if I expressed myself in writing, you won't have any other option but to take my words for their face value.

I'm in love with you, Taylor Mathews. I think I knew it from the moment we went toe-to-toe in that waiting room in Chicago. No one has ever challenged me the way you do, and it lit a fire in me that I quickly became addicted to.

But you need to find your happiness too, my sweet sassy. I want to be that happiness for you, not stand in the way of it. If I'm not it for you like you are for me, I don't want to hold you back from finding it. If you can't say that you love me too, then maybe you don't. Love shouldn't be difficult. Scary? Maybe. Probably. When I first realized how I felt about you, I was scared—but only because I had to confront the possibility of losing you.

Funny thing is, I still don't feel that I've lost you.

Because I never had you in the first place.

So...checkmate.

Looks like you've taken me down. I have no more moves to make...no more pieces to sacrifice. This knight can't fight any more battles to prove his fealty to you...his love for you.

I know, when it came time to wage the largest fight, I let you down the most. I let my mother abuse you—and I will forever be sorry for that. It's not easy for me to admit I've fucked up—it doesn't happen often, you know—but when it does, I go a little crazy for the chance to make it right. It's hard now, knowing things aren't right for you, but accept this as a fraction of my agonized apology. I made a mistake. People are typically given a chance to atone for their mistakes—but nothing about this journey of ours has been anything close to "typical."

Maybe that's why I have fallen so hard. And would still be willing to fall again—if you ever want to try again.

Yes, that's my way of holding the door open. Maybe by just a crack...maybe while my king still stands...

Maybe because we both know the queen holds all the power on the board.

You know where I live, where I work, and even where I play. You know the real me, Taylor. And when you figure out who the real you is, maybe you would like me to be a part of your life again. Until then, I wish you well and all the best.

Truly yours, if you decide you deserve me,

Mac

I lowered the letter with shaking fingers—and a jaw plummeting in raw shock. Then, before I gave in to the craving to tear the thing to shreds, wadded the damn thing up and hurled it across the room.

The backs of my eyes stung. The fire, so telling in its intensity and strident in its heat, had become a too-familiar occurrence in my life now.

A life I couldn't imagine without him.

A life I didn't dare think of letting him back into.

What the hell do I do now?

And *why* the hell was I even asking myself that? Not after that...that...

What the hell *was* that? A love letter? An apology note? An ultimatum?

And why did I care, when it enraged me to the point of trembling in sheer dizziness as I stood, wobbled across the room, and flung open the door of my bedroom?

My haven.

The one place I was safe...

Where I could flop on the bed, like I did now, and scream into the pillows until my throat hurt, my head throbbed, and the moisture behind my eyes became a defensive desert once again.

"When I've decided I *deserve* him?" I growled, staring up at my ceiling. There were so many other lines in that damn letter that needed to be screamed about, but that seemed like a damn good place to start.

Asshole.

Asshole.

I bolted off the bed and stomped across into the living room, grabbing up the epic "Maclain Charter" as I went. On my way over to the kitchen, I dared to read it again—almost welcoming the fury it stirred anew. This, I could deal with. The anger was my new shelter.

Dickwad.

Dickwad.

Where exactly did he get off thinking he knew anything about me or my happiness? I considered calling him and letting him have a piece of my mind, but that was what he was hoping for, so I calmly set my cell phone down on the counter. I pulled out a piece of paper to write a letter in response. Maybe putting my thoughts on to paper would help get them in order.

As I scrawled his name across the top, my cell phone rang. I snatched it up, expecting it to be him, knowing I would've read his decree by that point.

"You *fuck*. What the hell makes you think you can just say all of that and then—"

"Taylor? Taylor, honey? Is that you?"

My entire stomach surged into the bottom of my throat.

The line wasn't filled by the beautiful, husky voice of the world's biggest bastard-clown. It was the slurring, drug-addled voice of Janet Mathews.

I hadn't looked at the caller ID before starting my diatribe—and wished I had.

"Mom?" I croaked.

"Baby, I need your help."

"Of course you do."

ALSO BY ANGEL PAYNE

Cimarron Series:
Into His Dark
Into His Command
Into Her Fantasies

Temptation Court:
Naughty Little Gift
Pretty Perfect Toy
Bold Beautiful Love

**For a full list of Angel's other titles,
visit her at AngelPayne.com**

ACKNOWLEDGMENTS

Thank you to the readers and fans who have supported the Stones and their crazy journey so far. We hope you enjoy this new part of the saga!

So many thanks to our awesome beta readers.

Your feedback has been so invaluable!

Ceej Chargualaf

Kimberley Hellmers

ABOUT
ANGEL PAYNE & VICTORIA BLUE

USA Today bestselling romance author Angel Payne loves to focus on high-heat romance starring memorable alpha men and the women who love them. She has numerous book series to her credit, including the action-packed Bolt Saga and Honor Bound series, Secrets of Stone series (with Victoria Blue), the intertwined Cimarron and Temptation Court series, the Suited for Sin series, and the Lords of Sin historicals, as well as several standalone titles.

Angel is a native Southern Californian, leading to her love of being in the outdoors, where she often reads and writes. She still lives in Southern California with her soul-mate husband and beautiful daughter, to whom she is a proud cosplay/culture con mom. Her passions also include whisky tasting, shoe shopping, and travel.

Visit her at AngelPayne.com

International bestselling author Victoria Blue lives in her own portion of the galaxy known as Southern California. There, she finds the love and life-sustaining power of one amazing sun, two unique and awe-inspiring planets, and four indifferent yet comforting moons. Life is fantastic and challenging and every day brings new adventures to be discovered. She looks forward to seeing what's next!

Visit her at VictoriaBlue.com